SKINWALKERS

Book 2 of the VOLK Series

D. Werkmeister

"... old-world mysticism alongside the modern law enforcement intrigue that will satisfy fans of both fantasy novels and thrillers." — ***Kirkus Reviews***

Gruesome murders in the desert, Native tales of ancient shapeshifters, mysterious indications of Russian involvement, and a crack FBI team sent to untangle it all. Werkmeister's sequel to his wonderfully original novel <u>VOLK</u> is a page-turner pulsating with excitement. Terrific stuff! — **Carl Deuker, Award Winning Author**

"It was a glorious, hair blown back thrill ride! I loved it!" — **ARC Reader T. Hess**

"Wow! Skinwalkers is a heart-pounding thriller that will keep you on the edge of your seat with its bone-chilling plot twists. I can't wait to see what comes next." — **ARC Reader / Author B. A. Nichols**

Acknowledgements

I would like to recognize my editor, Sarah Davis. Thank you for trying to keep me on the grammatical straight and narrow. Thank you as well to my local writing group. Your thoughtful critiques were helpful beyond words.

To my former co-workers in the FBI, thank you for your camaraderie and friendship. And for providing me with years of anecdotes, characters, and stories, many that will never be told, but make me laugh to this day. Stay safe.

To the readers of VOLK, thank you for your support.

To my family, my wife, Amy, and my daughters, Catherine and Sarah, thank you. Your encouragement and enthusiasm have kept me going.

"Beware that, when fighting monsters, you yourself do not become a monster...for when you gaze into an abyss, the abyss gazes also into you."

Friedrich Nietzsche

PROLOGUE
The New World, 1595

Francisco Bestia woke shivering. He had been warned by his fellow priests that the deserts in this new country were blazing hot by day and near freezing by night. Reaching to pull his wool blanket up, he realized it was nowhere to be found. Barely awake, he felt along his body and was stunned to realize he was almost nude, his clothes mostly torn to shreds.

The fog of sleep gradually lifted, but before it cleared, he was a child back home in his small Spanish village. It was Christmas, and he had just finished a holiday feast with his family. Slowly, the images of his mother, father, and sister blurred away until he was fully conscious. The familiar acrid smell of smoke filled his nostrils, but there was another aroma under it. A sick, metallic smell of fresh blood. It was an odor he immediately recognized from his years with the conquistadors.

Forcing his eyes open, he propped himself up on his elbows. In the dim light of the dawn, several of his fellow Spaniards lay peacefully around the fire, still asleep. But as he looked closer, he realized something was wrong. The bodies were not in a position of slumber. He rose to his bare feet for a better vantage and immediately dropped back to his knees.

Death surrounded him. The entire foraging party, every man, slain. There was no sound save for the occasional pop from the dying coals of the fires. He looked where the horses should have been and saw a large heap of flesh with one hoofed leg sticking up into the frigid air. In the orange dawn light, he could see steam rise from the carcass. There was no sign of the other horses. Finding a wool blanket nearby, he draped it over his shoulders as he walked among the dead, offering blessings.

Moving among the corpses, he noted that several of them had drawn their swords and died with them in their hands. But he found no signs of combat. He had walked enough battlefields in the past several years to recognize a fight with the local tribes. None of those telltale signs were present. There were no broken weapons, no arrows, no lost clothing, nothing. Nothing except dead Spanish conquistadors.

The sun crested the hills in the east, and in the full morning light, he looked closer at the wounds suffered by the soldiers. They were ghastly: deep gouges, limbs removed, heads caved in. This wasn't the work of the local tribes.

At first, he could not remember any of it. He reasoned that perhaps he had been knocked unconscious during the attack or maybe his mind had blocked all memory of the horror.

He returned to the fire and added more wood. The radiant warmth of the renewed flame finally drove away the chill. He watched the coals glow a deep pulsing orange. As he held his hands out to warm them, he noticed the dark maroon stains up to his elbows. Despite the heat of the fire, a chill ran down his back. Troubling visions flashed across his mind. Men screamed in horror before they were cut down, their faces twisted in pain, their eyes full of terror. Faces he recognized. But most disturbing was a vague recollection of a taste. A wave of nausea washed over him as his body shuddered. His eyes tightly closed, he said a silent prayer.

When he opened them again, he focused on the fire. Trance-like, he studied the flames rolling around the wood and flickering skyward. A resigned peace settled on him. At that moment, he decided he was wrong. It had been the local tribes who slaughtered these men after all. That is what he would tell the commander back at *la fortaleza*.

CHAPTER 1

THE ARIZONA STATE POLICE cruiser rolled along the dark highway north on Highway 87. Trooper Roger Pearl glanced down at the clock on the dashboard, 3:00 a.m. He had four more hours on his shift before he headed back to the barracks. His mind drifted as he listened to the engine hum. He thought of the trip he had booked to Napa Valley. He was excited to see the look on Maria's face when he told her about the surprise vacation. It was a perfect place to propose.

He realized he hadn't heard anything on his radio for a while. It was unusually quiet tonight. Fine with him. He looked at his rearview mirror, no headlights, only the faint glow of the city on the horizon behind him. Ahead, past his own headlight illumination, was thick blackness. The desert landscape was only a shade less dark than the overcast night sky. It was a Friday night, actually Saturday morning now, and his patrol for impaired drivers had been fruitless. He told himself that was a good thing, fewer dangerous drivers on the roads. But his experience told him that just because he didn't see any that didn't mean they weren't out there. He had seen his share of fatal accidents over the past seven years to know better.

As he crested a slight hill, his lights reflected off the taillights of a car parked along the side of the highway. He slowed down, thinking it was probably a stranded motorist or someone too drunk to drive. Then he saw the dark streaks on the asphalt, skid marks. He pulled up behind the car, a red Jeep Wrangler, and saw it appeared to have stopped abruptly, facing off the road at about 30 degrees. He took a few seconds to survey the stop, no hazard lights blinking on the Jeep, probably not a breakdown. The spotlight from his cruiser created an arc of light across the cold, dark landscape. No driver, no passenger. Nothing. Something was wrong. He activated his red and blues, grabbed his flashlight, and got out of the car. A smell immediately assaulted his nose. He recognized the sick smell of open flesh.

Instinctively, he released the retention strap on his pistol and kept his hand on the weapon as he scanned the area with his flashlight.

I saw the police car approaching. Actually, I could hear the hum of the engine and tires rolling on the pavement long before I saw the lights come over the hill. Plenty of time to get into the shadows and watch. A few months ago, I would have slinked away if the cops showed up. Not anymore. I know what I am: a killer. No, I'm more than that. I'm a god.

I won't run tonight.

Trooper Pearl found the body in front of the Jeep, lying on the desert sand, stained dark with blood. He checked for a pulse but knew there wouldn't be one. Her eyes stared blankly into the night sky. She'd been mauled by some kind of animal.

"What the hell would do this?" he said to himself, as a ripple of nausea rolled through him. He shined his flashlight on the front of the Jeep and saw the grille and hood were damaged.

As he keyed his radio to call in the fatal accident, he heard it. Someone or something was moving in the distance. Shining his flashlight in the direction of the sound, he called out, "State Police!" The noise stopped. He wondered if his nerves were getting to him, his mind playing tricks. Was there really someone out there in the dark?

What he heard next, a deep menacing growl, sent a chill down his back. He drew his service weapon and scanned the night air again with his flashlight perched under the barrel of his handgun. A wave of panic tried to claw its way out of his chest. His movements with the flashlight became erratic, sweeping the beam rapidly across the cold barren terrain. The light passed over something before his brain could register it. Swinging the light back, he caught a glimpse of something moving fast behind his car. Now blinded by his own headlights, he squinted as he moved, keeping his weapon trained at the rear of his patrol car.

On the quiet highway, he saw it: some kind of animal crouched by his trunk, staring at him. The flashlight beam reflected off the eyes, and they glowed against sandy brown fur. He couldn't quite make out what it was, but it seemed large, too big for a coyote. Whatever it was, it didn't seem to be afraid of him.

Another deep growl echoed in the cold night air as it continued to stare at him. The panic he was barely containing before now broke free and flowed through his body like ice water. He fired at the creature, hoping to frighten it away, but it still didn't run. His blood ran cold as it stood up, towering over the cruiser. The flashing red and blue lights illuminated it, but his mind could not register what he was seeing. It continued staring at him, the glow of the eyes only broken by a split second blink before it started to move. He did not know what it was, but he knew it was deadly and now coming for him. He fired the contents of his magazine. Small trickles of blood appeared from the bullet impacts, but it never flinched. He could see the teeth bared now, gleaming white against the crimson stained fur that surrounded the mouth.

His flashlight slipped from his shaking hand while he struggled to retrieve another magazine. Muscle memory kicked in, and he slammed the magazine home and sent the slide forward. Before he could bring the weapon to bear, it charged.

It's done. I glance at the broken body lying at my feet and let out a roar. Hunting in the desert is liberating. The opportunities are scarcer, but I can really turn it all loose. Feels good. The stupid bravado of these people stuns me. This cop learned a very stern lesson, like the others.

The look in their eyes when they realize they are doomed is almost as satisfying as the taste of their flesh. I have to admit, it has turned out to be a pretty good night.

Before I return to my catch in front of the Jeep, I reach down and tear off the name tag. R. Pearl.

Detective John Lightfoot returned to the office at the Arizona Bureau of Investigation. He dropped his bag in a chair and hung his western cut blazer over the back. Rubbing the back of his neck, he stared at the large white board on the other side of the large conference room. He was exhausted. Not from being up since 4 a.m. when he got the call, he was used to that. It was the mental fatigue from the past several months that was eating him alive.

The TV down the hall suddenly interrupted the normally chipper morning broadcast with breaking news. He shut the door. It was going to be about the Pima Predator. Jesus, what a day.

He ran through the crime scene in his head. One civilian, identified as Caitlyn Jones: dead and half eaten. One state trooper, Roger Pearl: dead and torn apart. Sixteen rounds fired with no indication of their hitting anything. No blood trail, nothing. Dashcam footage retrieved from the trooper's car showed him exiting his vehicle, discovering the body of Jones near her disabled Jeep, and then, ostensibly, detecting someone else in the area and moving off camera to engage them. Nothing else on the video. No radio call. Despite the closed door, he could hear the press was having a field day with this.

It wasn't bad enough the press had hung a name on this psychopath, naming it for the first county a victim was located in. They had given every crackpot in the state a reason to call his office with their hunches, suspicions, visions, and ghost stories of who was behind the killings. Not helpful.

He took a sip of his coffee, now cold and bitter. The white board seemed to mock him. Across the top were photos and names of the victims lined up chronologically with their deaths. Below was a map of the state. Green and red lines crisscrossed the map, marking the addresses and final locations of the victims. If there was a connection between the victims, he couldn't find it. Only the condition of the bodies provided a common thread: mangled to some degree with signs of carnivorous activity. No one could identify a murder weapon and there appeared to be no effort to conceal the bodies.

No doubt there was a serial killer out there, but nothing like he had ever seen or heard of.

The door opened, and the breathless reporting from the television grew louder momentarily as his partner, Detective Ed Stackhouse, came into the room. The large man stood next to John holding a steaming mug of coffee. "Helluva morning."

"That it is," John said, still staring at the board.

"So with this morning, that makes eight," Ed noted as he took a sip of his coffee.

"Eight we know about," John pointed out.

"Well, he don't seem to be hidin' 'em, so that's probably a good number."

"True," John acknowledged.

"By the way, there's fresh coffee in the muster room," Ed said without looking.

"Thanks. Think I'm gonna need it."

They both stared at the board for a moment before the sing-song melody of John's ringtone broke the silence. He looked down and took a deep breath. He had been expecting this call, but still felt his stomach tighten. "Captain is calling," he announced.

FBI Special Agent Terri Watson's eyes focused on the rearview mirror, her blonde hair trailing from the back of her knit cap. One of the challenges of surveillance was watching something intently without appearing to be watching it. Parking past the target location and looking back in your mirror was a simple technique. The cold weather today in Philadelphia made their job a little easier. People sitting in running cars didn't seem out of place. Her partner, Philadelphia Police Detective Marc Peterson, was sitting next to her, watching pedestrians on the sidewalk bustle by, bundled against the cold November air. They had sent their confidential informant, Alex, source name VOLK, into the Europa Tea House about an hour ago.

Terri and Marc met Alex Stepanova over a year ago. Technically, she was a source, but their relationship was complicated. Terri had worked with numerous sources, some more affable than others, over the twelve years of her Bureau career. Alex was–different. Terri felt confident when she thought, I'm gonna guess no other FBI agent in the Bureau has a shapeshifter as a source. At least not one they know about. Terri and Alex both preferred the term shapeshifter. It felt less gothic.

To say Terri had been reluctant to accept that she and her partner were tracking a werewolf last year would be an understatement. Her science-based brain could not make the jump to a supernatural cause behind the killings in Philadelphia. However, the evidence became over-whelming, and when they confronted her, Alex confirmed it.

Since then, Alex claimed to have changed her hunting habits and had proven to be a valuable resource. Only Terri and Marc, along with fellow FBI agent Sarah Holmes and medical examiner Jerri Williams, knew the truth of their discovery. But Terri knew there were others. The Russian scientists and a few high-level Russian government officials knew there was a werewolf in the world as well. Their experiments in rapid cellular regeneration accidentally triggered Alex's transformation, after all. But at least they didn't know where she was.

No, Alex was definitely not a typical source. True, she was a wealth of intelligence on Russian matters. It was obvious she had an ax to grind against the people responsible for her transformation. She relished the opportunity for retribution. But there was more. Her unique skill set had saved Terri's and Sarah's lives that night from the cartel assassins. Was Terri's bond with Alex based on something more than their working relationship? Had she become a friend?

She pushed the thought aside and refocused on the entrance to the Europa Tea House in her rearview mirror.

A few weeks ago, they had received a tip about a car theft ring operating in the Philadelphia area. That alone was not unusual. Like most metropolitan areas, cars were routinely stolen. But this theft ring was different. It was receiving orders for specific cars from Eastern Europe and shipping them overseas. The operation was so efficient, the cars were often loaded into containers and en route to the port of Newark before the owners filed a police report.

Additionally, there had been several violent carjackings linked to them. Newer vehicles, with substantial anti-theft devices installed, were easier to steal at gunpoint than by stealth.

"You think she's ok in there?" Marc asked jokingly.

Terri laughed but didn't take her eyes off the mirror. "Yeah. I think she's good. I haven't seen anyone come flying out a window yet."

He chuckled. "Ya got any plans for Christmas this year?"

"No, not really. I might go to my aunt Bunny's in Bethesda. Not sure I can stand that though, so it might be Chinese food and Netflix," Terri answered.

"You know you're welcome to come over. I get the kids for Christmas day this year. They like you. Call you their aunt Terri."

"Thanks for the invite. I don't want to intrude, though."

"Naw. After they open their presents, they usually go hang out and play video games or something. Be nice to have someone to talk to."

She nodded. "I'll let you know."

Marc watched a woman in a long down coat push a cart of groceries past the car, her scarf-covered head tilted forward against the biting wind. "So where do you think she got the intel on this meeting?" he asked casually, already having a pretty good idea of the answer.

"I didn't ask, but I'm going to guess somebody's email got hacked." During the course of their relationship with Alex, they had learned she was an adept cyber hacker.

"Good bet. I think she likes this stuff, chasin' bad guys."

"No doubt. When she told me about the meeting she said she was free this morning to monitor it, if we wanted."

"No one better to send in there than her. Those goddamn ears of hers don't miss a thing. And don't even get me started on her sniffer," he said with a chuckle.

Terri laughed. "Right?"

Marc shifted in his seat. "So, while we're on the subject of shapeshifters and what not, you thinkin' what I'm thinkin' about this killer in Arizona?"

Terri took a deep breath as she kept her eyes on the mirror image of the cafe entrance. "It sure as hell sounds like one, if the reporting out West is accurate. That trooper never stood a chance."

Marc shook his head. "No. Poor bastard didn't have a prayer, if what we think is happenin' is really happenin'. They got no idea what they're up against."

Terri glanced at Marc. "But we might be able to help them now. By killing a law enforcement officer, there is now a federal nexus for investigation."

Marc thought for a second. "Maybe. But we're in Philadelphia and this, eh, thing is in Arizona. How do we go about doing that? Just pick up the phone and tell the cops they might have a werewolf on their hands?"

Terri refocused on the door to the cafe. "If this were a home game, we'd be in better shape. But Sarah started working with the Phoenix FBI office and Headquarters this morning, trying to get a temporary duty assignment for us to get out there. It's a little tricky, but we're counting on our own similar Alex-related crime scenes from last year to help with the justification."

Marc nodded. "Might work. Not too many murders fit this type of profile. Gettin' some boots on the ground out there might give us better insight."

He took a sip of black coffee from the paper cup he'd been cradling in his chilled hands and laughed. "I guess *then* we'll figure out how to tell 'em they got a werewolf on their hands."

"Yeah, that might be an interesting conversation," Terri admitted.

"Have you bounced this off Alex?"

"Not yet. I wanted her to be focused on this meeting today."

"Good call."

Inside the small cafe, Alex sat alone in one of the four booths. Several tables filled the center of the floor with only one occupied, near the door to the restrooms. Four elderly men spoke Albanian while playing a card game. An old television, mounted high on the wall behind the counter, was showing a European futball game between two teams Alex didn't care about. Fortunately, the sound was muted. A young man with wavy dark hair leaned against the counter, back to his customers, watching the game nonchalantly. The indifferent vibe he oozed clearly indicated he would rather be somewhere else. She noted the pleasant aroma of espresso and black tea was offset by the stale odor of unwashed men.

A man with thick gray hair and bushy eyebrows shouted as he threw his cards on the table and raised his arms in triumph. The commotion sent his cane, which had been hanging on the edge of the table, to the floor with a clank. The sound momentarily drew the attention of the only other patrons: two well-dressed men seated in the booth opposite Alex's.

She sipped her tea and casually pretended to read her book. She had chosen to bring a copy of Tolstoy today. It seemed appropriate. Her eyes were on the pages, but her attention was on the two men speaking in hushed tones. She occasionally jotted key bits of information in her notebook. To anyone caring to wonder what she was doing, she was in a world of her own, taking notes on a difficult novel for some class or book club.

From the corner of her eye she saw the two men leering at her. In a whisper, one made a rather rude comment regarding her appearance and what he would like to do to her. Lewd laughter followed. Consciously unclenching her jaw, she offered no indication she could hear their conversation.

The two men finished their meeting. The man who made the comment began sliding out of the booth. "Nikolai, you leave with the check, again!" the seated man said in Russian.

Nikolai laughed as he stood and made his way to the door. "You are a wealthy man, Sergey. You can report this business meeting to the IRS. Perhaps you need the deductions?"

She closed her book and rose to leave as well. The man gave her a lecherous smile as he held the door for her.

"She's out," said Terri.

Terri watched a middle-aged man in a gray down jacket exit after Alex, staring at her rear-end briefly as she walked up the street before mockingly shaking his head and walking the opposite direction. Terri recognized him as Nikolai Portnov, from his driver's license photo.

Alex continued to walk to their predetermined meeting spot, a shopping center parking lot five blocks away. Her clothes brushing over the microphone of the concealed recorder created a rhythmic whooshing sound.

After a few seconds, Alex spoke. "The man who exited right after me was one of the men in the meeting. I believe his name is Nikolai. The other individual in the meeting remains in the cafe. He has thick white hair, wearing designer jeans and a black leather coat, very high quality. He has expensive shoes as well. I believe his first name was Sergey." Her voice sounded tinny coming through the handheld radio on Marc's lap.

Terri got on her car radio to alert the agents in the van. "107 to surveillance team."

The radio crackled, "Go for surveillance team."

"See the guy in the gray coat, that came out with our source? Try to get some good shots of him and ID his car if you can. If not, don't worry, we really want to get the next one to come out. UNSUB has white hair, wearing jeans and a black leather coat. He's our mystery man. Try to get the tags of the car he gets into and some good photos as well. Thanks"

The reply came. "Copy. Will do."

Terri maneuvered the car onto the street and, after a few blocks, turned into the strip mall parking lot. Within a few minutes, Alex arrived and hopped into the backseat.

She removed the transmitter from her coat pocket and handed it to Marc. While he removed the battery and seated the small device back into its Pelican case foam shell, she turned to Terri. "You have changed your hairstyle, Agent Watson. I noticed before but did not have a chance to tell you. I like it very much."

Terri removed her knit cap and absently ran her hands through her recently trimmed hair. "Thanks. But how did the meeting go?"

"Oh yes, you were right. These men are involved in an elaborate theft scheme. The man with the white hair and dark coat who remained in the cafe, Sergey, seemed superior. He spoke fluent Russian. He gave orders to the one who walked out with me, Nikolai. The subordinate spoke Russian with a Romanian accent." She consulted her notes. "The superior instructed the other to quickly secure the remaining cars on the list so they can fill the last shipping container and get the order out. The underling stated some of these vehicles are hard to crack. He was told to not waste time and utilize the crews if necessary. I do not know what crews he was referring to. He did not elaborate." Alex closed her notebook.

Marc nodded. "Anything else you can think of?"

Alex paused briefly, "I do not like these men. I would like to eat them, when you have completed your investigation, of course. Would that be possible?"

It was a matter-of-fact question.

Terri hid a smirk as Marc again explained the do's and don'ts of the criminal justice system. "No, you can't eat them. We've talked about this. That's not how it works here."

Alex seemed disappointed. "These men are pigs and should be treated as such." She folded her arms across her chest as Marc continued to stare at her. Alex and Terri's eyes met in the mirror.

"Very well. I will not." Her lips formed a tight straight line. In her mind, she finished her sentence: "Unless it appears they will escape justice."

Terri decided to change the subject. "Hey, Alex, we'd like to get together for dinner tomorrow night, if you are available. It would be Marc, Sarah, and me."

Alex broke into a smile. "Yes, I would like that very much!" she gushed.

"Great. We'll want to talk about a case and pick your brain a little bit," Marc said.

"How wonderful! I do enjoy these forays into the criminal underworld."

"We'll want to know what your thoughts are on skinwalkers," Terri added.

Alex's brow furrowed slightly and the joy ran from her face. "I see. It is not totally unexpected though. Your inquiry is related to the grisly Pima Predator killings in the state of Arizona, is it not?"

Terri should have guessed Alex was already aware of the serial killings. She was a voracious consumer of news. "It is."

CHAPTER 2

*W*HY IS MY PHONE *alarm going off at 7 am? I know I turned it off. Somebody at Apple must have turned it back on remotely to torment me, make me question myself. They've done it before. Besides, I know they're listening to me.*

I want to put my phone through the wall but decide not to. It's still useful for work. Instead, I put it in the heavy metal box I found at a thrift store. I think it was for milk deliveries, back when that was a thing. My grandma used to have one at her ranch. The metal will block the energy waves, and it won't read my thoughts from there.

It is Saturday. I don't have to go to work today. Sitting on the side of the bed, I stretch. My limbs are waking up, and I can feel the power in them. Then I see the pill bottles lined up on the nightstand. With a sweep of my hand, I send them flying. I won't be taking these again. I have no need for them anymore.

So much to think about. The meal last night was good, despite that cop showing up. He died like he should have, but now I'm not sure it was a good idea. The cops are bumbling idiots. Nobody really cares about the people I've killed so far. They're just cattle. But now that I killed a cop, they're really gonna be pissed off. Not ideal at all, but necessary. My other half needed that.

I know the cops will be hunting for me. So what? People have always been after me. The difference now is I can say, "Bring it on, assholes. I will tear your faces off." I'm not a scared little kid anymore.

The paranoia, as my former doctor diagnosed, keeps me sharp. The thought of once being afraid of these people makes me laugh. Now they're afraid of me, as they damn well should be.

I always knew I was destined for something great. My teachers didn't see it. My family didn't see it. But I could feel it. The only one who could see it was Grandma. She knew. Now my other half and I are fulfilling our destinies.

What should I do today? I've spent the last several months compiling a list of mortal assholes who have wronged me. I strained my memory going back to my elementary school days, then middle school, high school, college, and my jobs. Those that were okay to me will live. Those that weren't will die. Pretty simple. It's not a complete list, but it's close, for now. I'm sure it'll grow as more of these idiots cross me.

I don't feel like working on my list today, as fun as it is; imagining their faces just before I end them brings a smile to my face. They'll know the wrongs they have committed and the payment is due. Looking at these medicine bottles on the floor, I realize I actually do need to add another name to my list. Yeah, Doctor Swanson, I think we'll have one more session to discuss my antisocial behavior.

Standing and stretching, even in this form, I can feel the strength flowing through me. I can't even see the places where the cop's bullets hit me.

Oh wait, here's a lump on my chest. One bullet hasn't been pushed out yet. I brace myself for the pain. A little dig in the flesh with a steak knife and voila, here it is. Looks like a bloody little mushroom. I do a fadeaway jumper right into the plastic bucket with the others. Nothing but net.

Looking down, the shallow wound where I dug the slug out is almost completely healed. Damn, I am amazing.

The incident on the road keeps coming back. Was killing that cop a mistake? I know they'll be after me like a fat kid chasing the Mr. Softee truck. But I'm smarter than them. They won't catch me.

I gotta mix up my hunting between the list and some randos to keep them off my trail. Sometimes I kill for food. Sometimes I kill for fun. Who am I kidding? It's always fun.

It'll take time to get through my list, and I have to be careful. Don't want to bring too much heat down. Even though I'm pretty sure I'm immortal at this point, I hear a voice in my head: "Be a good boy for grandma. Stay patient, Rutty. Stay patient."

I think I'll play some video games and post some thoughts on 8Chan today. Even a living god has to take a day of rest once in a while. I gotta think.

Alex checked the clock. Still over an hour before the food arrives. Of all the skills she possessed, cooking did not make the list. Agent Watson had asked to bring dinner, but Alex refused. She knew allowing Agent Watson to bring dinner would likely mean pizza. She didn't have anything against pizza, provided it was prepared well. But life is too short to not indulge in saporous cuisine from time to time. Thus, she ordered dinner to be delivered from a neighborhood Mediterranean restaurant she enjoyed. Their lamb was seasoned and roasted to perfection. The moussaka was absolutely delightful as was the freshly made hummus and warm pita bread. Her mouth had watered a bit as she placed the order.

Waiting for the food and her guests to arrive, a melancholy mist settled over her, as it often did in quiet moments. Deciding that doing something, anything, was better than steeping in pain, she moved to her expansive bookcase. Removing a few books revealed a small wall safe. After retrieving her secure laptop, loaded with TOR, The Onion Router, and other software gleaned from the dark web, as well as some she had written herself, she settled back at her desk. This was her weapon of choice for the personal war she was waging.

Her fingers rapped on the leather blotter, while the antiviral detection software ran. Finally, a green check mark indicated the device was free of any known infections. A thought flashed across her mind. How many times had someone she was targeting seen a similar green check mark? Most of them never realized their security had been compromised. Of course, most of them didn't know they were being targeted and failed to keep their software up to date. It takes discipline to maintain these protocols. Most people lack that trait. The difference between her and them: she knew she was actively being hunted.

Next she booted up her version of TOR. In short order, a hooded ninja icon appeared on the screen and gave a thumbs up. Now she was ready to connect to the internet.

"Let's see what my trap lines have to show."

The sound of rapid typing filled the quiet of the room. As was the case for the last several months, all her probing attempts had been blocked and, in several instances, a digital poison dagger had been thrown back at her. Her security software had done their jobs well and stopped them. As expected, the FSB and Russian Ministry of Justice were not easy to penetrate.

"You gentlemen have upped your game, I see," she said to herself as her fingers deftly tapped the keys in a rapid staccato. "Well now, what is this?" A smile spread across her face.

The last probing action she checked was the simplest trap she had sent. A sophisticated trojan horse, concealed in an official looking invoice, sent to the manager of the supply department at the Ministry of Justice.

It required a little internet sleuthing to uncover a list of vendors to the Ministry. A little more digging on the list finally revealed a vendor that recently lost its contract. Their website graciously revealed the email address of the billing department. A few hours crafting the phony unpaid invoice with the embedded virus, and it was done.

She nodded approvingly at her work. It looked good enough that someone in the Ministry had opened it, downloaded the PDF invoice, and forwarded it to numerous superiors for resolution. Bureaucracy at its finest.

The trojan horse had opened back doors at every computer network it touched. She was in. Her typing paused while her eyes scanned the department nodes she now had access to. An audible gasp escaped her lips when she read, "Conviction / Incarceration Records."

Her head snapped at the clock. She still had twenty minutes before the food was due to arrive and thirty minutes before her guests. Willing her hands to remain calm, she typed the name Marinka Garin.

Within seconds, her mother's fate impassively appeared on the screen. A tightness gripped her chest and she became aware of her heartbeat. Scanning the record, she discovered her father's arrest and conviction record as well. Apparently, they had been tried together.

Without taking her eyes off the screen, she felt around the desk until her fingers found pen and paper. As if writing a shopping list, she noted the names and titles of everyone associated with the conviction of Marinka and Yerik Garin, then slid the paper under her desk blotter.

Before logging off, a GIF icon caught her eye. She hovered the cursor over the link at the bottom of the page. With the tap of the mouse, the image of a handsome woman filled the screen. Gray hair pulled back tightly, a stark, unsmiling face stared back at her. Alex thought the look reflected sadness and resignation. Her chest ached when she noticed a bruise on the woman's cheek. But it was the bright green eyes, accented with deep crows feet, that drew Alex in.

The room started to spin as a wave of memories flooded her mind, like a swarm of fluttering butterflies. Each beautiful and precious, but also fleeting.

The smell of fresh baked pirozhki and Mama, much younger, dark hair framing her features, taking them out of the oven. Handing me one, "Careful, Catherine, they are hot, my love."

Smile. A soft touch of my cheek. So beautiful.

Sitting on her lap. She is reading a book of poetry to me.

Peace. Joy. Soothing voice.

She is kneeling before me. I am sad, confused.

"Why are the children at school so mean, Mama?"

"Because they are jealous. You are extraordinary, Catherine, and they resent you for it."

Smile. Wiping tears. Comfort.

Mama and Papa, beaming. Both older, looking at my diploma.

"We are so proud of you Catherine."

Squeezing hugs. Joy.

A look of worry, lines on their faces.

"Please be careful, my love. No matter your cause, Catherine, there are always people who will wish you ill."

Concern in his voice. Strong hug. Love.

The doorbell chime rang in her head, snapping her back to the present. Robotically powering down the computer, she nestled it back inside the safe. She replaced the books on the shelf and moved to answer the door. Glancing at herself in the mirror, she realized she was crying.

"You ok, ma'am?" the delivery man asked, as he handed her the cardboard box. Steam rose from the aluminum covered trays. If the circumstances had been different, she would have enjoyed the savory aroma.

Alex gave a weak smile. "Yes, thank you. I have just learned my parents are dead."

A look of shock and sadness appeared on his face. He removed his tweed cap and bowed his head. "I am very sorry, ma'am. Peace to you and your family."

As he backed away, Alex caught his arm and handed him a twenty for a tip.

Closing the door, she said to herself, "How interesting, peace to my family. And what family is that, exactly?" Her old life as Catherine Garin, before her time as a white hat hacker, her arrest for treason, the medical experiments, and ultimately her transformation, was now truly over. It seemed silly, mourning over parents she only recently remembered, yet the hurt was intense. A hollow lonely feeling suddenly filled her.

Then it hit her. Catherine Garin's family was dead. But Alex Stepanova's *family* was alive and arriving in ten minutes.

Now, more than ever, she needed to be around them and feel alive. The heavy thoughts of her parents' fate went into its proper box. The soft memories that had found their way to her consciousness went into the box as well. She would take them out again, when the time was right, when she had time to process the pain. Deep down, she knew where that would take her. Dark thoughts, like spilled ink, were already forming.

She forced them away. Tonight was not the time to let the beast bay at the approaching storm. No, the rest of this evening was about–family.

Terri rang the bell as Marc and Sarah Holmes stood back on the sidewalk, methodically scanning the darkened street and parked cars for anything or anyone that seemed out of place. They were not expecting any trouble, but habits that might save one's life are good habits to keep.

Sarah was the third and final member of the FBI investigative team working with Alex. The top of her auburn bob barely reached Marc's shoulder as they stood back to back. At 5 feet 3 inches, she didn't look like an FBI agent. She looked like a gymnast. When she initially arrived at the FBI academy, several of her male classmates quickly dismissed her due to her diminutive size. However, after she scored a perfect 300 score on the fitness test, smoking most of those same male classmates in the 1 ½ mile run, she earned the nickname Mighty Mouse. Her reputation as a powerhouse was sealed when, in week 11, she arrived back at the academy on a Sunday night, sporting an entry number written on her right deltoid. While others had spent the weekend recuperating, she had competed in a triathlon. In the field, the investigative skills she honed as an analyst, before becoming an agent, had made her an invaluable member of the team.

Alex answered the door wearing a red blouse with a black and white herringbone patterned pencil skirt. Her green eyes danced and a genuine smile creased her face. She looked stunning, and Terri was a little taken aback. Alex leaned in and gave her a warm hug and a kiss on the cheek. She felt her face flush slightly.

"Please do come in. I have ordered dinner, and it just arrived a few moments ago," Alex said as she stepped aside, motioning her guests to enter. "Agent Holmes, how very good to see you. And Detective Peterson, a pleasure as always."

Sarah and Marc entered, each in turn receiving a strong warm hug. Terri thought she heard Marc's back crack.

Marc handed Alex the bottle of wine he had been cradling in his arm.

"I thought we were doing casual tonight?" Terri said, surveying the set dining room table complete with china and lit candles and thinking Martha Stewart would be jealous of this seating.

"Oh, dear Agent Watson, I know you and your brethren have an affinity for take-out Italian cuisine and eating Chinese food from cardboard containers, but there are times where dining on actual plates is called for. I decided this was one of those occasions."

Alex had transferred the delivered food to serving platters and set a lovely table. "Let me get my bottle opener for the wine and I will return in a moment," she said, moving toward the kitchen.

"Eh, it's a twist off," Marc pointed out sheepishly. "Sorry."

Alex glanced down at the bottle, "So it is," she said with a casual laugh. "Very well, let's all be seated then. We can discuss work while we eat, or would you prefer to talk over tea and baklava after the meal? I must admit, I am intrigued by this case you mentioned."

"Over dinner is fine." Terri said, as she surveyed the table. Something was off tonight with Alex. She seemed particularly gregarious and upbeat. Almost too upbeat.

Everyone filled their plates as Terri started. "So, Alex, as you know, there have been a series of killings in the Phoenix area. We would like to get your opinion."

Sarah handed Alex a folder with the press clippings and reports about the murders in Arizona. Terri and Sarah picked at their food while Marc ate with gusto. All three watched as Alex read the contents of the folder, eyes intently focused on the pages.

"Yes, I have read most of these already." Her expression turned more serious as she read the unreported details from the police reports. Without looking up from the documents, she pointed to the table. "The lamb on the kabobs is seasoned to perfection. Please, do not be shy. Eat as much as you wish."

Marc accepted the offer and Terri handed him the platter of kabobs. As expected the meal was delicious. Alex did have impeccable taste when it came to food.

Closing the folder, Alex glanced around the table before she spoke. "This is quite interesting. Without seeing the crime scenes, it is difficult to make a more educated guess. But based on the information provided, my assessment would be that there is likely a shapeshifter of some sort involved."

"That was our thought as well," said Terri. "We are attempting to get more details on the murder scenes through the local FBI office. The Medical Examiner here will try to get autopsy photos and reports as well."

Terri knew Dr. Jerri Williams had reached out to her counterparts in Phoenix earlier in the week, but there was no telling how long it might take to get those reports.

"There are legends of skinwalkers in the American Southwest. Are you familiar with these?" Sarah asked.

"I was not, but after Agent Watson mentioned them to me, I did some focused research. As far as I can discern, my lineage is from Mesopotamia and Europe, so I am not inherently familiar with them. But the reading

I have done on the legends appears to describe a shapeshifting phenom-
enon. Once one peels away the religious and magical overtones, it is
essentially a description of a New World werewolf. Now, is the creature
involved in these particular murders a skinwalker? I cannot say."

"Of course not," said Sarah. We are only guessing based on the location of the crimes and the historical context. Does anything about the
victims indicate a pattern to you?".

"At first glance, I do not see a pattern. Of course, no pattern at all can
tell us a few things."

Marc leaned in. "Yeah? Like what kinda things?"

"Well, if the killings are truly random, the killer may be reckless, prone
to impulse. He or she is not particularly discreet either. Murdering a state
trooper is a very rash action, one that indicates a lack of self control.
Perhaps even a misplaced sense of invincibility."

Terri scribbled her notes of the conversation as Alex spoke.

"Could be a younger person," Marc offered. "Their noggins aren't
finished baking yet and they don't tamp down some of those impulses.".

Sarah glanced over at him and gave him a nod of approval and grin.
"Marc's bringing his A-game tonight," she pointed out jokingly.

Alex smiled."Yes, very astute, Detective Peterson. There is another
possibility. The person or persons may be suffering from a mental illness,
perhaps schizophrenia, or some type of sociopathic disorder. Ratio-
nal thought may have been previously compromised and then further
compounded by the power of the transformation process. It is quite
intoxicating.

She grinned playfully as she took a sip of her wine.

Her mouth puckered slightly. Tilting the glass, she inhaled deeply
through her nose. Quietly setting her glass on the table, she stood. "You

know, I have a lovely pinot noir that I think would play well with the coriander and ginger in the–"

"We are planning to go out there and assist in the investigation," Terri stated bluntly

Alex turned, her brow furrowed. "No, no, no. You must not go." She spoke from the kitchen. "This is not your problem to deal with. I am sure your counterparts in Arizona will prove capable of handling this situation."

She returned with an unopened bottle of wine and set it on the table.

"Alex, as far as we know, we're the only people in the country that understand the true nature of the situation in Phoenix. We have a duty to assist," Terri said firmly.

Alex seemed exasperated. "I understand your noble sense of duty, Agent Watson, but this is exceedingly dangerous. You do not want to cross this creature. If we are all correct with our beliefs, this is a most savage adversary. He or she will have no reservations about attacking you. Unlike me, when we met that first night, I had enough self control and forethought to know killing law enforcement officers was not in my long-term best interest. This one has no such thoughts, as exhibited by the fate of one very unfortunate state trooper."

A silence fell over the group.

Marc broke the tension. "Yo, for the record, we very much appreciate your discretion that night, Alex." He raised his glass in a toast toward Alex. Terri saw what he was doing. Alex usually responded positively to some flattery.

Alex took the cue. She smiled and raised her glass as well. "Thank you, detective Peterson, but actually I am the fortunate one. If I had reacted in a more impulsive manner, it would have been my loss. I would have missed out on our delightful conversations, and, I hope I am not speak-ing out of turn, I would have missed out on our collective friendship."

"You are not speaking out of turn. You are our friend," Terri con-firmed with a smile as Marc and Sarah nodded in agreement.

Despite who she was, she was their friend. Terri took another sip of the wine Marc brought, hoping her taste buds had dulled since the first exposure. They had not. The wine was still bad. Note to self, she thought. Next time, I'll bring the wine. Where did he get this stuff?

"It is interesting that another one of my kind has apparently appeared. I wonder why now?" Alex asked as she deftly removed the cork from the bottle of pinot noir.

"It's possible this has been happening all along, but no one recognized it. If we didn't know you, like we do, we wouldn't consider that expla-nation in the least," Sarah pointed out.

"True. This one seems stationary. Perhaps he or she was recently trans-formed?" Alex stated.

Terri jotted "Stationary. Roots in the area? Recently changed?" in her notebook.

Marc brought the conversation out of the hypothetical and back to the more pressing matter.

"Okay, so let's say we get out there to help those poor bastards. Whatta we need to know? I mean, we can't just sit back and wait for it to die of old age? Does that even happen? I mean, are you guys immortal?"

"Detective Peterson, as always, I do enjoy your directness! You ask a very good question. I do not know in my own case, since I did not come to this situation in the natural way. But I know others before me did in fact die, so I would say no to the question of immortality."

"Well, that's a start at least," he said. "Look, we know bullets are worthless. Howda we defend ourselves, if necessary?"

Alex thought for a moment. "From what I can recall of my previous incarnations, humans have attempted to dispatch my kind for centuries. Sometimes they met with success, but more often they did not, and paid a butcher's toll for their efforts. To your question, it seems the old weapons have proven to be the most useful."

Marc's face fell. "Uh, whatta you mean, like crosses or somethin'?"

Sarah shot him a look, "I told you, that was just in the movies and only for vampires, not werewolves." She glanced at Alex, "Sorry, shapeshifters."

Alex smiled and nodded. "Yes, you are confusing your movie tropes, detective. A Christian symbol, or any other religious symbols for that matter, will mean nothing to this creature.

I am talking about slower moving weapons, edged weapons, arrows, spears, intense fire. Things of this sort. These have been the manner in which humans have defended themselves against my kind over the centuries. I will tell you, as painful as it is, a single mortal wound will not be sufficient to kill this creature. It will require several blows to cause enough damage to overcome the healing properties."

"How is it that bullets don't do it but swords or spears do?" Marc asked.

"I cannot explain my physiology. I can only describe the effects. A bullet striking my flesh, and, in all likelihood, the flesh of our Pima Predator, will only penetrate a short distance. A slower moving weapon will penetrate deeper and slice."

"Like oobleck," Terri said, looking up.

"Oob what?" Marc asked.

Sarah nodded slowly. "I think Terri is onto something. Oobleck is a non-Newtonian fluid. It doesn't follow the rules."

"Would you guys speak English?" Marc asked, exasperated.

"An oobleck is a liquid some of the time," said Terri. "You can slowly push your finger into it and it moves. If you smack it, it instantly turns into a solid, stopping your hand like a brick."

Marc looked around the room. "Am I the only one here that's never heard of this oobleck thing?"

Terri looked at Alex. "So when your flesh is struck by a bullet, it has the ability to instantly stiffen. But as you describe it, a blade moving slowly won't cause that reaction."

Alex nodded. "I believe that is an accurate assessment."

Terri wrote the information in her notebook, while at the same time she tried to imagine how any of it was helpful. Getting close enough to one of these creatures to use the weapons Alex was describing was not very appealing.

Sarah asked, "What about silver? That's mentioned in a number of old myths and stories. Is there anything to it?"

"Silver does have interesting properties," Alex agreed.

"Silver ions are antimicrobial. There may be something there." Terri added, looking up from her pad briefly. "We should talk to Jerri about that."

"I cannot confirm the effects of silver weapons on my kind," said Alex. "You see, they would have been on the receiving end of such implements, and not have had the knowledge of what type of metal was deployed against them."

She continued. "There is also one creature that can destroy a shapeshifter." She looked at Terri. "Another shapeshifter."

Terri met her look, and the silence was back. Sarah and Marc noticed the looks between the two women.

Terri knew what Alex was insinuating. A chill ran down her back. Her jaw locked firmly in place. She did not reply.

Sarah glanced at Alex and Terri. After an uncomfortable few seconds, she tried to break it. "OK, maybe the play is, we get out to Arizona, identify this killer, get Alex on a flight, and we collectively take this guy or gal out?"

Alex remained focused on Terri as she spoke, "I do like the way you think, Agent Holmes. That course of events would be much preferred to having you face this alone."

Turning to Sarah, she said, "I would happily assist you in dispatching this creature. I cannot stress enough how dangerous it would be for you, even collectively, to face this killer. They are not to be trifled with, in any manner."

"So that's it," said Marc. "We get a seat at the table in Arizona and have the 'Alex ace' up our sleeve the whole time. If, or when, we find this ne'er-do-well, we step back and bring in the big guns. We all come back like conquerin' heroes. I like it."

His effusive description of Alex's role appeared to catch her off guard. 'Was she blushing?' Terri thought to herself.

Alex stood. "So it appears we have a plan. Now, who would like some baklava and tea? Or would you prefer coffee? I have a wonderful Turkish roast I discovered at a small shop in Center City. It is very robust and quite strong. I think it will pair beautifully with the honey and walnuts."

Alex watched from the window as her friends walked to their car. The warmth of the evening still embraced her. Despite the discovery she had made earlier, it was one of those brief moments in life where things seemed right. She had been surrounded by people she cared for deeply and knew cared for her. There was a singularity of purpose among them.

She remembered watching Terri's face as the flickering candlelight cast its glow on her. She looked beautiful. Alex felt her heartbeat quicken slightly at the thought.

The soothing embrace of friendship and camaraderie slowly faded in the silence of her home. The bittersweet memories of her mother and father finally kicked open the lid of their box and floated freely in her mind.

"I did love. And I was loved," she said quietly to herself. Years of agonizing uncertainty had been erased in flash, only to be replaced by a new pain.

"I'm so very sorry, mama."

Alex watched the taillights of the car disappear around the corner, and a new terror gripped her chest: an image of one of her kind standing over the torn and bloodied bodies of her friends, roaring in triumph. She closed her eyes to force the thought away, but the impression it made remained.

"I will not let this happen," she swore.

After the meal, the three of them helped Alex clear the table and load the dishwasher. As they departed, Terri couldn't help but notice a different look in Alex's eyes. Was it sadness?

The cold night air braced them as they walked to Terri's car. There, they sat for a few moments while the engine warmed and discussed the working dinner they just had with Alex.

"On a scale of one to ten, how screwed are we if we get out to Arizona and have to tackle this asshole alone?" Sarah asked.

Marc stared out the windshield. "I'd say eleven." He turned to Sarah in the backseat. "You haven't seen Alex in her full form, have you?"

Sarah shook her head. "No, I have only seen her mid transformation. That was pretty scary."

"Yeah, in full form, she's damn-well terrifying. She's a killin' machine. Stronger than anything you've ever seen. Faster and more agile than any animal. And then consider that these here pop guns we carry don't do a goddamn thing but piss her and her kind off. If this thing in Arizona is anything like her, you've got yourself a very bad day ahead if you cross paths with it."

Terri remembered their first encounter with Alex fully transformed. She killed two men that night right before their eyes, tossing them like they were rag dolls. An involuntary shudder ran through her as she pulled the car onto the street.

"He's right. We stand almost no chance against one of these alone. We need to have the right plan and the right weapons. I'll talk to Jerri tomorrow about the silver angle. Maybe there is something there that can help us."

"Yeah, she's our best shot. Not like we can talk to anyone else and ask them how to kill a werewolf," Marc observed.

"Hey, what was up between you and Alex tonight?" he asked, turning to Terri.

"She was giving you some kind of stare there," Sarah added from the backseat. "It was around the part where she was mentioning a shapeshifter can kill another shapeshifter.".

Terri hesitated as she thought briefly about spilling her secret. This was the perfect time. But the words wouldn't come. What would they think? Would their relationship change? She needed to think this through better. "Look, she's odd. What can I say?"

Marc looked at Terri, as if he expected her to keep speaking. When she didn't, he turned and looked out the passenger window. "She is that. Damn glad she's on our side, though."

Back at her condo, Terri lay on her sofa. Max her tabby cat jumped on her stomach and started to knead. She absently scratched his head between his ears and listened to his purr. It was comforting.

She thought about the day when Alex told her she sensed Terri had the 'gene' for lycanthropy. Gene or curse, call it what you want, apparently Terri had it. Alex told her the gene would lie dormant until it was triggered. The catalyst for that? A wound from another lycanthrope. Talk about your movie tropes.

She knew what Alex was insinuating at dinner, and the idea terrified her. Was she really a shapeshifter? And if so, what did that mean?

She glanced at Max, his eyes closed in feline bliss while he rubbed her hand with his whiskered cheek.

Despite Max's best efforts, the weight of the dinner conversation pressed on her. She knew she was in a Hobson's choice. Either she was going to be risking all their lives at the hands of a monster, or she had to become one herself to stop it. They had a plan, but what if Alex wasn't there in time? What if the skinwalker was too strong for her? Would she be forced to watch her friends die, before she, too, was killed?

And if she heeded Alex's call to become a shapeshifter herself, what then? There was no going back. Would she crave flesh? Become a killer? Would she lose herself? Lose her memories of her father?

That Hobson was a real prick, she thought to herself as she closed her eyes and focused on Max's purring reverberating in her chest.

CHAPTER 3

J OHN LIGHTFOOT MANEUVERED THE unmarked blue Dodge sedan onto the shoulder of Highway 87. A ribbon of yellow crime scene tape clung to a rock, whipping in the wind like a striking snake. He glanced over at Ed, packed into the passenger seat, as he put the car in park. Ed let out a groan of relief as he popped the seat belt release and unfolded his large frame onto the roadside. He had played defensive end at University of Redlands, and John always thought if he was a little bigger, he might have been at a Division I school and possibly gotten a look from a pro scout.

"Tell me again, why we comin' back out here?" asked Ed from behind his dark sunglasses as he panned the bleak landscape. "The crime scene guys have been all over this place. If there was anything here, they'd've found it.".

"I know. I just want to take another look. Somebody killed our trooper. I want to walk the ground again, see if we can figure out how it happened. Something just doesn't feel right."

Ed nodded. "Okay, I get it man. We'll give it another walk through."

A slight gust of dry wind caused John to reach up and secure his white straw cowboy hat. "So the jeep was about here," he said, standing in front of his car, holding his hands out.

"And the body of Caitlyn Jones was in front of it." Ed said, pointing to the area of road adjacent to where John was positioned.

"Roger got out of his car and walked around to the front of the Jeep." John mimicked the actions of the trooper from the dashcam video. "He sees the body, leans down, probably to check for vitals, and then he looks up. Why?"

"Something caught his attention. Maybe he heard something? Whoever had killed that girl was still here," Ed said, looking out across the desert.

"Right, then he drew his pistol and moved to his right, staring at his car. Was somebody behind his car?"

"Yeah, you could see him lookin' that way, shieldin' his eyes." Ed walked over onto the asphalt. "The shell casings were all around here." He pointed to the yellow centerline of the road.

"And his body was found on the far shoulder of the road," John said, walking to the location where Roger Pearl's remains were recovered.

A tractor-trailer horn blared, and Ed jogged off the pavement as the big rig roared past. "Sixteen shots, all from 'bout same spot."

John joined Ed at the rear of the Dodge. He peered out across the landscape. "What the hell happened here that night, Ed?"

"Best guess is, he surprised the killer at the scene. The killer then moved around behind his car and–" Ed paused.

"And then what? They did a sweep out there, looking for the slugs from his pistol. They didn't find any. How did the killer survive that barrage of fire? No blood, no nothing. And then get on him and tear his throat out? It just doesn't make sense." John shook his head.

"I dunno, John. I knew Roger from the academy. He was a good dude, competent as they come." Ed looked at the ground.

"All right, so we know what Roger did that night. Let's try to figure out what the killer did." John walked back over to the spot on the road where the body of the girl was found. "He's here, crouched over the body, when he sees the headlights. What does he do?"

"I'd hustle into the desert. Get away from the headlights." Ed said, walking a direct line into the desert from the road. John followed and scanned the ground.

"He wouldn't have to go too far to avoid the lights," John noted. Within a short walk, the two men discovered a small gully 80 yards from the road.

"Yup. I'd hop right in here," Ed said as he slid down the small embankment.

The two men walked south along the dry gully. "Now at some point, the killer comes out and moves back toward the patrol car," John said. "Why? This old creek bed runs for miles. He probably could've just made his escape. Why did he come back?"

"He wasn't done with his first victim, the girl," Ed said, just realizing the thought as he said it. "Damn."

John smiled. "I think you hit on something there, partner. He wanted to do something but was interrupted by Roger."

"She wasn't sexually assaulted. So it wasn't that." Ed suddenly got a funny look on his face, like he had just smelled something rotten.

John saw it and knew what he was thinking. "No, it wasn't that. You saw the girl's body."

"Goddamn. He was gnawing on her when Roger came over the hill, and he wasn't done. What kind of sick sonofa–"

John cut him off. "Ed, look at this." He was pointing at a stone in the gully wall.

"What the hell is that?" Ed asked, removing his sunglasses and squinting.

"I don't know, but let's get a picture of it," John said cautiously.

Ed took out his phone and focused on four large scratch marks on the rock, the photo marker John held up for scale in the photograph showed almost twelve inches across.

CHAPTER 4

Dr. Jerri Williams had just gotten off a phone call with her counterpart in Phoenix. The early signs of a stress headache throbbed like a distant drum. She leaned back in her chair and closed her eyes, hoping the dull ache behind her eyes would ease.

While she tried to relax and let the pain pass, it dawned on her that people aren't too different from the other animals that populate our world. Case in point, when two dogs meet for the first time, they often feel a compulsion to sniff each other's rear-ends. There are perfectly plausible explanations for this from animal behaviorists, but the bottom line is the dogs focus on the non-expressive end of their counterpart to glean some information. The other end is the one that can bite you, but they still want to focus on the derriere.

And then there are professionals. Her experience has been that whenever professionals, doctors in her case, from the same area of expertise meet for the first time, the conversation inevitably devolves into an establishment of position. Who is more senior? Who has the most relevant experience? What schools did each attend? This formality is always guised as pleasant small talk, but in reality it is the recognition of hierarchy among the peers.

Jerri had grown weary of this routine. She had done this dance too many times with too many counterparts over the years. In addition to wasting time, it often led to fellow doctors, usually male doctors, walking away with a false sense of superiority in their educational backgrounds, prestigious residencies, and otherwise general privilege. They would hear of her pedigree and fill in the blanks that she scratched and clawed her way into medical school. They would imagine she struggled with several early classes and had to work long hours to keep up with her more fortunate classmates. This was all true. But they wouldn't learn that through hard work and sheer willpower she had become one of the top professionals in her field. They wouldn't learn her keen and curious mind would put most of them to shame.

Her counterpart in Phoenix, Dr. Stephen Jones, had just wasted thirty minutes of her time with this dance.

Actually, she thought, if he follows through and provides me with the reports, photographs, and tissue samples he promised, the whole thirty minutes will not have been wasted. Only twenty minutes.

They had corresponded by email several times, so he already knew who she was when they spoke about the murders in Jones's city. He also knew, from these correspondences, similar murders had been committed in Philadelphia. And finally, he knew Jerri was hoping to get her hands on material that might help him. Despite coming into the conversation with all that foreknowledge, Stephen Jones insisted on doing the hierarchy dance.

He attended Arizona State University for pre-med on a golf scholarship, then attended Stanford University for his MD, and a residency in Los Angeles at Cedars-Sinai.

He finished with, "I still like to get out now and again and swing the sticks a bit. I'm not a consistent scratch golfer anymore, goodness no, but on a really good day, I can still break par. Not too shabby for a part-timer!"

Somehow, with all that juice behind him, he still ended up looking at dead bodies, same as me. Interesting, Jerri thought.

At some point, he asked Jerri about her background, but she could tell he wasn't really listening. In his mind, the hierarchy had been established.

Eventually, they got down to brass tacks, and he finally admitted he had no clue about the spate of homicides Jerri was calling about. He promised to send her the materials she requested, and then sheepishly admitted that it seemed some of the hair and tissue samples tested had gotten contaminated with animal DNA.

She was not surprised by this in the least. In fact, she expected it. This strengthened her belief that the Pima Predator was a werewolf, or at least a shapeshifter of some type. Of course, she couldn't let him know this. So she graciously told him cross-contamination can happen in the best labs and she would be most appreciative if he could send the items along quickly. She really wanted to tell him that if he focused on this job more than his handicap, he might be able to advance an investigation someday, but she held her tongue.

She knew Dr Stephen Jones wasn't going to miraculously extricate his cranium from his rectum, particularly in regards to this case. He would never be able to recognize the clues before him and make the correct conclusion. No, for while Dr. Stephen Jones was trying to establish himself as the alpha doctor in the room, Jerri was making her own observations. Was he smart? Her father always warned her not to confuse an education with intelligence. Did he have an intellectual curiosity and an open mind? How hard did the man work? What kind of character did he have? Maybe these introductory rituals were useful after all. One just had to know which end was the important one.

There was a knock at her door, and Jerri opened her eyes to Terri Watson poking her head in. "Hey Jerri, do you have a few minutes? I want to bounce something off you."

Jerri smiled. "C'mon in, Agent Watson. I was just on the phone with the ME in Phoenix. He's a piece of work, but he promised to get me the materials." She decided not to belabor her opinion of her counterpart.

"Good deal. Any time frame?"

"He said he'd have them out in a week or so. And, he also mentioned some of the samples appeared to be contaminated with animal DNA."

Terri's eyebrows went up at that news. "Well, I think we're now all in agreement about *what* the killer is. We had dinner with Alex last night, and she's convinced as well. And that brings me to the topic of my visit. What do you know about silver?"

Jerri gave her a suspicious look. "And why are you asking about silver, as if I don't already know."

Terri laid out the plan they hatched with Alex.

Jerri wasn't impressed. She stared across her desk at Terri. "You're not serious, are you?"

Terri let out a sigh. "Actually, I am. You said before, doing nothing is a choice. We can't sit by and do nothing while one of these creatures is tearing a path of destruction through Arizona. We're the only ones who understand the threat. Now we need to figure out what we can do to stop it."

"Look, you and Marc were damn lucky with Alex. It seems she still has some sort of moral compass. I have to imagine, that is a rarity among her kind. What I've read from out West, this one is much less–discerning in its dining habits."

Terri looked at her shoes. "Yeah, that was Alex's assessment too."

"But that isn't going to stop you, is it?" Jerri asked.

"Look, we have every intention of only locating it and having Alex come out to deliver the coup de grace. But if we get confronted, we need to have something to give it a bloody nose and, hopefully, turn it away. Alex suggested 'old' weapons. Edged weapons will cut and penetrate. I saw firsthand with her that they hurt. But the healing is so fast that real damage is prevented. We wondered, if the legends are true, could silver hinder the healing process?"

Jerri blinked twice. "Old weapons? Like swords?"

"Yes, something along those lines."

"So, if I hear you correctly, you are contemplating going mano a mano with a monster armed with what? Swords? You know what? That sounds like suicide to me."

"We are not looking for a fight, Jerri. But we need to be prepared for the unexpected."

Jerri tilted her head to her right. "And just where are you going to get damn swords anyway?"

"There's a blacksmith in Central Pennsylvania that can forge whatever we want. Marc found him on the internet. Said he got pretty good Yelp reviews," Terri said somewhat optimistically.

"Good Lord. I can't believe we're having this conversation," Jerri said, shaking her head in disbelief. "But here we are nonetheless."

She took a deep breath and let it out in a huff and smiled. "So let's see if we can't figure out a way to save your collective butts. Now, silver does have well-documented antimicrobial properties, particularly the silver ion. There just may be something to the old stories."

Terri took out her notebook and started to write as Jerri spoke.

"In humans, it wouldn't matter, but in the case of werewolves and what have you, it may disrupt their cells' ability to rapidly heal. I don't understand what happens in their bodies that allows them to do that.

Believe me, I'd love to know. Probably win a Nobel Prize. But it is likely caused by some mutation that can cause rapid cell regeneration. Perhaps that mutation is disrupted by the silver ions. This is just pure speculation, though."

"I see what you're driving at, the rapidly growing cells may be hindered by the silver, as its antimicrobial properties kick in," Terri said, her eyes lighting up a bit.

Jerri nodded. "Right, similar to how chemotherapy kills the fast-growing cancer cells." She saw Terri's face cringe slightly, before she looked away. "Are you ok?"

Terri closed her eyes. "Yeah, I'm fine. I just–I watched my dad die of cancer. The chemotherapy was awful. I just got a flash of those days. God, it's been twelve years, you'd think I would be past it by now."

"It's all right, honey. Some things we never get over. They'll come back to us at the darndest times," Jerri said.

Terri looked at her hands. "I know. I'm good."

Jerri looked closely at her. "You know, if you need to talk about anything, I'm here. I'm not your doctor or a therapist, but I'm a good listener."

Terri smiled, "I appreciate it, Jerri. Careful, I may just take you up on that. Now, about this silver ion business."

CHAPTER 5

MARC FOLLOWED THE MAP'S instructions on his phone and prayed the signal didn't get lost. This part of Pennsylvania could best be described as abutting up against the middle of nowhere. He was a city kid by nature, but his time in Afghanistan and other parts of the world had taught him skills to navigate open spaces. But those skills involved maps and techniques of terrain association, neither of which were available to him at the moment. All he had was his phone to guide him on the narrow country roads that wound through forest and farmland.

The last directions from Google, when he had left the paved road several miles back, were to turn right on an unnamed road. A chipper voice from his phone announced, "Signal lost."

"Thanks for the update you worthless piece of–" Marc unleashed a gratifying stream of obscenities, a skill he learned in the Marine Corps. When finished, he peered at the wet gravel ahead.

Adding to the disorientation was a steel gray sky, dumping rain and sleet for most of the past three hours. He slammed his brakes as a gap in the trees appeared to his right. "Well, it's a road and it's unnamed," he said under his breath as he eased the sedan onto the tree-lined path.

Arched branches, long devoid of leaves, created a tunnel effect, tightening the claustrophobic feel. Surviving too many ambushes made being in a vehicle with poor visibility uncomfortable for him. The gnawing unease left him restless.

Leaning forward, he strained to see through the windshield during brief periods of visibility, as the wipers fought their running battle with the freezing precipitation. His efforts were finally rewarded when a rusted mailbox on a post appeared out of the rain. Rolling down the fogged window, he saw "K. Flanagan" stenciled on the side.

The quarter-mile driveway ended at a modest two-story farmhouse that could use a new coat of white paint. Behind the house was a small workshop with a sign hanging over the door, "The Celt's Forge." Silhouettes of an ornate celtic cross and some kind of medieval sword bracketed the name.

A short thick man with a full red beard, wearing a kilt and leather apron, appeared in the doorway as Marc pulled up. He waved at Marc and motioned him to come in. It had to be Kieran.

The smell of hot metal and sweat filled the small workshop. The propane forge roared as a block of steel glowed bright orange. Gripping a long steel handle with thick leather gloves, the man pulled the yellow metal from the flames. Expertly hefting the hot metal onto an anvil, he hammered away at it with a large hammer. Bright sparks flew from the now orange metal with each blow. Marc noted the man's forearms were the size of an average person's leg. After a few minutes, he put the metal, now a dull red, back into the forge and turned to Marc.

"You must be Kieran." Marc held out his hand.

"Aye, that I am." Kieran removed the leather gloves and clasped his hand in a strong handshake. "And you're the fella who ordered the seax blades, are ya?" Kieran still had a slight brough from his Irish homeland.

"Yeah, I'm Marc Peterson. We spoke on the phone a few days ago."

"Aye, I remember ya. A rush job, ya said."

Marc surveyed the workshop. The propane forge sat in the middle of the floor with an antique-looking anvil a few feet away, anchored to an ancient black timber and wrapped at the base in a log chain. A large belt sander lurked in a dark corner, like a droid from a science fiction movie. Several hammers, punches, tongs, and files hung above a worn wooden workbench.

"Quite a place ya got here, Kieran. A little off the beaten path though."

He laughed. "Aye, it is. I like it that way. I'm not much for people or cities."

Marc nodded. Despite the cursing on the drive here, he respected the appeal of the simple life this man had chosen. "I can understand that. Some days, I'm not so keen on 'em either."

The blacksmith smiled. "Right then. I've your stuff over here."

Marc followed Kieran to the back of the shop. On the table were three large knives and leather sheaths laid out on a dirty white towel. The single-edged blades were just over twelve inches in length and had the mottled pattern of two different types of steel forged together.

Marc surveyed the items. "Beautiful, but are they sharp?"

"Sharp? You can shave your arse in one pass with these, my friend!" Kieran exclaimed, taking one of the weapons and proceeding to clear a patch of ginger hair off his thick forearm.

"Perfect. They look great," Marc said, hefting one of the weapons in his hand.

"Now, ya said you wanted function over form, so they're not really for displayin'."

"I wouldn't say that, those blades look pretty fancy." Marc looked at the damascus pattern in the red glow of the forge. He squinted.

"Is that writing at the base of the blades?"

"Aye, it is! You've a keen eye." Kieran said, beaming. "I couldn't help meself. It's Nordic runes. No seax blade is comin' out of this forge without a wee bit of Nordic flare. This blade has Uruz, for strength and courage. This one, Algiz, for protection. And the last one has Tiwaz, for a righteous warrior."

He paused, then said, slightly disappointed, "Aye, I could've made the handles real things of beauty, but ya said that wouldn't be necessary. Can I ask what you've planned for these? Not that it's any of my business."

"Nope, it isn't." Marc smiled and pulled out a wad of bills from his coat pocket. "How much I owe ya, my friend?"

Having accomplished phase one of the plan for the day, Marc drove east and was greeted by the Philadelphia skyline shrouded in thick clouds. As expected, the Schuylkill Expressway was anything but. The artery was perpetually congested on dry sunny days. Marc knew the addition of any weather activity would bring the highway to its knees. So he crawled along until he reached the exit for route 23 in West Conshohocken. As a cop in Philly, he'd learned the backroads.

It was late in the afternoon when he reached the federal building. Fortunately, the parking garage was only a few blocks from his next destination. Jeweler's Row is a section of Old City where dozens of small shops advertise watch and jewelry repair, new and used rings, buy-sell-trade options. The one he was looking for had also listed precious metal plating as a service performed.

Pressing the door buzzer, he heard the lock disengage a few seconds later. Inside the small showroom of glass cases, the store owner, a thin old man with glasses resting on the bridge of his nose, eyed him suspiciously. He glanced at the duffel bag tucked under Marc's arm.

"Hi, I'm Marc. I called a few days ago about a plating job."

The old man's face softened and he smiled. "Yes, of course. I spoke to you. Something about some silver plating, if I recall?"

"Yeah, that's me." Marc set the bag on the counter and unzipped it to reveal the sheathed knives. "I wanna get these silver plated."

The old man reached into the bag and unsheathed one of the blades and looked back at Marc in disbelief. "Is this some kind of prank?"

Marc chuckled, "Yeah, I could see how ya might think that, but it's no prank. I need these plated with silver."

The old man shrugged. "It's your money. I require half the cost up front and it'll take a week or so."

"No problem. Here's my number. Gimme a call when they're ready." Marc set his credit card and business card on the counter. The old man swiped the credit card through the reader and handed it back to Marc.

As he turned toward the door, the old man read the business card and asked, "What does a cop want with silver plated daggers? Oh, what the hell do I care? See you in a week."

Ross Gates rapped on the metal door frame before leaning against it. He had just climbed up four flights of stairs from the basement computer lab. A sheen of sweat glistened on his forehead. Ed Stackhouse and John Lightfoot looked up from their computers.

"Ross, my man! You all right?" Ed asked as he spun his chair to face the man.

"Yeah, I just took the stairs. Dang elevator's on the fritz."

John smiled. "Again? I think they're trying to help us get our ten-thousand steps in."

"Well, I probably need the exercise, so I shouldn't complain too much," Ross replied. He did need the exercise. His blue polo shirt started to show sweat in the armpits and strained against the force of his belly, threatening to untuck from his khaki pants. "Anyway, I got what we could from the Pearl body camera."

"Tell me you got something good for us," Ed implored.

"Well, I got something. It's a still image, all I could get off the hard drive." He handed over a thumbdrive. "Damn thing looked like someone took an ax to it."

John's face cringed slightly.

"Oh jeez. I'm sorry. That came out wrong. I didn't mean any disrespect. It's just that the camera was in pretty bad shape, and I mean, I've never seen a body camera damaged like–" Ross realized the more he talked the deeper the hole got, so he stopped.

"Anyway, I'm real sorry about the trooper. Wish I could have gotten you guys more."

John nodded slightly. "Thanks, Ross. We know what you meant. Appreciate you running this up to us."

"Sure thing. Good luck." Ross turned and headed back to the stairwell. At least he would be heading down this time.

Ed popped the thumb drive into his computer, and John walked around behind him. Both men squinted as they stared at the screen.

The only image was a blurry still of two half-crescent-shaped shadows smeared upward against a haze of gray. Ed strained his eyes to make any sense of what the camera had captured.

"Crap. I was hopin' there was something here, but this is useless," Ed said, leaning back in his chair.

John reached down and took the mouse and modified the image. With the image rotated and the contrast increased, the shadows now didn't appear to be mere shadows anymore.

Ed leaned forward, "Does that look like what I think it looks like?"

"If you're thinking of claws, then yes. Where's that picture we took at the scene, the one in the gully?" John asked.

Ed pulled his phone out and opened the image. Holding it up next to the computer screen, he said under his breath, "Oh hell no. This can't be."

John suddenly remembered being a child back on the reservation and hearing a ghost story his grandmother would tell him. It scared him then. And it scared him now.

The rhythmic buzzing of his cell phone on his desk drew him away from the monitor. A 215 area code number appeared on the screen.

"Hello, Detective Lightfoot? This is FBI Special Agent Sarah Holmes from Philadelphia. Have you got a few minutes?"

CHAPTER 6

Doug Bowman left work a little late. There were some efficiency reports to wrap up, and the glitchy software corporate pushed out was not very intuitive. He knew he was no computer whiz, but these new upgrades were awful. Did anyone who developed these things actually try to use them?

He was happy to finally be heading home. His wife had just texted and asked him to pick up some food from Comedor Guadalajara. They had to eat quickly to get their son to the rink by 8 pm for hockey practice. That was fine with him; the old practice schedule had them on the ice at 6 am. That was brutal.

While he eased his pickup out of the lot and onto the street, focusing on the cross traffic, he never noticed the midnight-blue SUV behind him, the one that pulled out of a parking spot at the same time he did.

Rush hour traffic was trailing off, so the drive to Comedor only took a few minutes.

The place was busy tonight. A family of five sat near the hostess station waiting for a table to open up. The youngest, a boy about four-years-old, looked up from the phone game he was playing and stared at Doug in that slightly unsettling impassive gaze children can have. Doug smiled at the child, but the boy simply looked back down at his game.

After he paid, a smiling waitress brought Doug several bags nestled in a cardboard box. The aroma of the food stirred his appetite. He reached in and tore off a piece of hot tortilla from an open bag and popped it in his mouth as he pressed out the door.

I'm practically giddy with excitement. This is what I was made for.

I don't have to wait long before it emerges with a box of food. As it presses the key fob for the lock, I step out.

At first, it is startled, then it recognizes me and smiles.

It starts to speak, but the transformation starts. The smile drains from its face. I am not who it thought I was. I don't have to unleash the full beast, not for this ant. Just a partial transformation is enough to shock it. I wonder what I look like? Does its face register shock because it recognizes a living god?

The shape stepped out of the shadows, and Doug almost dropped his order. His heart skipped a beat initially, but then he looked again.

"Oh, hey. You gave me a scare. Grabbing some grub on your day off, too, eh? This place does a nice–"

The words trailed off. Something was wrong. The eyes seemed to stare through him. They caught the light in a way that made them glow, like a cat or a deer. The head rolled around once and Doug heard the vertebrae crack. When the face stared at him again, it was–different. Only when the mouth opened and he saw the teeth did he realize just how different.

He wanted to run, but his feet stuck firmly to the ground.

I grab its face with my hand and smash the back of its head against the truck door, leaving a dent. The box of food drops onto the ground as its arms go limp. My teeth tear at its throat. Its blood fills my mouth and drains onto the parking lot asphalt. The task is done, and I feel the transformation reversing.

I walk back to my car with one of the bags of food. No sense in letting it go to waste. He won't be needing it. The smell of blood and beef, seasoned with cumin and chili powder, fills my car. I am suddenly ravenous. I shove a handful of the hot food into my mouth. The food is excellent, but the addition of Doug's fresh blood makes my head spin. It's delicious! Why have I never tried this before?

Sarah stopped by Terri's desk. Financial records were spread and stacked over most of the surface. She knew there was a system there somewhere. She just couldn't see it.

"Hey, I talked to that Arizona detective, Lightfoot. They are getting some assistance from the local field office in Phoenix, but after I explained the similarities to the cases we had in Philly, he welcomed the idea of us coming out and to assist. I talked to our man on the desk at FBI HQ, and he's down for it too. He said they would cut the TDY orders to Phoenix as soon as they can free the travel funds up." TDY stood for Temporary Duty. It always bothered Sarah that the Bureau lingo included the Y at the end.

Terri looked lost for a second, and her brow furrowed. "That's good news,"

Sarah read the hesitation. "I thought that was the plan?"

Terri dropped her voice. "It is. I–I just don't like the thought of trying to handle this on the fly."

Sarah knelt down and whispered, "I get it. Lightfoot and his partner, Stackhouse, sound like they're on the ball. Everything I've heard about them indicates they are very good investigators, but they don't know what they are looking for. They need help."

Marc walked by and noticed the impromptu meeting at Terri's desk. "Hey, is this just a girls' meetin', or can I join in too?"

Sarah looked over her shoulder. "Sure, you're practically one of the girls now," she said with a laugh.

"Thanks, I think."

Terri silently shuffled some paper on her desk.

"Everything OK, Ter?" Marc asked.

Terri stood, looked around the squad area, and put her coat on. "Let's go out and get some coffee."

Sarah knew this was code for, 'We need to talk about some serious crap that is not for the rest of the squad to know.'

Nestled around a small round table in the corner of their favorite Old City coffee shop, the three leaned in close over their steaming brews as they talked.

"Look, I know I was gung ho on the plan. As Sarah said, identify and locate." Terri hesitated. "But this could get very dicey. Fast. I'm just having second thoughts. I don't want to wind up on the Service Martyrs Memorial Wall, and I don't want to see your names there either."

She looked down at her coffee.

"I hear ya, Ter," Marc said. "We're all gonna be very careful. Plus, I got a surprise for ya. How do you feel about some knife-fighting classes?"

"Knife-fighting classes?" Sarah asked, turning to Marc.

"Yeah, I splurged and got us some insurance." Pulling out his phone, he showed them the pictures of the weaponry he had purchased.

"Holy crap, Marc! Are those made of silver? What did these cost you?" Terri asked.

"Nah, silver is too soft to make a blade out of. These are forged damascus steel, 150 layer count."

"Sure, whatever that means," Sarah noted, as she looked at the picture on his phone.

"Not important. The beauty is they're tough as hell, sharp as a razor, *and* silver-plated." Marc grinned.

Terri nodded. "Silver-plated. Very smart. Hypothetically, that might work. The steel cuts, minute amounts of silver enters the wound, and, if we are right, slows the healing process. Did you come up with this whole thing on your own?"

Marc beamed, "I did. Not too bad for a knuckle dragger, right?"

Sarah gave him a punch in the arm, "You only drag those knuckles for effect. You're actually pretty smart. I'm onto you now!" Sarah was genuinely impressed with Marc's plan.

"So who's teaching the classes?" Terri asked.

"Eh, look, I'm no expert, but I studied in Okinawa for a bit, while I was in the Marines. I can teach the basics. I don't think we got time for formal classroom instruction."

Sarah shook her head. "Will the wonders never cease?"

Terri laughed—a real laugh finally, Sarah thought. It was good to hear. Terri had seemed a little distracted since the dinner with Alex, and Sarah was worried about her. But things seemed to be shaping up now.

Terri felt pretty good walking back into the squad area. Marc and Sarah's confidence had buoyed her. The addition of the silver-plated blades meant they might have some additional protection if needed. And the pumpkin spiced latte seemed particularly good today.

She was almost at her desk when her boss, Supervisory Special Agent (SSA) Jeff Tyler, motioned for her to come into his office. Jeff had taken over the squad when Jim Martin retired last September. Terri understood one of the constants in the Bureau was change. Agents transfer in, agents transfer out. Supervisors retire or move up, and new ones move in. There was a near constant slow churn.

Like his predecessor, Tyler was what she would call an "agent's supervisor." He had done the job on the street as an organized crime agent for fifteen years before getting the desk. It was his dream job and he wanted to see the squad continue to thrive.

"I'm just finishing your file review," he started. As the SSA for squad 1, he had to periodically review the cases and sources of all the members of his squad. For younger agents, he often offered suggestions. For cases awaiting prosecutorial actions, he called over to his counterpart at the United States Attorney's Office and tried to grease the wheels to speed things along. For experienced agents, the file review process was mostly perfunctory.

"So what's going on with this auto theft ring caper?" Jeff asked, as he set his reading glasses on the desk. "Looks like things are moving along well. There was some good source reporting. I like that. I don't want to see us lose momentum on this. Particularly since these goons are becoming increasingly violent in their larcenous endeavors."

"Completely agree, boss. I didn't get a chance to include it in the review, but I'm working on a pole camera installation on the junkyard in the Northeast. Pretty sure it's a front. Paperwork is almost done and ready to route to the tech squad for installation."

A pole camera was a stationary camera placed to watch a particular address or area. The video images could be monitored live or recorded and reviewed later.

"Tech guys said the install might be a little tricky but they can cook up a plan to do it. I can review the data when I get back from Phoenix in a couple of weeks," Terri pointed out.

He sat back in his chair. "Yeah, about that. Sarah told me it looks like orders for you guys will be coming down the pike soon. Two weeks can be a long time if this case is moving quickly. I'm going to reassign it while you are on TDY," Jim said, bracing himself.

She tried to put on her poker face. "Okay, I think Ned would be a good landing spot. He's uber-organized and diligent. Augie or Jack would do a good job with it too." Terri had opened the case and wanted to see it through to prosecution, but she understood his point. She wasn't happy about the case going to someone else, but she knew the agents she had listed were very good.

"Actually, they're buried. like most of the squad. I'm going to give this to Anthony Jackson."

Terri's poker face disappeared, and she bristled. "Oh come on boss, not AJ. He's under assigned because he couldn't investigate his way out of a paper bag."

She'd had several run-ins with AJ since he had come to the squad. He was what older agents referred to as a 2/20. They have two years in the Bureau but act like they have twenty. On top of that, he was a misogynist. The combination made him utterly repugnant to her.

"Look, I know he can be difficult, but-"

"Difficult? He's an asshole," she said before she could catch herself.

Jeff stifled a laugh. "Maybe, but he's our asshole, and we need to see if he can grow and handle the work we do on this squad. This case is straightforward and he should be able to manage it. Get him up to speed, and file the case transfer paperwork."

Terri stood to leave. "Will do, boss. But if he gives me any attitude, I won't hold back."

"I would expect nothing less," he said with an exasperated smile.

Terri stepped out of Jeff's office and a smile crept across her face. The faint refrain of "The Victors," the University of Michigan fight song, marched across the squad area.

AJ furiously hammered his keyboard and cursed. "Goddamn it."

Even though he was from Boston, AJ had attended college at The Ohio State University. To drive that point home, he adorned his cubicle with copious amounts of OSU paraphernalia. Knowing this and understanding the heated rivalry between OSU and Michigan, someone had recently loaded an MP3 file of the Michigan fight song onto his computer and set up a series of random rules to trigger the music. A small University of Michigan flag also appeared in the lower right corner of his screen and waved majestically while the music played.

The frustration coming from AJ's cubicle was delicious to Terri.

Glancing at Ned across the squad area, she detected the slightest grin creasing his lips. Their eyes met briefly, and she nodded silently. He nodded back. Good man, that Ned.

Terri waited for the final verse to end and the little flag to disappear before she pulled a chair over to AJ. She didn't want to distract him from his anguish.

"Nice song you got there, AJ, but you really shouldn't play it during the middle of the day. People are trying to concentrate around here."

"Funny. Is this your handiwork, Watson?" he asked accusingly.

"Me? I wish, but I'm not tech-savvy enough."

"Yeah, you're right. Chicks and tech don't mix well," he said with a sneer. "So did you just come over to gloat?"

"No, I have some real work to discuss. I'm going on a TDY, and the boss wants me to transfer a case to you."

"Really? What, some dog case you can't crack?"

Terri held her tongue. She was going to try to play nice.

"No, this is a real case. It's all teed up for you. I'll go over it now and send you the case file this afternoon."

CHAPTER 7

A LEX'S BREATH FORMED INTERMITTENT clouds before her in the cold damp of the early December air. She was most enjoying the evening stroll home. However, tonight was one of those times she missed being in a more natural environment. The ambient noise and light pollution of the city created an unnatural world she sometimes found offensive. "But, one cannot just walk to a wonderful restaurant, if one resides in the forest," she reasoned.

She had just finished a satisfying meal at a nearby Polish restaurant, and her mind played the meal over in her head. She had started with some tartar and a delicious beet soup. Then for the main course she had kotlet schabowy and potato pancakes. The food was hearty and savory.

The owner, a lovely woman with a deeply creased face from the old country, was impressed with Alex's appetite.

Alex commented to her in Polish, "It is easy to have a large appetite when the food is so delicious." The old woman had smiled broadly at the compliment and told Alex to please call her *Baba*, grandma in Polish. Alex could tell she pleased Baba greatly by speaking her native tongue. She offered Alex a free dessert of makowiec, which Alex graciously accepted.

Her mind wandered as she walked along the damp sidewalk, recalling her conversation in Polish. She inhaled deeply, enjoying the smell of wet leaves and rain. Using languages from her past incarnations often triggered a memory. Lost in her thoughts, one started to emerge, like a figure walking out of a fog. She consciously relaxed her mind to see what might appear from the mist.

She could see a dozen or so soldiers from the Grand Army approach on horseback. The sunlight reflected off the sabres hanging at their sides as they expertly rolled with the movements of their steeds. Small dust clouds kicked up behind them as they trotted toward the farm. There was a young girl, possibly a daughter, whom she rushed into the house. After telling the girl to remain quiet, the woman in the dream stepped out of the farmhouse and waited for the soldiers to arrive. Alex could feel the anxiousness in the woman. The beast stirred in her, anticipating the battle to come.

Suddenly it vanished, yanked away by a voice only a block away or so. It was feeble and pleading for mercy.

Cigus Varney lay on the sidewalk, blood trickling from his left temple area, where he had been pistol whipped. He looked up in terror at the three men standing over him. Before he could react, the one with the pistol kicked him in the side and laughed. The air rushed out of his lungs and a sharp pain followed when he tried to fill them again. Cradling his arms across his ribs trying to protect them from another blow, he gasped weakly, "Please. Take it. Here are the keys." He tossed the keys to his rental car at the feet of the men.

"Yeah, we'll take it, but gimme your wallet too," one of the men without the pistol demanded.

Cigus reached back and retrieved his wallet, feeling a sharp pain in his ribs as he twisted. With a shaking hand, he held it out. "That's all I have."

The man scanned through the wallet. "Damn, old man, you're broke." He took out the few bills and stuffed them in his pocket. "What else you got?

"My suitcase is in the car. That's it. Please take whatever you want and let me go," he pleaded.

"That won't do, old man," the one holding the pistol said menacingly.

The third man, who appeared to be younger than the others, spoke up. "Why don't we just go? We got the car."

"Shut up! He seen us and he's gonna go to the cops," the man holding the wallet snapped.

"No, I won't go to the police! I won't report this. Please, I beg you."

The man with the pistol pointed it at Cigus's face.

Sure he was going to die, Cigus closed his eyes. Then he heard a female voice, calm but forceful.

The three men stared at Alex, forgetting their tormented prey for the moment. She continued to stride toward them. The one with the pistol laughed and swung the weapon toward her. The one holding the wallet dropped it on the ground and reached into the pocket of his jacket. The third one watched nervously, stepping backward a pace.

She spoke in a voice as smooth and cold as ice. "If you leave now, I won't harm you. But I am warning you, this is my favorite coat and a new blouse. I like them both very much. If you pull that trigger and put a hole in them, I *will* tear your lungs out." Her voice grew deeper and raspy.

"Fuck you, lady."

She registered a metallic click as the man pulled the trigger and the hammer snapped forward. She instinctively dodged slightly, but the weapon failed to fire. The man looked down at the pistol in surprise. She charged.

Snatching the wrist holding the pistol, she yanked the man off balance. Viciously driving her hand into his throat, she lifted his feet from the ground. The blow drove him backwards onto the cold damp pavement. His skull struck with a deep hollow thud. A sinister halo of black blood pooled around his head as unblinking eyes stared into the night sky. He didn't move again.

Looking back over her shoulder at the second man, a glint of light caught her attention as he pulled a knife from his jacket pocket. He brandished the blade with a shaking hand. His eyes wide with fear. The voice trembled slightly as he spoke, "I don't want to hurt you lady, just let me go."

Her eyes fixed on his. A smile spread across her face as she rose from her crouch. The smell of fear oozed from his pores.

"Oh no, you had your chance to leave. You chose to stay and play. So let's play, shall we?" she growled as she stepped toward him.

Swiveling to her right, she easily dodged the wide arcing slash. Before he regained his balance, she lunged. In one fluid motion she twisted his wrist and pulled his arm straight. A sickening pop occurred as she crushed the back of his elbow, separating the joint.

He fell to his knees as a shriek started to form in his throat. The sound was stifled when a strong hand clasped over his mouth.

Staring into his eyes, she spoke. "You have lived a life of violence, preying on those weaker than you. What a waste." A violent twist left his head hanging unnaturally. The limp body slumped forward.

The third man stood frozen. She sensed his terror. His breathing was shallow and fast, his heart racing. In a flash she was on him. Clasping his throat, she pulled his face to hers. Her grip on his neck tightened, then relaxed slightly. "You are barely a teenager," she gasped.

"I'm not part of this! I barely know these guys. They're from my neighborhood and asked if I wanted to make some money tonight. That's all. They said some European guys with funny accents were payin' them to get some cars. That's it. I didn't know they were going to do this!" He held his hands up over his head.

She eyed him closely. "You are young and have a future, I hope. I will spare you tonight because I feel you do not enjoy this life. You will leave now and not tell anyone what you have seen. Do you understand?"

"Yes. Thank you," he squeaked out.

"Do not thank me yet. If I have erred tonight in letting you go unscathed and we meet again under similar circumstances, I will not be this generous." She sniffed him. "What is your name?"

"Donte Crenshaw. My, my mom calls me DC."

"I will remember you, Donte Crenshaw. Now what are you going to tell people about what happened here tonight?"

"Nothing. I, I met up with these guys but left early. I didn't see a thing."

"Good answer."

She released him. He glanced down, one last time, at the two broken men sprawled on the street, before he spun and ran into the darkness.

Alex surveyed the scene. The gray-haired figure sitting up on the sidewalk clutching his side, stared at her. He attempted to speak, but his eyes rolled up into their lids, and he crumpled over.

"Now, what to do with you two?" she said to herself. Her head snapped as the sound of an approaching truck echoed off the buildings.

Carefully collecting the gun and knife with a gloved hand, she placed them in the men's coat pockets. Hefting a body under each arm, she quickly made her way to the corner.

Upon her return to the scene, she retrieved the old man's car keys and wallet from the street, and strode toward him.

The gym was busier than usual. Terri was surprised there were so many workout misfits like her at this hour. She had just finished her run on the treadmill and powered down the video screen, having watched a documentary on space exploration while she logged her miles. Wiping off the equipment, she heard her cell phone ring.

"Hey, Alex, what's up?"

Alex's voice was calm but had an undercurrent of urgency. "Agent Watson, there is a man in my house who is in need of assistance, and I am unsure what to do."

Terri froze in the doorway to the locker room. "I'm sorry, did you say there is a man in your house?"

"Yes. I believe he needs help," Alex stated.

"Is he hurt?" asked Terri

"Yes. He is currently unconscious," Alex confirmed.

There was a slight pause before Terri asked the obvious question. "Um, did you--?"

"No, Agent Watson *I* did not harm him, I found him. But actually, I did have to dispatch two men to save him. He was being most savagely attacked on the street by these men and I believe there was an intention to kill him."

Terri grabbed her gym bag from a locker and started running for her car. "Sit tight. I am on my way."

Three blocks from Alex's home, Terri saw the red and blue lights reflecting off the parked cars and damp pavement. Several police cars and an ambulance were on the scene. An older uniformed officer directed traffic. Flashing her badge, she asked, "Hey, officer. What's going on?"

The officer seemed unperturbed as he leaned into Terri's window. "Looks like a traffic accident. The driver of this here box truck says these two guys flew out into the street, right in front of his truck," he said, pointing to the restaurant delivery truck in the middle of the street with its flashers on. "He says it happened so fast, he couldn't stop. Ran 'em full over. Says they looked like they were airborne when they shot out from between two cars."

He chuckled darkly.

"Wow, that's odd," Terri said casually.

"Yeah, driver seems sober and all, so I don't think he's makin' it up," the officer said, shaking his head. "Recovered a Smith and Wesson 9mm handgun and a knife so far. There's a cop here used to work in the 12th district. Said he recognized one of the flyin' squirrels. Suspected in a bunch of armed robberies. So maybe these guys were running for a reason."

Terri nodded. "Thanks, Officer. Looks like you have it well in hand. Have a good night and stay safe," she said as she rolled up her window.

She eased up the street and around the corner. Several blocks later, she squeezed into a spot.

Alex was waiting for her at the door when she arrived. "Thank you for coming, Agent Watson. Please come in." Alex noticed Terri's sweaty gym attire. "Did you run here, Agent Watson?" she asked.

Terri glanced down at her wet shirt and running shorts. "No, just came from the gym. Where is he?"

Alex pointed toward the living room.

Terri stared at the unconscious man lying on the couch. The pale figure looked to be in his seventies. A purple lump the size of a plum jumped from his left temple. Leaning over the man, she thought his breathing sounded ragged.

"Can you do anything for him?" Alex asked. Terri detected the slightest hint of emotion in her voice.

"He looks rough. I am not an EMT or doctor." Terri's mind raced. This guy should be in a hospital, but that would get very complicated very quickly. She thought about driving him to the ER and dropping him at the door, but he didn't look like he should be moved. There was only one medical doctor she could think to call.

Jerri Williams knocked and stood nervously at the door to the Pine Street address Terri had given her. After several seconds, Terri opened the door. Jerri followed her inside and found the patient on the sofa. A woman with short dark hair knelt beside him, holding his hand. When the woman turned, Jerri was struck by her green eyes.

The woman smiled and stood. "Hello Dr. Jerri Williams. I have heard many good things about you, and I am honored to meet you in person. I am Alex Stepanova."

Jerri shook Alex's hand warily. Her fear and shock must have been evident.

"I see by your expression you know me as well, Dr. Williams," Alex said with a slight nod. "At least you know of me. Please, enough of these pleasantries. I do not wish to hinder your healing efforts." Alex motioned to the elderly patient.

Jerri opened his shirt, a large crucifix necklace lay on his chest. After several minutes of silent examination, she said, "There is an obvious contusion on his head. I'm guessing he has a concussion. There is also a large area of bruising on his ribs. There may be fractures there as well. His heart rate is steady and his extremities show reactions, so I don't think there is spinal injury. I am concerned about bleeding on the brain. Many elderly patients are on blood thinners. That blow to the head could be serious. How long has he been unconscious?"

"Approximately thirty minutes." Terri replied.

Jerri let out a breath. "Look, I am a medical doctor, but I haven't practiced on a living patient in a decade. As you know, the cases I work on now are already well beyond any healing."

"I appreciate that, Jerri. But there was no one else we could call. What can we do?"

"Well, I am inclined to try to wake him up. I can better determine his condition then. Do you have any ammonia?" Jerri asked Alex.

"Yes, I believe I do, in the hall closet. I'll only be a moment," Alex said as she disappeared up the stairs.

Pacing nervously, Terri whispered, "Is it possible that he may have memory loss from the concussion?"

"Yes, even if he wakes up, he may not remember the events immediately prior to his injury. Why do you ask?"

Terri gave Jerri a wide-eyed look and a slight nod toward Alex, who had returned with the ammonia and cotton.

"You see, Dr. Williams, I rescued this poor soul from a trio of men who were in the process of robbing him and showing every indication of wishing to murder him. The poor man may have seen some things–things that may be hard to explain."

Jerri suddenly caught on. "Ah yes. I see. Well, there's only one way to find out."

She waved the soaked cotton ball under the man's nose. His head jerked slightly and his eyelids fluttered open, much to her relief.

"Hello. I am Dr. Williams. Can you tell me your name?"

The man's eyes rolled around briefly before settling on Jerri's face. "Cigus. Cigus Varney," he croaked out.

Jerri asked him several cognitive questions: what year was it? what city was he in? who was the president? He answered them all correctly. She then asked, "Do you remember what happened?"

He thought for a second then looked around the room and found Alex. He stared at her then said, "I was saved by an angel."

"Oh, shit." Terri murmured under her breath.

•

Terri held her paper coffee cup with both hands, enjoying the warmth. Outside, the sky was mottled gray. Wind-whipped rain pelted the tall windows. It wasn't freezing, but it was the kind of cold that penetrated your bones and chilled you from the inside out. Jerri sat next to her, looking tired as she sipped her coffee, waiting for it to both wake her and warm her.

Terri looked up and saw Marc and Sarah approaching her remote corner table of the cafeteria.

"Yo, Dr. J, what brings you to the Federal Building? Sure can't be the food."

Marc unwrapped his breakfast sandwich from its wax paper and took a bite. "It's 7:30 in the morning, how the hell can this thing be dried out already?" he asked incredulously, looking back at the kitchen. "Sorry, just had to let you guys know that the food here hasn't improved. You're smart to just get some joe. So what the hell happened last night?"

"We have a situation." Terri proceeded to relate the events of the previous night.

Sarah sat unblinking, mouth hanging open. Marc looked down at his partially eaten breakfast sandwich and pushed the tray away.

He looked over his shoulder then whispered, "So, if I got this straight, she killed these three guys and brought the victim to her house?"

"Yes," said Terri. "Well, technically, she said she killed two of them. The third one was just barely a teen and had no stomach for this stuff, so she let him go."

Sarah thought for a second. "Well, now there is a silver lining. I mean, she only killed two of them and spared the youngster. Plus, she rescued the victim and seems to be concerned for him. I, for one, think this shows some real personal growth here."

Jerri almost spit her coffee out. She wasn't used to Sarah's wry humor.

"Okay, so what about the two stiffs? Who's got the homicide ticket?" Marc whispered.

"There isn't one, at this time. It's being written up as a traffic accident, truck versus pedestrians. At least that's what the cop I talked to last night was thinking."

"I checked the logs at the Medical Examiner's Office this morning on the way over. Listed as probable traffic accident," Jerri whispered.

"Well that's a lucky break." Marc said, as he sat back in his plastic chair.

"What's the prognosis for the patient?" Sarah asked.

"Well, he seems to be out of any life-threatening danger. His concussion and broken ribs should heal on their own. It will just take some time and rest, hopefully," Jerri said.

"So best guess, how long before he can be released back into the wild?" Marc pressed.

Jerri glanced at Terri before she spoke, "It depends on how well the patient heals. Some people are just good healers and others not as good. On average, I think ten to fourteen days for the floor and up to thirty days for the ceiling."

"Well, that's a problem. We're due to head out to Arizona in a few days." Marc noted as he leaned forward, elbows on the table.

"How much did this guy see of Alex in action?" Sarah asked.

Terri took a deep breath. "He saw enough that he thinks an angel saved him."

"Oh, shit." Sarah laid her head on the table.

"Yeah, that's what I said too. Once he's on his feet a little bit, I plan to give him the 'national security confidentiality' talk. But in the big picture, you two are going to head to Arizona without Alex and me. We'll follow as soon as we have this situation locked down."

"So, Sarah, looks like we're going to have our butts swinging in the fresh breeze with no backup for a bit. You good with that?" Marc asked.

"Guess I'll have to be."

Marc looked out the rain covered window. "Ya know, all of a sudden, this cold don't seem so bad."

CHAPTER 8

B RIGHT LIGHT STREAMED THROUGH the oversized windows as
the steady flow of traffic outside created an almost hypnotic background. The din of the lunch rush at The Toasted Owl Cafe buzzed and
provided a welcome distraction for John Lightfoot–something he and
Ed desperately needed right now. The normalcy of the vibrant crowd
reminded them the world was still alive and generally good. Suze, their
server, set their drinks and straws. "Burgers should be coming right up,
boys."

"Could I get a little hot sauce?" John asked.

"Sure thing, hon," Suze drawled.

John looked out the window at the street scene while thoughts rolled
in his head. One thought, a memory actually, kept rising to the surface.

"What're you thinkin', partner?" Ed asked as he took a sip of his Dr
Pepper.

John looked down at the table and pushed his straw through its paper
cocoon. "You don't want to know."

"Try me. 'Cause I don't have a damn thing," Ed pressed.

John looked up and leaned in. "I'm thinking about those scratch
marks we found in the desert."

Ed nodded. "Uh huh."

"When I was a little kid on the rez, my grandmother would tell me stories, Navajo stories. One of them scared the hell out of me. I guess that's what it was supposed to do, you know, keep little kids in line and out of trouble. Have you ever heard of the skinwalkers?"

Ed didn't say anything but took another sip of his soda and slowly shook his head.

"Well, let me tell you what I remember from her stories. They're called *yee naaldlooshii*, he who goes on all fours. They're spirits that can change a man into a kind of animal. They got red eyes, razor sharp claws and teeth. The story goes that they hunt people. Some legends say they're witches or medicine men who became corrupted by evil. They can possess a person and turn them into one as well. They're powerful, like, physically strong and huge. Almost impossible to kill." John paused. "That was the story anyway. I know it sounds crazy, but you asked."

Ed held his soda, the straw still in his mouth, staring at John. Finally he spoke. "You believe in these things?"

John shook his head. "I didn't. But I will tell you, the tribal elders won't even say the name, because they're afraid it might conjure one."

"You said you didn't believe. Does that mean you do now?"

"I don't know, Ed. I mean, we have eight half-eaten people across the area. And those images we got back from Pearl's body cam. They sure as hell looked like claws to me. I just don't know what I believe anymore." He hung his head.

"So maybe we're looking for someone who *thinks* they're one of these things? And acts accordingly. Wears some kind of claw gloves or something and feels like they need to nibble on their victims."

"Yeah, that makes more sense. Sorry. I was just getting caught up in my own head," John said with a weak smile.

"Course, that don't explain how a trained state police trooper empties his magazine at somebody and still ends up dead on a lonely highway." Ed pointed out. "Panic? Body armor? I can't explain that."

"That one's a mystery. When we catch this asshole, maybe we'll get the answer."

Ed nodded and saluted with his red acrylic glass. "I like that you said 'when.' Power of positive thinking, my friend."

Suze delivered their order. "Here you go, boys. Two double cheeseburgers and fries." Reaching into her apron pocket, she pulled out a bottle of Tabasco. "And hot sauce. Anything else I can get you right now?"

"We're good. Thank you," Ed said, flashing a smile.

"So when do our new friends from Philadelphia arrive?" Ed asked between bites.

"They think next week. Have to get permission from their HQ and funding approved."

Ed nodded. "Coming out here right before Christmas. Interesting. What's with the urgency on their part, I wonder? I mean, I appreciate it and all."

"Yeah, I hadn't thought of that," John noted. "Hey, what do you think about that case from the parking lot last night?" John asked, as he dipped several fries into the ketchup, hot sauce, and black pepper mixture he had created on the side of his plate.

"The robbery gone wrong?" Ed asked.

John jabbed a few fries into his ketchup. "Yeah. Bowman was the guy's name, Doug Bowman. Something about it doesn't feel right."

Ed nodded. "I know what you mean. His wounds didn't look like they were caused by a—anything I can think of."

John took out a small notebook and started writing while holding his hamburger in the other hand. "I'm gonna ask the ME to take another look at that one."

"You think it could be our man?" Ed asked with a slight rise in urgency. "He was all there, though. I mean, he didn't look like he'd been mauled or anything." Ed paused for a moment. "You know he worked at the distribution center where my baby sister works. He was her supervisor."

John set his burger down and his eyebrows shot up. "Oh shit. I didn't put two and two together on that. I'm sorry."

"No sweat. In all the hubbub, I think I forgot to mention it to you."

"How is Trina doing?" John asked.

"She's hanging in there. Shocked, like everyone I guess. She said he was a pretty good dude." Ed said.

"I can believe that. How long has she been there now, five years?" John asked before taking a bite of his cheeseburger.

"Actually, it'll be six next month. She said they treat her pretty well, and she mostly likes the people she works with, so that helps." Ed seemed distracted now.

"Hey, It's probably just like it was initially written up, a robbery gone wrong. Nothing more."

"Yeah. But you got me thinking now." Ed replied quietly, looking down at his plate.

John felt like an idiot. How could he have missed that the victim from last night worked at the same place as Ed's sister? He knew why Ed was upset. Nobody wanted to think their loved one was one step removed from a serial killer. He wrote off the *faux pas* to fatigue. It was a reasonable excuse, but it still bothered him. "I'm sorry, Ed. Let's change the subject. How are your parents liking the sun, sand, and surf?"

Ed appreciated the change. "Oh yeah. The gulf coast of Alabama is treatin' them well. They've become complete beach bums since movin' there. Drinkin' margaritas every damn evening, watchin' the sunset. They text me pictures just to rub it in," he added with a laugh.

"Think they want to adopt another son? Me and the family could use a vacation."

Ed snorted a laugh. "Oh man, they love you, John. I don't think you got to be adopted to visit. They got the room, too. When I was there last year, they showed me the spare bedrooms in their condo. One bedroom has bunk beds with dinosaur wallpaper. I think they were hintin' that they want me to settle down and give them some grandkids."

In the ten years they had been partners, John had seen Ed date several knockouts but never anyone long term. John finished his bite of burger. "Not very subtle."

"Nope. That they are not. I told Trina she better get married soon, take some of the pressure off of me. How about your fam? Is Cheyenne still looking at Arizona State?"

John nodded "Yup. Wants to study environmental science. And since she's become a self-declared eco-warrior, that seems like a good fit."

Ed grinned. "I can see that. She's always liked bugs and stuff. What about Dak? I know he's only a sophomore, but any thoughts on college?"

John chuckled as he shook his head. "If he's had any, he hasn't told his mom or me. He's running track this year and, as far as I can tell, he has no idea what he wants to do."

And I wouldn't worry too much about Dak. He's a good kid. He'll figure it out. I mean, after all, you did."

John laughed. "I wouldn't say I figured anything out, especially lately."

At that instant, both of their cell phones alerted at the same time. John's stomach tightened. This couldn't be good. They were instructed to return to the office.

Ed drove while John called the office. In a hushed tone, Trooper Cantarino informed him that the captain was pissed off that some FBI agents were coming out to assist in the Predator investigation.

John disconnected from the call. "Well, despite completing the necessary paperwork and obtaining all the appropriate signatures, apparently, our captain has just realized a group of FBI agents are coming to town in a few days to share notes."

"And let me guess: now he's afraid they're gonna crack this sucker wide open and steal his glory?" Ed said with a sarcastic chuckle.

"You are an astute investigator, Detective Stackhouse," John noted.

At least they were able to finish most of their lunch.

The cemetery is quiet and almost deserted. There's a burial at the far end from me. Five people in black stand by the fresh earth mounded next to the casket. Must not have been very popular. Nobody's near me so I have the rest of the place to myself. I've always liked to come here, even before Grandma died. Most kids liked to play in parks or playgrounds. I liked the graveyard.

Sometimes, I hear the voices. As a kid, they'd tell me which kid at school to watch out for or which one to punch. I remember coming back from recess in fourth grade, and Tim Knight was standing behind me. The voice told me Tim was talking smack about me, and I needed to stop him. I turned and hit him square in the nose. Once I showed him that I was onto him, he steered clear of me. Maybe I should look Tim up and have a get-together someday?

Today I'm here to talk to Grandma.

She was the only one who believed in me. She said she saw something in me that reminded her of herself. I loved spending time at her ranch. She always had a small herd of angus there. Before they disappeared, Mom and Dad tried to keep me away from her. I think they were scared of her. But I'd go to her house on my bike whenever I could.

The day she showed me her collection of trophies was special. I remember the look of pride on her face as she opened the door to her shed. It looked like the storage room for a museum.

"What is all this?" I asked.

"This is our history," she said proudly.

"I don't understand?"

"Here, take this in your hand," she said, handing me an antique pocket watch. The crystal was broken and the clock face stained with a rust color.

As the cool brass touched my palm, I felt it. Like a dream, but I was awake. I saw a man, I don't know who, riding a horse toward me. His horse reared and threw him to the ground. I watched the animal gallop away. I moved toward the man, still lying on the ground. He looked shocked and scared. A pistol appeared and a flash of light. Then I was on him. He screamed. I felt my teeth tear into his flesh. I never felt so alive before that moment.

She reached over and took the watch from me. The vision was gone, and I was standing in the shed again.

"So, you do have the gift," she said smiling.

"Who was that?" I asked.

"I don't know. It really doesn't matter who the man was. They're just cattle."

"Were you the– hunter?"

"No, dear me, that was my grandfather, Henry Bestia."

"So these go way back," I stated, looking around the shed.

"Yes," she laughed, "I have added many items, but these go back gener-ations. I am just the keeper now. Too old to hunt like I used to. Now when I feel the beast awaken, I go to my herd." She pointed to the field with her cattle.

I thought for a moment about the feeling I had holding the watch. "So, when can I hunt?"

"You're still a little young. It won't be long though."

She closed the door to the shed. Putting her arm around me, she steered me toward the house. "Now, how about some fresh strawberry shortcake?"

What a day that was.

I'm now reminded of the day she passed. I visited her in the hospice home. Lying in the bed, frail and weak, she gasped, "It's time." She took my hand to her lips. I thought she was going to kiss it, but she bit me. Hard. Hard enough to break the skin. Her eyes sparkled as she licked the blood from her lips. "You're a killer now," she said with a wide smile.

She died later that afternoon.

Standing over her grave, I can hear her. "Be careful, my boy. The hunters are after you."

"Don't worry, Grandma. I know all about them. I'm a pretty good hunter myself."

CHAPTER 9

T ERRI HELD THE RUBBER knife just as Marc had shown her, left arm bent with the blade almost parallel to her forearm, as she faced her opponent. In this case the opponent was several trash bags stuffed with loose paper suspended from a rope. Duct tape repairs marked the previous slashes and stabs.

Standing with her feet spread, knees bent, and her weight equally distributed on the balls of her feet, she focused on the suspended Hefty bag man's center.

"From here, you can move forward, backward, or side to side. As you do that, you can slash with the weapon. Let the blade do the work. You can thrust as well, like a boxing jab, very quick. The key is to not over do any maneuver and get off balance. Give it a try," Marc encouraged.

Terri had watched Sarah get her feet twisted as she whacked the bags with the rubber implement. Now, she shuffled her feet, careful to not cross them, and slashed the "weapon" across the black trash bags. Sliding to the side, she slashed again across the back before stabbing it several times. Small puncture marks appeared in the dark plastic.

Marc grinned. "Good footwork, Ter!"

"Show off," Sarah said jokingly.

Terri smiled broadly. Kali knife fighting was a martial art and thus shared many similar concepts with the training she already had: balance, focus, conservation of motion. She was actually enjoying it, until she remembered why they were doing it.

"I think that's enough for today," Marc announced.

"I second that motion; my shoulders are burning," Terri said.

"Same. It doesn't seem that heavy, but swinging this big-ass rubber knife for a long time gets to a girl." Sarah rubbed her shoulders.

"I don't feel so bad now that I know you're whipped, too," Terri said with a smile.

Sarah stretched her arms over her head. "This is a whole different kind of workout than I'm used to. I need to get home and pack anyway."

"I'll box up the real deal knives and FedEx them to Phoenix. We'll pick them up there. God willing, we won't need 'em and they'll turn into conversation pieces."

"Amen." Sarah said, crossing herself.

Terri checked her phone, "I need to swing over to Alex's place. She texted about her house guest while we were fending off the Hefty garbage bag man."

"You want some company?" Marc offered.

"No, I'm good. If she's got anything hot, I'll let you guys know." Terri really did want Marc with her but decided it was the coward's path to use him as a shield. She suspected Alex wanted to talk about her predisposition toward lycanthropy, as Terri referred to it. Alex wouldn't do that with Marc present, but that was only delaying the conversation. Best to just face it head on like a woman.

Cigus looked as if he had just awoken from a nap as Alex entered the living room. She must have startled him when she unlocked the front door. Having finished her lecture for the afternoon, she hurried home to check on him. Normally, she would have enjoyed the discussion with her students on the reign of Ivan the Terrible, the first Tsar of Russia. He was a most intriguing figure. But today, she had been distracted by thoughts of a portly gentleman sleeping on her couch. She did remember to tell her students there would be no more classes for the month. In lieu of a final exam, a paper explaining the structure of early Russian society was due on December 15.

He sat stiffly on the sofa. A grimace appeared on his face for a moment as he adjusted himself. She handed him a cup of broth. He cradled the oversized blue mug in both hands as he sipped the warm liquid. Her appetite awakened slightly at the aroma of the umami emanating from across the coffee table.

He glanced at her over the lip of the mug and set it on the table. "Thank you for the broth, Miss Stepanova. It's very good."

"You are most welcome. It is not homemade, of course, but a high quality bone broth nonetheless. And you may call me Alex, if you wish," she said as she continued to study him.

"Thank you, Alex," he said with a reserved smile. "May I ask, why are you staring at me?"

"I wish to understand you."

"Well, the easiest way to do that is to talk to me. You won't learn much from just observing me," he said with a laugh.

Alex smiled. "Yes, of course. How rude of me. So, where to start, Mr. Cigus Varney? I see you wear a large crucifix under your shirt. Are you a man of faith?"

Cigus glanced down at this chest. "I was. I was a Jesuit. Perhaps, we should start somewhere else?"

Alex detected a flash of discomfort wash over his face and noted the past tense. She wanted to know more, but obliged her guest. "Well, then what brought you to Philadelphia? I took the liberty of examining your wallet and discovered you are from Chicago."

"Yes. My sister died last month, and I was here settling her affairs. I grew up in Philadelphia and planned to return home. I was taking a walk around my childhood neighborhood, when–it happened."

"I see. Do you have any other family?"

"No. I have no wife or children. My sister was my last living relative. I guess I am now truly alone in the world," he said. A tinge of sadness hung in his silence. "So. If you would indulge me, I would like to get to know you as well, Alex."

She shifted in the chair slightly, "Certainly. I think that is fair."

"So you are a teacher?" he asked.

"I am a professor of history."

"How wonderful. Do you have any family?" he asked.

"No, I do not. It appears we are alone together, Cigus Varney." She gave him a polite smile.

"Yes, it seems so. Well, I am happy to have met you. Were it not for you, I believe I would be no more." He paused. "Speaking of our meeting, what happened to the men?"

"Well, as you put it, two are 'no more.' The third one hopefully is on a better path," she stated directly.

"I am not a man of violence or revenge. I am sorry for their souls. A year ago, I would have said a prayer for them and asked God for forgiveness." His voice trailed off.

Alex examined his face. His aura was generally warm and kind, but his face revealed hints of conflict and turmoil.

"How does that make you feel? Killing two men?" he asked gently.

Alex was caught off guard by the question. After a little thought, she replied, "I have a hard heart. I am not troubled by it. But please know, I do not kill wantonly, Cigus. It was necessary to save you." The ease she felt in this man's company was as refreshing as it was unsettling.

His gentle brown eyes found hers. "Where does this hardness, you describe, come from? Were you hurt as a child?"

Absently, Alex answered in Latin, "*Non habeo pueritia.*" *I have no childhood.*

Cigus perked up, "You speak Latin?"

She smiled. "I speak many languages, some living and some dead."

Cigus took another sip of broth. Replacing the cup on the table, he asked, "Alex, this may sound strange, but are you a divine being of some sort?"

She threw her head back with a laugh, "Oh Cigus Varney, I am the furthest creature from divinity you can imagine."

He held up a hand. "Hear me out. Before I lost consciousness on the street, I saw– something. I saw you, but then it wasn't quite you. I saw the way you moved, the speed and strength. And your voice was different, deeper. Don't tell me I was imagining the entire thing."

Alex looked away. "The human mind is not infallible with its perceptions. Perhaps you only thought you saw those things, due to the grievous wounds you suffered."

"I remember you gave them a warning, and then–" The old man paused. "I am confident in my recollection. You are different, aren't you?"

Alex looked back at Cigus. "I sense your inquisitive nature about me may have more to do with your search for a faith you have lost, than an attempt to understand who I truly am. To that end, I will tell you, I am not an angel. I am not a saint. I cannot restore what you have lost." Her tone was harsher than she intended, and she regretted it immediately.

A pained look came over him, and he sat still for a few moments. "Yes Alex, you are very observant. I did lose my faith. Too many years of watching an institution run by old men work only to preserve their power and status. To protect themselves and the institution from the sins they committed. One day, the words I recited rang hollow to me. I knew my time as a priest was over. It's not so easy to walk away from what you thought your core was. It leaves one feeling – hollow."

Alex nodded slightly. "I understand."

"Since then, I have been searching for a sign, if you will, that there is something beyond us. Something beyond our own consciousness." He smiled weakly. "And when I saw you, vanquishing those who meant me harm, I thought perhaps you were the sign."

She softened her tone. "I am sorry. I am not your sign. You should know, I have a particularly dark view of religion. To answer your question, I am different. I have certain abilities. But along with these abilities, I am somewhat–cursed might be the best word. I come from a long line of people with these same traits. From them, I have fleeting memories of those who lived before me." She stopped. "You must think I'm mad."

"No. I don't. Please continue," he encouraged.

"You see, I have a recollection of times long ago. Times before old men seized the reins of religion to drive their chariots of control. I have memories of entire pantheons of gods emerging only to give way to the 'one true god.' And my ancestors bore witness to the corruption of that deity as well. I do not know if there is a God, but my perception is that religion was always about men gaining dominance."

She paused and looked at her hands on her lap. "I am sorry to tell you these things."

He had a look of contemplation on his face as he sat silently for a few moments. "I see. I am not as perceptive as you, but I think you truly believe what you say." He paused. "Tell me, Alex, then what are you?"

She felt a strange connection to this old man and his earnestness. His questions didn't have any motive behind them other than simply trying to gain an understanding. She decided she liked him. "Sitting before you, I am not entirely what I appear to be. As I said, I carry memories of past lives deep in my being. So, in a sense, you could say I am ancient," she said with reflection.

She looked down at her lap and continued, "However, I am reluctant to tell you what I truly am. I like your company, Cigus Varney. I fear you will not look at me the same again or you will run away in fear, if you knew my true nature." She then said in Greek, "*Ánte psófa.*" *Let it go.*

Varney recognized the Greek phrase. He leaned back on the sofa, studying the woman sitting across from him. "Alex, I don't wish to pry. You can tell me what you choose. But I will tell you that I will not be shocked by anything you say. And as for running away, I am in no shape for that!" he said with a slight laugh, gently patting his broken ribs. "But let me ask you a different question. How do you see yourself?"

'Who was this man?' she thought. It was as if he genuinely wanted to know what she felt. As refreshing as that was, she did not have a good response. She had asked herself this question many times over the years. The answer was as elusive then as it was now.

She reflected on the things she had done, the people she had killed. Each one justified, in one way or another at the time, but brutal killings nonetheless. "I do not know how to answer your question, Cigus. I know what I am, in the physical respect, but I am very unsure about my actual being. At times, I have been a dark instrument of death and retribution. Other times I feel like I am a vessel of salvation and justice. Is it possible to be both?"

"Yes, yes, it is possible. Have you ever heard the saying, 'There is no saint without a past and no sinner without a future'?"

She shook her head.

"We are both, divine and damned, at the same time. That duality of our natures leads to a struggle we must constantly wage."

Alex sat silent.

"If I may point out, the fact you ask these questions of yourself, shows you know the path you are on." A warm smile appeared on his face, pushing his ample cheeks up near his eyes.

Alex smiled back. "I do appreciate your thoughts on this. If I *were* a religious person in the least, this might qualify as a sacrament of confession," she said with a laugh.

"Very true. Religious or not, it is helpful to talk. I mean it, I will not judge you, Alex. You may talk to me about any topic you wish. It is the least I can do to repay the debt I owe you."

She leaned across the table and took his hand. "You owe me nothing, Cigus Varney. I am happy you are still in this world."

By the time Terri arrived at Alex's, she could hear laughter through the door. There was a lightness to Alex she hadn't heard before. It was nice to hear.

Upon entering, she immediately noticed Varney's color had improved. His cheeks were a light red, and his eyes were clear and sharp. "It looks like someone is feeling better."

"Yes, thank you. I am feeling much better. I believe it is due to the wonderful care I have received under Alex's watchful eye," he said with a nod to his host.

"That's very good news. But my visit today isn't just a checkup. There's a matter I need to discuss with you, Mr. Varney. I don't know if you remember us meeting the other night. I'm Special Agent Terri Watson of the Federal Bureau of Investigation."

"Yes, I do recall meeting you. You were most kind."

Terri nodded. "Well, the reason I am here is to talk to you about the events of the other evening."

Cigus appeared uncomfortable. He glanced at Alex who was cleaning some dishes in the kitchen.

"I understand you may have witnessed some–things, or at least think you witnessed them."

Cigus nodded solemnly.

"I'm not going to ask you what you saw. But I want you to understand, there are matters of national security at play here. I would ask that you please keep any observations you may have made to yourself. There are certain facets of the events that evening we do not wish to be known outside this house. There is a danger. I cannot get into the details with you, but it is real and present. Do you understand?"

Technically, this wasn't a lie. There was more than a grain of truth to her words of caution. The revelation of Alex's presence to a certain foreign power could trigger a bloodbath on the streets of Philadelphia. It was a fine ethical line she was trying to walk.

He nodded. "Yes. I understand. She is quite remarkable, isn't she? Do you know she speaks Latin and Greek?" he asked.

"Yes, she is remarkable."

Terri was now worried. She caught Alex's eye in the kitchen, who gave her a slight "sorry" shrug. She turned back to Cigus.

"So we understand each other?"

"Yes, I believe we do. I do not wish to bear false witness. But I am an old man, and it seems my memory is fuzzy. If asked about the events leading to my injury, I simply do not recall."

"I don't want to put words in your mouth, but I appreciate your understanding." Terri rose to leave. "Alex, may we talk outside for a bit?"

Standing on the steps in the crisp afternoon air, Terri's anger boiled over. "First of all, what the hell are you doing in there? Speaking Latin and Greek to him? What else did you tell him? I mean, I am trying to keep you safe, and you're yucking it up with some stranger about how he was saved by a mythical creature," Terri hissed in a whisper.

Alex tried to reply, but Terri cut her off. "I'm not finished. Secondly, you cannot simply kill people in the name of–whatever. That's not how this works. We've talked about this. You're lucky that nobody is missing those two. Their deaths look like some kind of half-assed traffic accident. But this could have been really fricking bad."

Alex glared at Terri. "Are you finished, Agent Watson?"

Terri paused for a second. "Yes, for now."

"During the course of our relationship, you have implied you would like me to be more human. Exactly what part of *human* would you like me to be? The part that lies, cheats, is prejudiced, wages war, tortures their fellow man? That is a large percentage of these people. My kind have thousands of years of experience dealing with them. So do not lecture me about the virtues of the way things are to be done." She paused and took a breath. "In the matter of the other night, I did not fully transform nor did I consume those men. I did what I did to save a life."

Terri rubbed her forehead. "Oh, for Christ's sake, I know that, and I appreciate it, Alex. I am not angry at you for saving him." She motioned to the front door with her thumb. "I just wish the details could have been handled a little better."

Alex nodded. "I understand, but when I am presented with a violent situation, I will act. It's instinct. I will not apologize for who I am."

Terri shook her head. "I'm not saying do nothing. Maybe just don't kill them next time. Just give them a good thumping or something."

Alex looked up at the sky and sighed. "I suppose, given the circumstances, I could have simply *thumped them*, as you call it."

"Good. That's all I'm asking. I'm not saying they didn't deserve what they got, but you have to think about your security. Keeping you out of the spotlight is my biggest concern."

Terri felt like she made her point. Now onto the current situation. She lowered her voice even further. "And along those lines, how much does Cigus know?"

"I assure you, Agent Watson, I have not revealed myself to him. He is a delightful companion, and we have had extremely insightful conversations about faith and life and other existential topics. But I have not explained my nature to him."

"So he doesn't know—everything?"

"No. He suspects something but cannot bring himself to believe," Alex whispered.

Terri let out a deep breath. "Okay. So I overreacted. Sorry."

"Perhaps I overreacted as well." Alex sighed. "I have been on edge lately."

She paused a moment before continuing. "I recently discovered my parents died in a Russian labor prison. It seems they were arrested by the FSB shortly after me. I imagine their convictions were a foregone conclusion, as well as their ultimate fate," Alex said, her voice halting.

Terri felt her face register in shock. She had suspected this might be the case. Family members of those found to be revealing Russian state secrets were often arrested in retaliation. Hearing Alex say the words, and sensing the pain behind them, hit her hard. "I'm really sorry, Alex."

"Thank you, Agent Watson. I cannot help but feel it was my fault."

Terri didn't have a good response. "I've learned bad things happen to good people all the time. You were trying to do what you felt was just. They didn't deserve that. You didn't kill them; the system did. You know that, right?"

Alex closed her eyes and nodded. "I have found memories of them, particularly my mother. They are sweet and warm and painful, all at once."

Terri knew the type of pain Alex was feeling. "I'm happy you have those memories, and I know how that feels. When I think of my dad, it's like the joy is swirled with sadness. It's just part of the deal." She reached over and took Alex's hand. "Hey, we're alive, and, as long as we have these memories, the ones we loved are not really gone."

Alex held her hand and laughed. "Thank you, Agent Watson. You are most kind."

Terri smiled. "I can't take credit for it though. I read it on a card in a CVS once."

Alex laughed. "Even so, Agent Watson, the sentiment is much appreciated."

"So, Cigus seems to be doing much better. How quickly do you think we can get out to Arizona?" Terri asked, changing the subject.

"Yes, he is much improved. Although he is still unsteady on his feet. He has mentioned he feels dizzy sometimes when he stands. I am optimistic that in another few days he will be strong enough to care for himself, and we may depart."

"That'd be good. Marc and Sarah fly out tomorrow morning. I don't like them out there alone, so the sooner we can join them, the better."

"I too wish to be with Marc and Sarah. I fear for their safety, as you do." Alex stared at Terri. "You know where these protective instincts we feel come from, don't you?"

"No. Don't say it. We were having a nice moment there, and now you want to bring this up." Terri shook her head. "I knew it. I damn well *knew* you were going to bring it up. My answer is still a firm no."

Alex sighed. "Yes, you have made that clear on multiple occasions. I only bring it up because of the dire situation we will be wading into. Together we can protect Marc and Sarah and stop this threat. You have so much potential power at your disposal, if you will only take it."

Terri blurted, "Potential? To become a werewolf? Then what? Become a killer? Crave flesh? "

Alex's jaw clenched and her green eyes seemed to glow. "Is that what you think of me? Is that what I am to you? A monster?"

"Oh shit, I'm sorry Alex. That came out all wrong. I didn't mean it like that."

"Then how did you mean it?" Alex snapped.

Terri stammered. "Those are *my* fears. You've managed to control the beast side. What if I can't? What if I become a different person? I kinda like who I am."

Alex was silent.

Terri put her hand on Alex's shoulder. "Look, you are an amazing woman. You're intelligent, strong, and beautiful. I didn't mean to hurt you. I count you as a friend, Alex. And sometimes friends argue and say stupid crap."

"Yes. I suppose they do. And for the record, Agent Watson, I like who you are as well."

"Okay, so we're good?"

"Yes, we are good." Alex reached up and put her hand on Terri's.

Terri felt her hand warm under Alex's before she pulled away. Her face suddenly felt flush. It was time to go. She started down the steps but stopped and turned. "Hey, just curious, how did you find the information about your parents' conviction? We checked the public records and there was no mention."

A slight smile came to Alex's lips. "You do not want to know."

Terri thought for a second. "Yeah, you're probably right about that."

***

Lying in her bed that night, Terri kept thinking about the confrontation with Alex from earlier in the day. After much tossing and turning, she finally drifted to sleep, with her cat, Max, lying at her feet.

Suddenly, Alex appeared and took her hand. They walked into a forest, where thick green moss covered the ground. Columns of sunlight streaked through the thick canopy. Alex, now nude, lay on the soft forest floor. Terri removed her clothes and knelt down, softly running her hands across Alex's body. She felt Alex's hot flesh tremble under her touch. Alex reached up and brought Terri's mouth to hers. Electricity ran from her lips throughout her entire body.

Suddenly she jolted awake, surprising Max, who gave her a sleepy blink before putting his head back on his paws. Glancing around her bedroom, she realized she was alone. A slight wave of disappointment came over her. Alone. Was this what her life was destined to be?

Growing up as an only child with a single parent, she had learned to be comfortable being alone. When her mother left the family, it was initially rough. She didn't understand why her mom ran away. Dad tried to explain it as best he could and reassure her that he would always be there for her, but there was a hole. Eventually, she realized the eggshells she had walked on for years around her mother were replaced with bedrock. But she always felt like the odd man out with classmates. Maybe she kept everyone at an arm's distance because she didn't want them to see her pain? Maybe they kept an arm's distance because they *could* see her pain? Whatever the reason, she was left to heal her wound by herself. She adapted as well as a child could, and, by all standards, functioned well in the world. But on the edge of dream space, when it was most peaceful and tranquil, the wound sometimes ached as the loneliness crept in.

She adjusted her pillow and put her head back down. The dream left her uneasy. Thoughts and images of Alex now churned nonstop.

She used a trick she learned as a young girl to purge her mind of nightmares. Though this wasn't a nightmare, her racing mind still needed to be calmed. She took several deep breaths and forced herself to focus on scientific formulas and math problems. It was Terri's comfort zone. Soon, she and Max were again asleep.

CHAPTER 10

MARC AND SARAH LANDED at Phoenix International, collected their luggage and made their way to the rental car bus. Stepping from the air-conditioned building, Marc felt the sudden slap of hot dry air, and it immediately reminded him of Iraq and Afghanistan. A wave of anxiety washed over him as a tremor shook his right hand.

"Wow. Compared to Philly, this is some heat," Sarah remarked.

"Yeah, but they'll tell ya it's a dry heat," Marc said, flexing his hands as he surveyed the controlled chaos of the airport departure area.

"So is an oven. Just sayin'," she said as she removed her jacket, folded it, and shoehorned it into her already full shoulder bag.

They loaded their bags in the trunk of their rented Toyota Camry. Upon starting the engine, they quickly gained a greater appreciation for the invention of air conditioning.

Just as Sarah was convinced they had missed a turn when their destination was announced with a large sign bearing the name FBI Phoenix Division. In a nod to FBI history, a large thumbprint adorned the sign. Local flora decorated the island holding the sign, including saguaro cacti, which someone had delicately wrapped in a red bow. Located about twenty miles from the airport, on the northern edge of Phoenix, it was one of the newer offices the Bureau had been constructing over the last several decades. Ever since the Oklahoma City bombing of the federal building, the Bureau started moving their field offices into secure, fenced, standalone buildings. The location seemed to have been selected with an eye toward privacy, as there were no other structures nearby.

At the front desk of the FBI building, they were met by a young agent, Brad, wearing khakis and a blue polo shirt who escorted them into the office.

Brad felt compelled to conduct an impromptu office tour, pointing out the different squad areas, while guiding them to the violent crime squad supervisor. Unlike their home office, everything was pristine and uncluttered. The smell of new carpet still hung in the air.

Supervisory Special Agent (SSA) Mike Carson was an intense but affable man in his early fifties. A former SWAT team member, he still appeared very fit. The overhead fluorescent lights shone off his shaved head as he stood from behind his desk and shook their hands. "Welcome to Phoenix, the Mecca of Maricopa county," he told them.

Sarah seemed perturbed. "So wait, if this is Maricopa county, why is this killer called the Pima Predator?"

Mike chuckled. "Well, the first victims were found on a ranch, just across the border with Pima County. Some chucklehead in the press tagged the doer as the Pima Predator, and it stuck."

Sarah nodded. "It does have a certain linguistic ring."

"Yeah, it's probably better than my name, the Arizona Asshole. But that's why I'm not a writer."

Not a man that minces words, Marc thought.

"So, you guys think you have some angle on this creep out here? The state and local guys have been beatin' the bushes pretty hard and come up with diddly squat so far. We've been helping out, even before the murder of the trooper, and honestly, we haven't got much either," Mike said matter of factly.

"We hope so. We had some similar murders in Philly last year. Hopefully we can find a connection," Marc answered. He noticed a Marine Corps plaque on the wall behind Mike.

"Look, I'll be blunt. My squad is busier than a one-legged man in an ass-kicking contest. We don't have the time to run your butts all over the state. You'll have a desk here to work from, if you want it. I have a Bu steed for you, so you'll have a car as well. That's about it, as far as resources go."

Marc chuckled to himself. The Bureau had its own language, which he enjoyed learning. The first time he heard an official FBI car referred to as a Bu steed, he had to stop and think for a second.

"You can do what you need. But I'll tell you one thing. We have worked damn hard on building a good relationship with the local guys. Don't go and fuck that up. Understood?" Mike continued.

"Understood. Thank you for the desk. Appreciate the offer of the Bu car, but we got headquarters to pony up for a rental car. We'll stay out of your hair as much as we can," Sarah said. Marc saw a slight cringe on her face as the words left her mouth.

Mike rubbed his smooth head and laughed. "Not much danger of that."

"Were you in the Corps?" Marc asked.

"Yeah, 2nd ANGLICO."

"ANGLICO, 'Lightning from the Sky and Thunder from the Sea.' I was 3rd Marines, Infantry. Semper Fi."

"Semper Fi, Devil Dog," Mike flashed a broad smile. "I knew I liked you for some reason!"

"I'm a Philly Detective, but still a grunt at heart. So with any luck, I know how to avoid steppin' on toes with the locals," Marc said.

Mike came around the desk. "Very well. Go forth, and don't screw up. And especially don't get yourselves killed. The paperwork involved in that is crazy. Although, I read up on you both. I think you know how to take care of yourselves. That was some real hero stuff with those cartel guys last year." Mike looked directly at Sarah as he spoke.

Marc looked at her too. "Yeah, I feel pretty safe with Sarah next to me."

Mike smiled. "Goddamn right. I would too."

Sarah blushed and responded, "Thanks."

Marc noted her reputation was preceding her wherever she went in the Bureau. He could tell being the center of attention still felt uncomfortable to her. She'd need to get over that.

Mike's demeanor softened a bit. "Look, seriously, if you guys need anything, give me a call." He handed them each his card. "I have my cell with me all the time. I have to, I never know what these Neanderthals are going to get into next," he said as he leaned over and looked out over his squad.

The Criminal Investigative Division of the Arizona Department of Public Safety building is a nondescript three story building designed in the function-over-form, standard government, block-style construction so prevalent in the 1970s. The reception area consisted of several rows of chairs bolted to the floor and an old man with white hair seated behind a plexiglass window. He wore a scowl of disdain for all who entered his realm. The worn Happy Holidays placard that hung below his window and fake white Christmas tree in the corner looked like they had both seen their best years a decade ago.

Sarah guessed if you took a blindfolded person into the lobby and revealed it to them suddenly, they would guess "government building" before the cloth hit the ground. Only the Arizona Department of Public Safety seal on the wall distinguished it from similar lobbies in Pennsylvania or any other state.

Scrolling through her emails on her phone, she asked, "What was that angel thing you and Mike were talking about back at the FBI office?"

"ANGLICO, Air Naval Gun Liaison Company. Guys that call in and direct fire from planes and ships," Marc answered.

"Might be a good thing to have around if we locate our boy or girl out here." Sarah said with a nod.

Marc chuckled. "Right? Hopefully we don't need anything that heavy."

The door adjacent to the plexiglass window opened, and John Lightfoot appeared. He was six feet tall with raven black hair pulled back in a short ponytail. He wore a button down shirt and western style blazer with jeans and cowboy boots. "You must be Agent Holmes and Detective Peterson," he said as they rose. The old man behind the plexiglass peered at them over his glasses, and Sarah thought she detected slightly less disdain in his gaze.

Following John, they passed through the heavy door into a wide hallway that matched the lobby in its taupe-colored sterile drabness. "Stairs ok?" he asked. "The elevator's been wonky lately. Hate to get you stuck in there on your first day here."

"Stairs are fine. We've been sitting most of the day. Feels good to walk a little," Sarah admitted.

John nodded. "I know. I hate flying."

After climbing the three flights, they entered another unremarkable hallway. This one at least had signs of life, doors with name plates, conversations, and the smell of microwave popcorn wafting down the hall.

"This is Ed and my office," he said with a point of his finger toward a door as they walked down the hall, "and we have a spot for you guys just down there. It's small but you can use it as home base while you're here." He stopped at a door that had a handwritten sign in calligraphy that read: "Abandon hope all ye who enter here."

"And this is the war room. It was a conference room, but we commandeered it for this case," he said, opening a door.

Boxes of records lined the walls. Notebooks and files covered the large wooden table. A whiteboard stood in the corner. Sarah recognized part of it immediately, a map of the area marked with photos. A massive Black man got up from his chair. She guessed he was easily six-foot-four and close to two hundred and forty pounds of muscle.

"Hi, I'm Ed Stackhouse. Welcome to hell," he said with a slight laugh and a wave of his hand.

Marc and Sarah shook his hand and looked around the room. Holy crap, she thought to herself. Where to start?

John saw her head scanning the room. "Tell you what, why don't you guys drop your bags. We can get some coffee and compare notes. I think that may be the best way to get you up to speed."

"Sounds good. Coffee'd be great," Sarah said, wandering over to the board, studying the map.

She was still staring at the map when John returned. "Here's some coffee. Hope you like it strong."

Sarah grinned as she looked at her mug. It had a smiley face with the caption, "Be nice today...or else" and a pair of handcuffs.

John must have noticed her reaction. "We have a bunch of random mugs in the breakroom."

"I like it," she said, taking a sip. Before he had a chance to ask if she took milk or sugar, she asked, "When can we get out to look at each site?"

"This afternoon, if you want." Ed responded.

"Good, obviously, in chronological order," she said, eyes tracing the lines on the map to the photos.

John whispered, "She's all business. I like that."

Marc nodded back.

The door to the conference room swung open. A uniformed trooper with captain's bars on his epaulets stormed into the room. He was tall and lean with salt and pepper hair buzz cut short. He did not smile as he spoke. "So these are the FBI experts?"

John made the introductions. "Yes, sir. Marc Peterson and Sarah Holmes. This is Captain Cutler."

"Nice to meet you, sir," Sarah said, holding her hand out.

He looked at her hand, then around the room. "I'm gonna tell you straight up: you're here to observe and advise. This isn't your investigation. My people work for me, not you. If I hear you're overstepping your bounds, I'm calling the SAC and getting you removed so fast, it'll make your head spin. Clear?"

Sarah lowered her hand. "Crystal clear."

Cutler nodded as an awkward silence followed. "All right then." He looked at John. "Keep me apprised. I have a meeting." He turned and exited.

Marc looked at John and Ed. "Wow. I wasn't expectin' a big wet kiss on the cheek when we got here, but I wasn't expectin' that either."

John laughed. "Sorry about that. He's not always that prickly."

Ed stood. "Nope. Sometimes, he's worse. Want to get going?"

Marc and Sarah compared notes as the four of them drove from crime scene to crime scene. Where was the body located? What was the estimated time of death? When were the remains discovered? What were the condition of the remains? Approaching the spot on the highway where Trooper Pearl and Caitlyn Jones were found, Sarah asked, "Have you requested a psychological profile from the Behavioral Analysis Unit at Quantico?"

Ed looked back, "BAU? Yeah, we got that in after about the fifth or sixth victim. We keep updating them with details whenever a fresh one pops up."

"What was their assessment?" Marc asked.

Ed glanced back. "You can almost guess, I bet."

Marc closed his eyes and touched his temple, in his best psychic impression. "I'm gonna say, a white male, between 18 and 45 years old, antisocial tendencies, and a mommy fixation."

"Damn, did you read the report?" Ed laughed.

"Naw, that is pretty much what they all say, I think. They're usually accurate, but not overly helpful sometimes."

John pulled over onto the shoulder of the highway. Putting the car in park, he pointed out, "This was the location of the Jeep and State Patrol Cruiser. After we finish here, there is something in the gully over there I want to show you." Ed gave him a look and shook his head.

"I'm going to save you all some time. Johnny thinks we have some kind of skinwalker spirit thingy running around. There was a scratch mark on some rocks out there. Not sure if it's still there, but we have a photo of it."

Marc glanced over at Sarah, who met his look. "Let's go take a look," she replied, not offering any leaning one way or the other to the skinwalker theory.

Marc and Sarah squatted down and looked at the gouged stone closely. She took out her phone and took photographs as well. "I've got no bars out here."

John nodded, "Yeah, reception gets pretty spotty."

"Once we get back to the city, we can send these to Dr. J and Terri, back in Philly," Marc noted.

"What do you think, Ed?" Sarah asked the big trooper.

"I think we have some fool who *thinks* he's some kind of creature. Running around with metal claws and whatnot. I'm not into the supernatural stuff."

"Understood," Sarah said with a nod.

John rubbed the back of his neck, "I didn't say I believed it. I just said there were stories when I was a kid. It's probably just like Ed said."

Sarah felt there was more to John's thoughts on the matter, but she decided she would talk to him about it privately. "All right, I think there is one more. The most recent one, at a Mexican takeout place, right?"

"Yup, last week. He was initially listed as a regular homicide, but upon a deeper examination, the ME agreed with us that it's one of ours," John pointed out.

"And after that, we will conclude our murder tour for the day," Ed commented, as they walked back to the car.

Day one was in the books, and Sarah's head was swimming with the overload of information. Catching up on months of investigative activity was no small task. Marc had an expression that seemed appropriate to the moment: it felt like drinking from a firehose. She felt mentally exhausted, so when John offered to drive them back to their hotel, she was quietly relieved.

The drive to the Fairfield Inn was short, so she knew she needed to act fast.

Glancing at Marc, she said, "Hey John, you and Ed mentioned something this morning I wanted to follow up on."

"Yeah? What's that?" he asked while stopped at a red light.

"Those claw marks in the desert and the legends of the skinwalkers."

"Aw, I was just throwing out old stories it reminded me of. Kid's stuff."

"You know, a lot of old legends have a basis in truth. I'm not saying they're real, but there may have been something in the past that sparked it," she offered.

"Well, maybe that's true, but this is now." He paused. "You don't think there's a real connection, do you?" he asked.

"We don't want to rule anything out without givin' it a good shake first. Do you know any local tribal members we could talk to about those legends, like an elder or somethin'?" Marc asked.

"Yeah, I think I can set something up. I'm not really close to the tribal council or anything, but there is one 'old head' that might be willing to talk to you. He's a friend of my family."

"Great, the other two members of our group are arriving in a couple of days. Think you can have something set up by then?" Sarah asked.

"You guys are serious. You really think there could be a connection?" he asked as he pulled the car into the Fairfield Inn lot. His face was a mixture of amusement and shock.

"Let's just see where it takes us." Sarah said as she climbed out. "See you tomorrow."

Back in his room, Marc broke out a bottle of Glenlivet Scotch he bought at a nearby liquor store. Fishing a few ice cubes from the plastic bucket, he dropped them in the glass. They made a satisfying, almost playful, clinking sound before he poured two fingers of the amber colored libation. Swirling the ice in the glass a few rotations, he took a sip. The warm feeling in his stomach was satisfying.

"Guessing you don't have an IPA in there do you?" Sarah asked.

He shook his head. "Sorry. I'll try to get some tomorrow."

"You know, they have streets named after you: One Way," Sarah said with a laugh. "I guess I'll take one too, as long as you're pouring." She sat in a chair near the window checking her phone. "Jerri got the pictures from the desert and wants to talk."

Marc poured her two fingers on the rocks and added a splash of water as Sarah got Jerri on the phone.

"Hey Jerri, you're on speaker. So, Marc and I are here in Arizona, as you know, and the detectives brought us out to one of the crime scenes and, well, you have the pictures." Sarah took a sip of the Scotch and made a sour face as the liquor bit her throat. She set the glass on the desk.

"Yeah. Those pictures. I can tell you it is not from any animal, wild or domestic, in the Southwest. The scale is way off, way too big. But I'm guessing you guys already knew that."

"Hey Jer, Marc here. How does a claw that size fit with the bodies you examined in Philadelphia? The ones tied to Alex?"

Jerri paused, "It looks to be about the right size. The wounds we saw back here from her attacks would be consistent with something wielding a claw like that."

There was silence. Sarah finally spoke, "Right. That was what I was afraid you were going to say. So, we're likely looking at a creature similar in size to Alex then, correct?"

"Correct. You guys need to be very careful. Understand?"

"Yes, ma'am. We have every intention of steering clear of this guy or gal until we have the resources to make a difference," Marc assured her. He glanced over at the bed. The seax blades, still encased in bubble wrap, lay next to the opened FedEx box.

"Don't you ma'am me, Marc. Listen, I also got the lab reports back on the samples from there. They're consistent with what we saw with Alex last year as well. The DNA resembles human in a few places but predominantly animal otherwise, again the closest match is–"

"Yeah, I remember. Wolf, right?"

"So you do listen to me? Yes, the closest match is canis lupus. They're not 100%, but it's the closest in the database. This is the real deal. So you guys better collectively watch your asses, ok?" Sarah could hear the concern in Jerri's voice.

"Don't worry, Dr. J. We'll be alright," he said as convincingly as he could.

The call ended and they each sat quietly for a moment, thinking.

"Thoughts on the day?" Marc finally asked.

"I don't know. With Alex, there was a pattern, right? She selected men who were bad, violent or something. So far, there doesn't appear to be anything close to a pattern."

"Not one that we can see anyway. I'm not buyin' these are all random. Think about it, if you suddenly found yourself with all this power, wouldn't you want to settle some scores?" he asked.

"Yeah, I think I see what you're getting at. Somewhere in this pile of carnage are people our killer probably knew." Sarah said, nodding slowly. "Which ones, though?"

Marc took out his notes from the day. "All right, Trooper Pearl: wrong place at the wrong time. Eliminate him from the list completely. The other victim that night, Caitlyn Jones: there were signs of predation on her, right?"

Sarah looked over her notes. "Yes. Signs of predation. In fact, John and Ed believe the killer went back to the body after getting rid of the trooper. They didn't elaborate why, but it could be that his or her meal was interrupted."

"That's what I was thinking. All the others were consumed to some degree as well. Now what about the last one, the guy at the taco shop. No sign of predation. Was the act interrupted or was this just a killing? Our doer's been pretty careful about attackin' people with no spectators around. Why kill this guy in a parking lot?"

"I think that may be our first lead, Detective."

CHAPTER 11

AJ EASED HIMSELF IN the chair. The squad 1 area was quiet. Everyone else on the squad had been out late the night before on surveillance of a mob meeting in South Philadelphia and wouldn't be coming in until later. The banter that normally filled the morning was replaced by silence and the low hum of the hard drive as it replayed video the pole camera had captured the night before. The entrance to the junk yard on Aramingo Avenue, in crisp black and white on the monitor, remained almost unchanged on the screen until the clock on the monitor read 0237. Then the headlights of a vehicle appeared on the screen followed two seconds later by the appearance of a dark-colored SUV.

AJ tensed and leaned toward the screen. The car pulled up to the entrance of the junkyard as a man appeared briefly inside the fence. The figure walked to the gate, unsecured the lock on the chain and allowed the car to enter.

AJ paused the video and highlighted the area of the tag and zoomed in. On a notepad, he scribbled the letters and numbers.

Tearing the page off as he stood, he half-jogged down the hall to the radio room. Michelle Connelly had just taken her spot at the communications desk for her shift. An array of three computer monitors formed an arc nearly surrounding her. AJ quickly filled out the form requesting a registration check on the license plate he noted from the video. He could have done it himself at one of the other terminals along the far wall, but he knew Michelle could log into the system and have the results printed out before he could have adjusted the chair.

"Whatcha got?" she asked, taking a quick glance at the form.

"Standard run: registration, wants and warrants on the owner and a check for stolen vehicles."

The keys clicked in rapid succession as she logged into the necessary databases and entered the tag number. Within seconds the printer jumped to life and started spitting paper. "There you go. Looks like it was just reported stolen this morning."

AJ scooped up the printed papers and mumbled "Thanks," as he walked out the door.

Damn, this case Terri handed me might actually bear some fruit, he thought, as he made his way back to his desk.

Alex was already gone when Cigus emerged from the spare bedroom upstairs. He held the handrail as he carefully placed each foot during his descent. His recovery had progressed to the point that he could climb the stairs the night before. Getting into a bed and off the sofa in the living room gave his spirits a lift. But the trip down the stairs was actually more treacherous, he discovered, and a bit terrifying. He hadn't anticipated that. His right foot eventually touched the landing and he breathed a sigh of relief. He made his way to the kitchen and found a note from Alex. She had run out to do some shopping and planned to return in a few hours.

He filled the tea kettle with water and placed it on the burner. While he waited for it to heat up, he perused the kitchen. Earlier, Alex had given him a tour and shown him where she kept her collection of teas. It was a rather impressive assemblage. There was a tea for nearly every occasion. With a nod to his ancestral home, he selected a fine Irish morning blend. He loaded the mesh infuser with loose leaves and set it into his mug.

As he checked the drawers and cupboards, he noticed a distinct lack of cooking apparatuses. There were some assorted pots and pans, basic utensils, and of course tableware. But that was the extent of it. Alex had casually mentioned that she was not much for cooking. The pristine condition of the cookware bore testament to this.

At last the kettle started to whistle. Cigus poured the steaming water into his mug and watched as it began to turn a dark brown. He unconsciously massaged his ribs while he let the brew steep. The bones were healing fine and actually didn't hurt anymore, unless he tried to move too quickly. But the habit of rubbing them was still ingrained. At last, the tea was ready and he made his way to the living room with his mug.

Putting pen to paper, Cigus began to write in his journal. His conversations with his host had left him with many questions. Using his Jesuit training, he sorted these questions then applied information Alex had told him about herself. When he paused to take a sip of his tea, he realized it was now cold.

With a slight groan, he stood and made his way back into the kitchen to microwave his cup of tea. As the brew warmed him from the inside out, he saw a pad of paper and pen on the counter. He started to compile a shopping list. A little walk in the crisp mid-December air would do him good, as long as he didn't have to navigate too many stairs.

Karl Jaeger was working late at his home office. He knew he should be in bed by now. At 91, he needed more rest. If his assistant saw his desk light on, she would surely come in and shoo him to bed. The last several months had been very troubling for him. The Russian incident, as he referred to it, had reared its head last year. The reemergence of that foe forced him to expend increasing resources, both personally and organizationally. The damn Russian fools had been caught playing God a decade ago. And apparently God didn't like it.

He sipped his brandy as he stared at the dossier opened on his mahogany desk. The intelligence report was scant. His operative was fortunate to collect what he had, as the Russian security services had done their usual lockdown with well practiced efficiency. A single blurry picture, a still from a surveillance camera, was attached to the inside of the folder. He had studied it off and on since he received it almost a decade ago. Despite the poor quality of the image, a large beast charging down a sterile white hallway was clearly visible. Abomination.

Peering at the image with a magnifying glass, he used a light switch on the wall as a reference. As he had done many times, he estimated her height. The answer was always the same. She was larger than most. When he initially received the report and image, he had been led to believe the creature had been terminated. And then the explosive events from Philadelphia last year happened.

He finished his brandy, closed the file and locked it in his drawer. He had done all he could do. It was now up to the skill of his network and the blessings of God to move his agenda forward.

Before drifting to sleep, he said a silent prayer his FBI man in Washington would come through.

Already at his desk well before the commuters and carpoolers arrived, Robert had a few items to take care of before the morning meeting carousel began. As an FBI HQ supervisor, he knew this was the quiet time before the daily storm. It was still dark when he stepped from his rented condo in Arlington that morning. The crisp air burned his lungs initially as he walked the four blocks to the Metro stop. The Orange Line train pulled up just as he reached the platform. Getting a seat on the normally crowded train was a silver lining to the early hour.

After reading the message last night, sleep had been elusive. He was already monitoring several situations. The Pima Predator was the most noteworthy at the moment. The others were not named and had not garnered the attention of the press yet.

It was enough to keep him busy during his off hours. And then this new tasking had arrived from Vienna. This one was different. This one would likely require his direct intervention to identify and neutralize.

He started his computer and glanced at the pictures on his desk while he waited for it to boot up. His wife, Marjorie, holding their son, Aaron, smiled back at him. Aaron was going off to kindergarten, and Marjorie was giving him a hug. The memory of their funerals suddenly flashed in his mind. The most precious things in his world had been snatched away. He felt a pain in his chest as it all came back like a wave crashing on the shore. The horror, the anger, and the sorrow all exploded at once. Closing his eyes, he took a deep breath. He told himself it was the lack of sleep that rendered him vulnerable to these thoughts.

He believed everything happened for a reason. One could make the argument that violent deaths of loved ones have no reason. But it was that event that brought him into the Augur's fold. As a seer, the Augur opened his eyes to the dangers lurking in the dark. Through the Augur, he found a renewed purpose. A higher purpose.

Looking back at the monitor, he discovered his computer was now awake and patiently awaiting his login. After inserting his key card and typing his password, he was fully engaged with the system. He entered the search parameters: Philadelphia; Russian Organized Crime (abbreviated ROC); Eastern European Organized Crime (abbreviated EOC); Source Reporting, and a thirty-six month search window.

Immediately, a list of cases populated the screen. Scanning through the electronic files, he noticed a relatively new source had been providing some amazing intelligence. This intelligence spanned events in Russia, which he was pleased to see had been shared with the CIA, as well as some domestic criminal enterprises. Of particular note was the time frame the source became active and the information about a certain research lab in the hinterland regions of Russia. Very specific intelligence that seemed to match up with the information he had been provided with the night before.

He couldn't access the entire source file and thus did not know the identity of the source, but this was a very good start.

He was very fortunate. Working at the Transnational Organized Crime (TOC) - East section of headquarters gave him unparalleled access.

The Augur would be very pleased.

CHAPTER 12

Earlier in the day, Trina Stackhouse reluctantly moved some personal items into her new office. She set her Arizona Cardinals bobblehead next to a picture of her dog, a female brindle boxer named TeeKayOh. Both sat next to a picture of her family. Their joy lit up the frame. It was taken at her brother's promotion ceremony. He towered over them all; his thick arms draped around her mother's and her shoulders. The picture always made her happy.

As she looked around the office, the smile that had started to blossom on her lips shriveled. Being here and setting up shop was weird. It just felt wrong. Doug's funeral was a few days before and here she was, moving into his office. She wanted to advance in the company, but not like this. God knows, not like this.

The murder was a shock. Everyone uses that phrase about unexpected events, but this was an absolute shock. She remembered how she was home that night, heating some dinner, when Ed had called. As he told her about Doug's death, she shrieked and dropped the phone, scaring Tee. The next morning, a stunned silence swept the warehouse as the news percolated across the floor.

Since that awful day, she had struggled to fill his shoes. Her manager, Ron, was patient and took time to help her get her bearings with the reports. "You will do fine. Give yourself time to get into the flow. I'm here if you have any questions," he'd assured her.

Questions? That was an understatement. She'd worked the floor for years and been a team leader for several more. But this was entirely new territory. Feeling pressure to perform like never before, she fell back on the only tactic she knew: hard work.

Trying to make sense of the numbers and the damn computer systems, she'd been burning the midnight oil for the last week. However, glancing at her phone, she realized she might actually leave on time tonight.

Triumphantly pressing the enter key on the last upload, she exhaled. A shape in her doorway startled her. Rutledge, one of her employees, stared at her with a blank expression. She knew him to be a good worker, but also a little off-putting in his demeanor.

"Hey, what's up Rutty?"

Standing in the doorway, he said, "Hi. I just wanted to let you know I think you are doing a really good job, Trina."

She smiled. "Thank you. This is really hard for us all."

"It's a shame, what happened to Doug."

He closed his eyes and inhaled deeply through his nose. "Hey, did you change soaps, Trina?" he asked, matter of factly. "Anyway, I like it. Have a good night." Before she could say anything, he spun and left.

She stared at the door for several seconds. Trying to log out of the computer, she discovered her hands were shaking slightly.

Ezra Swanson sat at his desk, finishing the notes on his last patient session, Gloria Sanchez. A forty-seven year old female with acute agoraphobia. During their next session, they would try some exposure therapy and go to a supermarket together. She was reluctant to the idea initially, but, with some encouragement, he convinced her she could do it.

'Need to get moving if we're going to watch a *Sopranos* episode tonight,' he thought. His wife and he had recently started streaming the show. They were very late to the party because he had been reluctant to watch a show about New Jersey mobsters. But at his wife's urging, he relented. To his delight, he discovered a psychiatrist played a large role in the plot. It was now his guilty pleasure.

The sound of the front door caught his attention. His receptionist, Raymond, had left fifteen minutes ago. He called out, "Did you forget something, Ray?" When there was no reply, he followed with, "I'm sorry, it's after hours. Please call back during office hours tomorrow."

Still, there was no answer. He rose to go check the front of the office area when he heard it. A sort of growl, deep and rumbling. His first thought was that maybe a dog had gotten inside. Hurriedly moving to shut his door, he saw a shadow move across the floor. It wasn't a dog. Someone else was in the office.

The figure appeared in the shadows of the darkened reception area.

"Hello, Doc."

Ezra felt a ripple of unease move through his body.

"Don't you recognize me, Doc?"

Swanson peered at the shape, "Yes, of course. You missed our last appointment. I'm sorry, but this is after hours. Please call the office in the morning for an appointment. If you are in a crisis, we can call an ambulance." He pulled his phone from his pocket.

"Nah, I'm not in any crisis. I'm good, Doc. I wanted you to know that I had a breakthrough. I'm actually really, really good," the figure said grinning.

"Well, that is wonderful news. I am excited to hear about it. Perhaps we can schedule a time to talk?"

"No, I won't be coming back. I think I'll show you how well I am, right now." The figure let loose another growl that sent a shiver through Ezra. "Ya, see, Doc, I don't have those negative feelings about people that I used to have. Now I *love* people."

Ezra took a step backward. Something was wrong. Even in the low light, he thought the shape was–changing. He couldn't quite make it out, but the figure no longer resembled a man.

"Yeah, I love people now. They're delicious," the voice rasped.

Marc threw off the covers and rolled himself to the edge of the bed. Over many years, he had trained himself to immediately start moving when his phone rang in the middle of the night. Moving or not, it still took him a second to remember where he was. Blinking a few times, the hotel room came back to him. He glanced at the caller ID. It was Ed Stackhouse.

"Peterson here," he answered.

"Hey buddy, were you sleepin'?"

"Yeah, it's–" he checked his phone, 0219, "--what normal people are doing at two in the morning. What's going on?"

"We got another murder. John is heading to pick you and Sarah up. Should be there in about ten minutes. I'm heading to the scene now."

"Copy that. Who's the victim?" The cobwebs were cleared now as he put the phone on speaker and started to get dressed.

"Some doctor. Let me check my notes. Dr. Ezra Swanson."

"Okay. I'll wake Sarah and meet John downstairs."

A rapid series of loud raps at his door startled him. Then Sarah yelled out, "I'm already up and waiting on your sleepy ass. Let's go."

Ed chuckled, "I called her first, but I think you guessed that by now."

John filled them in on what he knew so far. Dr. Swanson's wife called it in around 1 a.m. She said she fell asleep watching TV, and when she woke up, she realized her husband hadn't come home. She tried his phone, but he didn't answer. That's when she called the police. She said this was his late night at the office and sometimes he stayed to finish paperwork, but he was never this late. Uniformed officers swung by the scene around 1:20 a.m. and saw the door was ajar. They entered and found the scene.

"What kind of doctor was he?" Sarah asked.

"Psychiatrist." John replied as he turned the corner. The early morning street was alive with red, white and blue lights.

Several police cars and vans from the Medical Examiner and Crime Scene Recovery Unit were crowded into the parking lot. Flood lights illuminated the exterior of the office complex, a sprawling collection of one-story buildings with large letters indicating which identical building was which. A news van was already on scene, shooting footage to be aired later when the city woke. The spectacle was all too familiar to John and Marc in their respective cities.

Ed met them as they pulled up and guided them through the police tape. At the door, they all donned shoe covers, latex gloves, and hair nets before entering. A uniformed officer posted at the door logged their names on a clipboard.

The scene inside the office was horrific. Ezra Swanson, or what was left of him, was literally scattered across the floor and walls. The photographers and videographers were just finishing up as they arrived.

"Holy hell," Marc muttered as he surveyed the room. As a homicide detective in Philadelphia, he had seen murder scenes before, a lot of murder scenes. But nothing like this. Blood stains soaked the carpet but were also splattered onto the white ceiling and eggshell walls.

Sarah was silent. She carefully walked around the room, trying to process what had happened here. Her stomach lurched.

Overwhelmed by the violence of the scene in the office, she made her way to the waiting area. There, she noticed the scheduling book for the practice lying on the floor.

"John, take a look at this."

John flipped the book open with the back of a pen and saw most of the pages were torn out. "Bag this and mark it for fingerprint analysis," he told one of the evidence technicians.

Suddenly, an officer called out. Another victim was found in the parking lot, a young male in his car.

The four of them made their way to the new location as the yellow crime scene tape was being unrolled around a gray Honda Accord. A body slumped over the center console. John shined a flashlight into the car, and Sarah saw the passenger seat was soaked in blood.

A cameraman from the news van ran toward the vehicle, rolling video as he approached. Running next to him was a blonde news woman breathlessly reporting into a microphone what she was seeing.

Ed found a young officer standing by his squad car. "Keep them the hell back," he barked, pointing at the news crew. "This is a crime scene, not a goddamn circus," he swore under his breath.

Back in the war room, Sarah dropped her shoulder bag and collapsed into a chair near the whiteboard. Plugging her phone into the charger, she saw it was only 4 p.m. Her stomach was a mess. Too much coffee and not enough food left her feeling nauseated and hungry at the same time, a strange combination.

Marc came into the room carrying several grab 'n' go sandwiches from the convenience store up the street. He tossed her a ham and cheese packed in a little cellophane triangle and a bag of Munchos.

God bless that man, she thought.

"Everybody get some chow," he said, handing out sandwiches and chips to John and Ed as well.

Sarah needed no encouragement. She had already torn open the plastic container. The spongy white bread, ham, and processed American cheese tasted like manna. She noticed Marc did not eat until everyone had started.

Marc washed down a mouthful of chips with a deep swig of water. "Okay, I'm just goin' to call it; that wasn't a random attack. Our doer killed the receptionist guy in his car, got the keys to the office to get to the doc."

John nodded. "I think that makes the most sense. There was no sign of forced entry and the keys were found just inside the door."

"Yeah, I can see that. But then what the hell happened? It looked like he was put in a blender without a lid," Ed Stackhouse said, staring at the ceiling.

Marc and Sarah exchanged looks. She spoke up, "I agree with Marc. This was a targeted killing. I think this one was emotional. Obviously, one would immediately think of a patient."

"Pulling surveillance video from all the cameras we can find right now. We also got teams out interviewing every person listed in his schedule book, but that only goes back a week," John affirmed.

"We need to see all the patient files," Sarah pointed out. The food was hitting her blood stream, and she started to feel more like herself.

"I know. Apparently they kept the active files in a locked closet at the practice. Old patient files were moved to a storage facility. The doc's partner is giving us a hard time about physician - patient confidentiality, though." John sounded exasperated.

"What the hell? His partner just got torn to pieces in his office, and this guy is giving us a hard time on the files?" Marc asked as he shook his head.

"We'll get 'em. We may need to knock out a search warrant application. That'll take some back and forth, though. Courts have been pushing back on government overreach with medical records lately," John pointed out.

Sarah thought he looked beaten down.

Marc frowned. "Can't imagine they would deny this search warrant, given the circumstances."

"Yeah, I agree. We just have to make sure all our ducks are in a row with it. Prosecutors don't like getting applications tossed back," Ed pointed out.

Sarah nodded. "In the meantime, can we get a list of employees who worked for the guy killed at the restaurant? Doug Bowman?"

"We've done that, already. We've talked to every known contact, employee, employer, ex-boyfriend, ex-girlfriend, neighbor, ex-neighbor, fucking mailmen, and every other connection you can think of for every victim. And so far it's added up to a pile of crap." John hung his head. "I'm sorry. I'm just frustrated."

"Don't apologize, we get it." Sarah said.

"My sister worked with Doug Bowman, the Tex-Mex guy." Ed said quietly. "We've talked to her about her co-workers, and nothing jumped out. We checked all the names of current and former people he worked with and came up with nothing but a few ex-felons who lied on their applications. We interviewed 'em, ran 'em every way we could and eventually cleared 'em." Ed set a sizable box of folders on the table. "Here they are. The ones with criminal records have a red tab."

"Thanks," Marc said as he hefted the box.

John stood, and the deep bags under his eyes were plainly visible. "Okay, I think everyone's beat. We're not going to get anywhere dead tired. You guys have some homework there. I'll run you back to the hotel, and we'll reconvene tomorrow."

"Yeah, I'll keep working on the warrant for the files. Best lead we've had in this case." Ed said, standing as well.

Marc took half the files and set them on the desk in his room. "I'll go through this pile and let you know if anything jumps out."

"Damn, we got a lot of material to cover," Sarah commented as she surveyed the stack.

"Reinforcements should be here in a couple of days. That should help," Marc pointed out.

"True. Once the alpha gets here, hopefully we can make some headway."

"Yeah, it'll be good to have Terri here," Marc said as he flipped open the first file and glanced at the contents.

"Right, but I was talking about Alex, the alpha," Sarah said with a laugh.

Marc chuckled. "You have a point. We got two alphas headin' our way."

Sarah thought about that for a second. "I don't want to know what that makes us," she said, shaking her head.

As she turned to leave with her files, Marc caught her arm, "Hold on a sec. I think it's time you started carryin' this."

He handed her one of the sheathed seax blades.

"Think so?" she asked reluctantly.

"I do. This guy–"

"Or gal," she pointed out.

"Or gal, is rampin' up or spiralin' down, depending on how you look at it. These killings are comin' fast and furious now. This last attack was all but a scream to come and get me. I got no doubt in my mind that the killer knew this doctor and knows we'll eventually find 'em."

"So, why do we need to arm ourselves like Viking raiders now?"

"You saw the news crew out there. We–you, me, John, and Ed–have all been filmed. What if your man decides to turn the tables and come after the pursuers? Just carry it in your bag. No one'll ever know your packin' medieval steel."

Sarah thought for a second then took the large blade and put it in her backpack. "Didn't think of that. I knew I brought you along for a reason," she said with a grin as she walked out the door.

CHAPTER 13

*W*HAT A DAY. *I feel good. Like, really good. My unscheduled session with the doc was very satisfying. After last night, it's like something woke up inside me. Everything is crisper, like things look in the light after a rain. Sounds and smells are so intense. I can hear my neighbors, Ted and Joann, getting ready for work. Not that I never heard them before, with these cheap ass walls. But now I can hear everything, even when they aren't yelling. Every damn word that comes out of their dull mouths sounds like they're in my apartment.*

When I came home last night, I paused by their door. I could smell the pizza they had for dinner. But I could also smell them. And then, when I focused, I could hear their breathing from the back bedroom. I imagined them curled up under their blankets, dreaming of some boring bullshit. A thought crossed my mind. Maybe I should pay them a visit? But I decided that didn't seem like a good idea. Hunting this close to home felt like an unnecessary risk.

These sounds and smells almost overwhelm my brain.

My brain. I can feel it working differently. I see the world in a whole different way now. All I think about is hunting. I replay my previous kills and await the next. Grandma, you didn't tell me about this part.

All I care about is satisfying my urges. And why shouldn't I? I'm divine.

Alex carefully removed the tags and folded her newly purchased clothes before placing them in her suitcase. She had never been to the American Southwest and decided she needed a new wardrobe for the occasion. The local REI store had been able to provide several combinations that were both practical and met her exacting standards. Several other items, which she had ordered online, had just been delivered.

The aromas emanating from her kitchen piqued her appetite. Cigus was feeling much better and offered to prepare dinner for them. He made it well known he was no gourmet. But what he lacked in skill he made up for in zeal and effort. He was a delightful presence.

She finished packing and appeared in the kitchen doorway. "I must admit, Cigus Varney, that meal smells wonderful. Is it shepherd's pie?"

"Yes! It's my mother's old recipe. One of my favorites," he said as he donned the oven mitts and removed the glass baking dish from the oven. "Now, I will warn you, I had no luck finding real shepherds at the supermarket, so I had to use beef and lamb instead," he joked.

"Yes, although savory, fresh shepherd is rather in short supply," Alex said with a laugh at her own inside joke.

The entree was hearty and satisfying, as all peasant dishes seem to be. Alex was quiet during the meal. When finished, she stood, thanked him for cooking and began clearing the table. Cigus stood in the kitchen door as she started to load the dishwasher.

"So, you are off to Arizona tomorrow?" he asked.

"Yes, my FBI friend and I are flying out in the morning," Alex said while placing the plates in the appropriate racks.

"I sense some trepidation, Alex. Am I correct that this is not a trip for pleasure?"

"It is not. It is a work trip. My friends may need my services," she said as the last of the flatware was loaded.

"And by services, am I correct to assume you do not mean your extensive knowledge of European history?" Cigus asked.

Alex paused. "Yes, that would be a sound assumption."

Cigus nodded. "I see. Whatever this trip involves must be extraordinarily dangerous then."

Alex closed the dishwasher door. Turning to Cigus, she said, "It may be. I worry about them, my friends. They have good hearts and intentions, but they may not fully grasp the danger they face."

"And you do?" he asked gently.

Alex didn't blink as she looked at him. "I do. I am intimately familiar with it. I intend to face it with them."

Cigus met her look. "Is it dangerous for you as well?"

Alex thought for a second. "Yes, I suppose it is."

"Both physically and spiritually?" he asked.

"What do you mean?" Alex asked, tilting her head slightly.

Cigus paused, then said, "We humans are strange animals. As a society, we ask young men and women to do unspeakable things in the name of security and patriotism. Many come away emotionally broken from the horrors they have done and seen. It's tragic, and I do not want to see this happen to you."

Alex started to say something but Cigus held up his hand and continued. "You said before that you have a hard heart. I disagree. I can tell you are good at your core, Alex. You have love in your heart. I can see it. Never forget who you are. You do what you must, but never forget the *why*. It is for the love of your friends that you expose yourself to this. And that love will bring you back."

Alex felt her eyes fill. "Cigus, there is something you should know–about me."

The old man looked at her with patient curiosity.

She closed her eyes. "When we talked before, I was reluctant to tell you about myself."

He smiled. "Yes, my dear. I recall. And I will tell you again, whatever you tell me won't change the way I feel about you."

Alex felt her heart catch as Cigus used the term "dear." She had not heard that term directed at her with love and sincerity in a very long time.

"Cigus, what you witnessed, the night we met, was true. I have a very dark and formidable side. I am descended from a lineage of–"

"Lycanthropes?" he asked quietly.

Her eyes shot open. "How did you know?"

He nodded. "I suspected it. My time as a Jesuit has taught me to always have an open mind."

"And you are not afraid?" she asked in amazement.

He shook his head. "No my dear, I am not afraid. I have gotten to know you. The real you, Alex. You are my guardian angel. How could I be afraid of that?"

Alex crossed the room and wrapped her arms around the portly sage in her kitchen. Cigus winced slightly at the powerful hug.

The early-morning traffic was light as Terri pulled out onto Pine Street. Cigus had walked Alex to the car and said goodbye to them both. He had a strange forlorn look on his face. Alex seemed a little on edge too.

She wondered if this was still fallout from the argument they had the other day? Or was it what was waiting for them in Arizona? Or was it something else?

She decided to test the waters. "You okay?"

Alex stared straight ahead as she spoke. "Yes, Agent Watson, I am just a little preoccupied. For some unknown reason, I am thinking about my family this morning. Thoughts of them have been rather pervasive over the past several days."

"Have you learned any more?" Terri asked as she watched a SEPTA bus pull into her lane.

"No, nothing noteworthy. I believe I'm still processing the ramifications of their deaths. Perhaps having Cigus with me has shown me what I have been missing; someone who accepts me unconditionally. It is odd, I did not remember my parents until I saw the pictures associated with their file. But I now feel a loss." Alex sounded distracted.

"File?" Terri asked.

"Yes, the FSB file," Alex replied, matter of factly.

"FSB file? As in the Russian secret police, FSB? How the hell did you see their FSB file?" Terri's voice rose.

Alex turned to Terri. "Oh, Agent Watson. I attempt to bare my aching soul to you, and you want to know about a file? Yes, the file was attached to the Ministry of Justice file I discovered in the Russian computer archives."

"What?" Terri jerked the car back into her lane.

"Rest assured, I was extremely careful. Once I learned what I needed to know, I have not attempted to gain access to their systems again."

Terri was practically screaming. "Did it ever occur to you that hacking into the Russian government network was *exactly* what got you jammed up the first time? Landed you in that lab? Got your parents arrested and killed?"

Alex looked down at her hands folded on her lap. "Yes, the irony of that did occur to me."

"Promise me, here and now, you won't do anymore crap like that without talking to me first," Terri said sternly.

"Yes, Agent Watson. I promise I will not make any attempts to access their systems without talking to you."

She paused. "Does that mean you care about me?" she asked playfully.

Terri could feel Alex's eyes on her. "Yes. And I also care about avoiding an international incident if they find you."

"I see," Alex said softly.

Terri glanced over and saw Alex biting her bottom lip. "What else? I can tell there's more."

Alex spoke quietly. "Yes, there is something else. I am hesitant to bring it up."

"If you tell me you've been reading Vladimir Putin's email—"

Alex laughed slightly. "No, we have discussed all the new developments on that front. This is more—personal." She took a deep breath. "You see, as I mentioned, I have been enjoying the company of Cigus and exploring my memories of my family. I realize it is important to have people in my life. People close to me."

"Uh huh." The crush of traffic on I-95 south was building and Terri focused on the impending freeway merge.

"I am feeling a yearning.," Alex said hesitantly.

Terri could feel her hands tightening like coils around the steering wheel. "Uh huh. What kind of yearning?"

"I think I would like to start a family. I have considered several options, and I have chosen Detective Marc Peterson to be the best option," Alex blurted.

Terri's eyes went wide and she spluttered, "What?! No. You can't do that!" The car drifted toward the center lane, currently occupied by a gray Honda Pilot, which unleashed a blaring horn.

Alex looked pained by Terri's reaction. She stammered, "Are you romantically involved with Detective Peterson? I am very sorry to have mentioned this if–"

"Me with Marc? No. But–"

"Perhaps I should ask Agent Sarah Holmes?" Alex asked.

"Sarah? No! I mean, I don't know about Sarah. But you can't do that!" Terri spluttered.

"Why?" Alex asked sincerely.

Terri said the first thing that came to her mind, "It is against regulations," she blurted.

"Oh Agent Watson, aren't we beyond that now? I believe there are several regulations we have bypassed. Certainly, this is a more minor rule that can be worked around," Alex pointed out.

Terri fumed. She didn't like being put on the defensive. "Yes there have been some regs we have had to bend and work around, but I–we have tried to maintain the integrity of the law at every turn. But this–this would go so far over the line that–"

She paused and thought for a moment and decided on a different approach. "Alex, having you two as a couple, beyond the regulatory red line, could be very dangerous for him. You can take care of yourself, but I know Marc. He would feel a responsibility to protect you."

Alex looked surprised. "Protect me? As if I am some vulnerable damsel that needs defending? That is as humorous as it is insulting," she fumed.

Terri willed herself to speak in a clear, even tone. "I didn't say it made sense, but I know him. He's a protector by nature. Look, Alex, he is a sworn law enforcement officer. You're an active FBI source working with Marc and me. Sleeping with sources is severely frowned upon. People have gone to jail over stuff like this."

Alex was silent.

Terri stared at the road and the crawling traffic ahead. She realized her heart hurt and she felt on the verge of tears. "I can't believe this. You fell in love with him? Actually, I can believe it. I get it. We all work together very closely. We spend a lot of time together. But I'm telling you, if you start a romantic relationship with him, you will be putting his career and life in jeopardy."

Terri didn't need to look at her to know she was annoyed. Alex did not like to be told no.

After several seconds, Alex responded. "Agent Watson, there are a number of areas I feel I need to address. Firstly, I am not 'in love' with Detective Peterson. I am not seeking a marriage or relationship with him. I said I wish to start a family, and I would like him to be the father, nothing more."

Alex took a breath.

"And if my role with your organization is an impediment, then I should think I could simply cease that position. Rest assured, I would continue to assist you and the others, as deemed necessary."

Terri's lips were pressed tight. Her face flushed under Alex's intense stare. For chrissake, she thought. I'm an emotional wreck.

Working with Alex was always going to be a challenge but she didn't see this one coming. She could make all the arguments she wanted, but in reality, she knew Marc was an excellent choice. She let out a heavy sigh.

"All right, in light of this development, I will complete the paperwork immediately to end your formal cooperation with the FBI."

"Thank you, Agent Watson," Alex said curtly. After a pause, she added, "I am sorry if this conversation was difficult, but I felt it was necessary."

Terri suddenly realized there was a major component that hadn't been addressed, "Have you spoken to Marc about this?"

"No. I wanted to ensure that any proposition would not impose upon our collective friendship," Alex reasoned. She had learned what she needed.

Terri nodded. "You know, there is a chance he may decline."

Alex looked straight ahead. "Yes, there is that possibility. But I truly doubt it. He is a man." Alex then turned to Terri to reassure her, "I will not discuss this further until this matter in Arizona is resolved. We do not need any distractions."

Terri released a deep breath. "No shit. Everyone's gonna need to keep their head in this game." Terri said the words, but her own head was still spinning.

Having the matter resolved for the moment didn't ease the pain in her chest. Focus on the job, she told herself.

While sitting in the American Airlines gate area of the Philadelphia International Airport, she rolled the situation around in her head. With this new revelation, Terri knew she had a responsibility. A responsibility to protect Marc. He was a big boy and normally this wouldn't even be a consideration. But this was not a normal situation. Alex was anything but a normal source. If she really set her mind on this path, who knew what kind of influence she could use to get what she wanted. Not to mention, it was Alex's choice to be an FBI source and if she wanted to terminate that situation, she could. Damn it.

Closing Alex as a source wouldn't mean they couldn't continue to work with her. They just couldn't use her information in any documents. Writing anything in her true name was way too risky. There might be some hot intel from Alex they would have to forgo writing up, but that was a small price to pay. They would just have to find other ways to report any intel, if that situation presented itself. It was a doable situation–not ideal, but doable. Not to mention, the mission for Alex on this trip, would not go into any reports.

She excused herself to use the restroom and once out of earshot of Alex, she called her supervisor, Jeff, back at the office. "Hey boss. Yeah, I'm at the airport now. Can you close a source down for me?"

CHAPTER 14

S ARAH WATCHED AS THE Bu car pulled up to the Arizona Criminal Investigative Division building. Mike Carson had sent Brad, of the earlier office tour, from his squad to pick Terri and Alex up at the airport. The young man was all smiles as he got out of the car and unloaded their bags. Sarah laughed a bit as Alex, dressed like a movie star in that casual but refined way certain people can pull off, emerged from the back seat. She wore low-waisted jeans with a thick leather belt, a buttoned down steel-gray loose long-sleeved blouse, rolled up at the sleeves and open at the neck. Brad asked if she wanted him to bring her bags inside. From behind her designer sunglasses, she politely declined. Clearly, he had no idea who was sitting in his backseat.

"How was the trip out?" Sarah asked Terri.

"Memorable," Terri said flatly. She shouldered her work bag and rolled her suitcase toward the door.

Alex hefted her bags and strode toward the door, pausing by Sarah, "Hello, Agent Holmes! Shall we get to work?"

Inside the war room, John Lightfoot greeted them. After introductions, he explained Ed and Marc had stepped out to get some lunch for the group. Alex set her luggage down and immediately went to the white board while Sarah and John proceeded to bring Terri up to speed on the investigation. As they spoke, John glanced toward Alex, who was engrossed in the timeline and victim information on the board.

He whispered, "Who is Alex again?"

Without looking back, Alex replied, "You could say I'm a person familiar with how your killer thinks."

"What, like a criminal psychologist? A behaviorist?" he asked.

"Yes, let's say that. May I see the crime scene photographs?" she asked as she turned to John.

He glanced at Sarah and Terri who nodded their approval. He retrieved a stack of manila folders and set them on the large table. "Here they are, in chronological order."

Terri opened her notebook and sat next to Alex. Together they reviewed the photographs and reports. The gruesome scenes were shocking and disturbing. Alex pointed out certain details while Terri noted the observations and asked follow-up questions. Sarah stood behind them, adding what she had gleaned from the files about each victim. John sat across the table from the trio of women, at first a little skeptical, but then began listening intently to Alex's thoughts.

Alex commented, "None of these attacks are from the rear. It appears the killer is always facing the victims. There is likely an emotional significance to seeing the victims' faces."

"Do you mean, like an enjoyment?" Terri asked.

"Yes. The killings aren't enough on their own. I believe the killer wants to see the expressions on their faces." Alex confirmed. "The killer isn't simply killing for food–"

At that moment, Ed and Marc charged through the door. "Tex-Mex express is here!" Marc announced with fanfare.

John, hanging on Alex's words, asked, "What was that last thing? They aren't simply killing for–what?"

Alex saw Terri's eyes go wide.

"I am afraid I misspoke. I am rather hungry and allowed my stomach to speak," Alex said with a laugh. "The killer is not simply killing out of compulsion, was my thought."

"I took the liberty of ordering you a grande steak burrito," Marc said as he handed Alex a paper bag.

"Thank you Detective Peterson, that was very thoughtful of you," Alex said as she smiled and unwrapped her foil entombed meal.

"And for you, I guessed on the chicken taco platter," he said, handing Terri a large bag.

"Much appreciated." Terri replied distractedly.

While the group bounced ideas and theories around over their lunch, Alex silently devoured her burrito with great gusto. Her green eyes sparkled as she savored each bite.

Ed looked over at Alex. "So how do ya like the burrito?"

She finished the last bite and wiped the corners of her mouth. "It was exquisite."

Ed grinned. "Yeah, it comes from a little mom and pop place up the road, Rito's. They do a real fine job there. Been around since before I can remember."

Alex continued. "I am not partial to fast food, but I detected the meat was well seasoned and not frozen. The tortilla was also fresh and pillowy. Someone prepared this food with great care, paying attention to the details."

Ed leaned back in his chair and looked at Alex. "Can you tell me how such a refined lady, such as yourself, got all mixed up in tracking serial killers?"

"Well, Detective Stackhouse, looks can be deceiving. You see," she said, deadpan, "I'm a reformed serial killer, myself."

Terri almost choked on her last bite of chicken taco.

Ed paused for a moment and then broke out into roaring laughter. "Okay, you got me. Dumb question. I deserved that," he said after catching his breath.

Alex simply smiled back.

John spoke up. "So, I've set up a meeting with a tribal elder for tomorrow. I still don't know what you expect to get out of it."

"We don't want to rule out any possibilities," said Terri. "Some background might be helpful."

"Yes, some historical context regarding the skinwalker legends would be helpful," Alex said as she leaned forward, elbows on the table.

"Are you coming too, Ed?" Sarah asked.

Ed shook his head. "No thank you. I'll take a pass on the ghost stories. I'm gonna do some followup interviews of folks in the office complex where doctor Swanson worked. See if anyone saw anything. Maybe our killer staked out the place beforehand and somebody saw him. Surveillance video from the night of the murder showed a youngish-looking, Caucasian person wearing a hoodie and baggy sweats entering the building. Kept their head down, though, so we got no shot of their face."

"I take it then you don't put much faith in the Native American legends?" Alex asked.

Ed took a swig of his Dr Pepper. "Naw. Our killer is flesh and blood, same as you and me. He's smart, but he ain't no boogie man or spirit. I respect all the beliefs of John's folks, but I don't subscribe to 'em when it comes to killers."

"Actually, I don't know how much I subscribe to it either. But so far, we got jack squat working the conventional angles. I'm open to anything at this point," John said, tapping his pen on a pad of paper.

"Let's just see where it goes," Marc said.

Alex nodded. "Yes, I am most interested in the meeting,"

"How is the court order for the psychiatric records coming?" Sarah asked.

"DA has the application and affidavit. Like we thought, he said this is a hot button issue. Courts don't like cops poking around in people's medical records without a good reason," John said.

Sarah finished her chicken burrito and chimed in. "I get that, but this seems like a pretty damn good reason."

"One would think so. But at the DA's urging, we had to up the probable cause and do a rewrite. Last thing we need is evidence tossed under an appeal," John pointed out.

Ed spoke up. "I'm on call tomorrow for any changes we need to put in there. Another reason I won't be takin' the field trip."

"Hopefully it all looks good, and we get it to the judge and she signs it in the next couple of days. Fingers crossed," John concluded.

"Seems like a good time to have our talk with the tribal elder. We're sorta dead in the water without those records," Marc noted.

John nodded. "Yeah, and along those lines, we have some law-enforcement-only matters to discuss. So, if you don't mind, Alex, we'll get you to the hotel."

Alex stood and smiled politely. "Not at all, detective."

"Just so you don't feel left out, we got some homework for you too. I've made copies of the crime scene and medical examiner reports you can take back there to review in detail. Please keep them safe. We don't want anything getting leaked to the press."

Alex nodded as the corners of her mouth hinted at a grin. "I can assure you, the files will be safe with me. I know how to protect secrets."

"I can drive you over, Alex," Ed offered as he stood.

Terri glanced at her phone as Ed and Alex left the conference room. A scowl crossed her face.

"Everything okay?" Marc asked.

"Yeah, just got a text from AJ," Terri said guardedly. "I closed Alex as a source, at her request, and apparently that word traveled faster than someone yelling free food in the breakroom. Christ on a crutch."

CHAPTER 15

D RAINING HIS PROTEIN SHAKE at his desk in the Philadelphia FBI office, AJ was feeling smug. He checked his heartbeat on his smartwatch. 63 beats per minute, perfect recovery. He'd finished his workout 30 minutes before in the office gym having established a new personal best bench press.

His search warrant affidavit regarding the Eastern European auto theft case was almost finished. The pole camera footage of the late night activity at the junkyard was just what he needed. He was able to get copies of the stolen vehicle report from the PD and interview the vehicle owner. He'd just gotten the call from the Assistant United States Attorney working the case that there was enough probable cause for a search warrant. He just needed to finish the affidavit and, with any luck, he and the squad would hit the junkyard within the next week. It'd be a nice stat for him. Reluctantly, he reasoned he'd probably have to put Terri down for a stat too, since she handed the case to him. She could be prickly, but she didn't steer him wrong.

He'd read the case file when he first took over the case and noted a source, code name VOLK, was a wealth of information. Then he heard that she closed the source today. Why did Terri close him? Always on the lookout for a good source, he'd texted Terri about possibly contacting

VOLK and reopening him. The reply was as blunt and acerbic as if she was standing in front of him: "No. Do NOT attempt to contact or reopen this Source. Find your own."

Even with Terri's rebuttal, it was a very good day.

His desk phone suddenly rang. The number 202-324-1000, the main trunk line from FBI HQ, appeared on the caller ID.

"Squad C1," he answered, officially.

"Is this Anthony Jackson?" the male voice asked.

"Yes," AJ replied warily.

"Good. I'm Glenn Curtis from the HUMINT desk at HQ. Got a favor to ask. We're looking for some good sources on Eastern European criminal networks. We can see you have a hot case that has some really good intel from a particular source, VOLK," the man said cheerfully.

"Yeah, I'm just finishing a search warrant affidavit on that case. Should make some headlines when we take it down," AJ replied. He took a quick scan around the nearly vacant squad area before propping his feet on his desk.

"Hey, that's excellent. Just to let you know, the Assistant Director in Charge over our unit has taken notice of you. There might be a spot for you down here. He thinks your skills might be underutilized there in Philly," the man said in a quiet tone.

AJ smiled. "That's great. I feel the same way," he said.

The man continued, "So, I just saw this source was closed. We want to meet with her, and see if we can reopen her. If you could pull that source file and get me the details, we can come up and talk to her. The Assistant Director is hot on this project."

"Her? The source is a woman?" AJ asked.

The voice on the other end of the phone paused. "Yes, unless I am mistaken, the source in question is female."

AJ realized he had never looked at the file or been involved in any surveillances with the source. His cheeks warmed with embarrassment. "Right. That source. I was thinking of a different one."

"Okay, then. Get me the basic biographical details: true name, DOB, POB, address, phone number. Once we have all that, I'll then let the Assistant Director know and we can schedule a time to come up and meet with you and her," the man said with authority.

"Got it. I got a few things on my plate here right now. Can I get this to you tomorrow?" AJ asked.

"That'll be fine. I'll be on the street all day tomorrow, so call my cell with the info when you have it," the man said.

AJ jotted down the number and hung up. It was about time someone took notice of him. He'd always felt he was destined for a position of leadership and having an Assistant Director taking you under their wing was a great first step.

For a fleeting moment, he thought about the text from Terri. "Screw her," he said under his breath as he made his way to HIU, the Human Intelligence Unit office, the local repository of all source files.

Robert hung up the phone and took a deep, calming breath. Seeing that the source was just closed was a fortunate byproduct of his daily monitoring of the situation, made all the easier from his position in FBI HQ. Maybe he should have waited a few days to call Philly? Too late for second guesses. But that wasn't why his hands were shaking slightly.

He'd almost screwed up the call. Knowing the source was a woman, and revealing that to the agent in Philadelphia, was amateurish. He wouldn't let it happen again. Hopefully, there wouldn't be a need for a next time. He'd baited the hook and cast the line. The only thing left to do was wait. His father had always told him, all good fishermen are patient.

With any luck the Philly agent wouldn't try to call the real Glenn Curtis directly at his desk. If he did, it wouldn't be the end of the road for his efforts. They would probably just chalk it up to a simple case of miscommunication. Maybe a small red flag would go up in Philly, but most likely not.

If AJ called the cell number, as instructed, it was a VOIP number Robert had established and virtually untraceable. It was a bold move, but risks were necessary. He knew the next 24 hours would be filled with anxious waiting for his burner phone to ring.

He needed a walk to clear his head and to complete another task. The small cafe, only two blocks from the Hoover building, was busy with the mid-afternoon crush of government bureaucrats. Men and women lined the counter in their cheap business attire getting a dose of caffeine and a confection to carry them through their mundane afternoons. The smell of fresh baked pastries filled the air. He reached into his shoulder bag and retrieved a cell phone, one of three burner phones he had purchased in the past six months. Scrolling through the functions, he selected 'mobile hotspot' before setting it on the table.

While it connected to the cellular network, he took a sip from his blue and white paper cup, decorated with pseudo Greek patterns. He suppressed the urge to pucker his lips as the unpleasant taste of stale coffee filled his mouth. During his last trip to Europe, he discovered Viennese melange, a wonderful espresso with steamed milk. He much preferred it to this swill. If all went according to plan, he'd be back there soon, enjoying his coffee in an Austrian sidewalk cafe. Actually, he thought, not *if* but *when* all goes according to plan.

But for the purposes of today, the bitter taste of American-style coffee would have to suffice. He let out a sigh. Sacrifices must be made. He produced a second phone, set to WiFi, and selected the mobile hotspot. He typed a simple email: "Contact made. Expect details tomorrow."

The entire event took less than five minutes. He powered down all the devices, loaded them back into his brown leather bag, and exited. He tossed the nearly full paper cup into the first trash can he passed on his way back to FBI Headquarters.

Karl Jaeger had gone to bed early that night. His heavy curtains blocked out the Austrian sunlight and muted the traffic noise from the streets below. His mind drifted through the vivid dreams.

He was a young man again, strong and handsome. The warm Italian breeze on his face was replaced by the cool air of a stone corridor. The black uniforms he and his comrades wore were crisp and clean. The totenkopf on their caps occasionally caught the light from the dim overhead bulbs and gleamed triumphantly in the sparsely lit corridor. The sound of their boots clicking on the stone floor echoed through the hall as the man led them to the rear of the Vatican archives. As the man with the vestments opened a heavily decorated door the scene suddenly changed. Karl was now wearing civilian clothes and seated across a plain wooden table from two Americans of the OSS. One of the men smiled and offered Karl an American cigarette. As the match sparked, it was accompanied by a dull buzzing sound.

The notification from his cell phone and sudden intrusion of blue light into his bedroom chased away the dream. His barely conscious mind reminded him that he had set his alerts to only allow a few select numbers through during the night. The message awaiting him must be important. His blue eyes fluttered open and eventually focused on the screen. It was some promising news from his man in Washington DC. Pleased with the message, he set the phone back in its place on his nightstand. Closing his eyes once more, he hoped to rejoin the dream that was interrupted.

The investigative trio met in Marc's room upon retiring for the night. "Here you go, Ter. Sarah and I have started carrying the blades in our shoulder bags. I think you should too. I didn't want to pass this around in front of Alex."

He handed Terri a leather sheath containing the weapon.

"I understand." Removing the weapon from the sheath, she was immediately struck with the workmanship of the seax style blade. It felt heavier than the rubber knives they had trained with but was well balanced and easily maneuverable. The blade flashed as it caught the light and Terri felt a pang of familiarity. Rolling her wrist, the blade arced before she locked it against her forearm.

"You seem pretty comfortable with it," Sarah noted.

"Well, Marc trained us pretty hard on these. Muscle memory, I guess."

Terri held the blade under the light. "Is that writing?"

Marc grinned. "It is. Kieran, the guy who made 'em, went full Viking. He included some Nordic runes. I think he said that one was–"

"Tiwaz," Terri said, surprising herself.

"Yeah, it represents a righteous warrior. How'd you know that?" Marc asked.

"I don't know. I must have read it somewhere," Terri answered quickly.

"How about mine?" Sarah asked as she pulled the blade from her bag.

Terri studied the engraved rune for a moment. "Algiz, I think. For protection."

Sarah ran her fingers over the symbol. "Algiz. I'll take it. And Marc's?"

He retrieved his blade from his go bag and handed it to Terri. A quick glance and she handed it back to Marc. "Uruz, for strength and courage."

"That's some memory you got there, Ter. I struggled when my kids gave me a word of the day calendar last Christmas," Marc said with a chuckle.

"Yeah, I can't even remember where I learned that. It's weird how the mind works."

She sheathed her weapon and put it in her shoulder bag. Where did she learn runes? A vague memory of her mother teaching her when she was young suddenly bobbed in her mind. It left her feeling a little off.

"All right," she said quickly as she entered the hotel hallway, "I'm gonna crash. I'm beat. See you in the morning."

Back in her room, Terri was in a near panic as she pressed her back against her door. She closed her eyes and took several deep breaths. What the hell just happened? When she read the symbols on the blades, it felt like an out-of-body experience.

Her mother had definitely taught her runic symbols. She could see her mother drawing them out on flash cards and quizzing her. But she had no idea why she *remembered* them. Memories of her mother were always upsetting, and this one was no exception. They were almost always painful to some degree: a cutting remark or soul-crushing indifference.

But this one was troubling for a very different reason. This memory was–pleasant: the two of them sitting on the floor of the living room bonding, her mother smiling when Terri got an answer correct.

She retrieved the blade from her bag and ran her finger over the engraved symbol. Why had her mother taught her this? Why, decades later, did she recall it? Was her mother preparing her for something?

Okay, just hold it together, girl. This is not the time or place to lose your crap, she told herself.

CHAPTER 16

A BRILLIANT RED MORNING sky spanned the horizon and gave the desert an alien glow. Alex gazed out the window through her sunglasses. The beauty of this landscape called to her. Almost unconsciously, she closed her eyes and inhaled deeply. She recognized Terri had brought her own shampoo and soap from home, as had Sarah. Marc was using the hotel amenities but did bring his own aftershave balm. John smelled the same as yesterday, only fresher.

"I'm callin' shotgun on the way back. Goin' on record and callin' it now," Marc announced, wedged against the backdoor.

John took his eyes off the road and glanced in the mirror. "Hang in there, buddy. It isn't too much further."

Terri chuckled from the front seat. "What, only another hour or two, right, John?"

"Sure, laugh it up, Ter. I feel like a canned sardine back here," Marc said as he tried to adjust his position.

John grinned. "Just another twenty minutes or so, buddy."

"Now, who are we meeting with again?" Terri asked.

"Sicheii is an elder and an old friend of my family, grew up with my father. He comes from a family of powerful shamans. Had a stroke a few months ago and isn't in great shape. But if anyone can tell us about the legends, it'd be him. I talked to his granddaughter, Chooli, to set up the visit. Known her since she was a little girl. She's taking care of him, and she thought a visit would be good for him."

After another thirty minutes, a cloud of dust enveloped the car as it came to a stop in front of a small house. Alex saw an old man sitting in a wheelchair on the porch of the house. A wooden ramp had been installed over the steps. His cheeks looked hollow, and the lines on his face were deep and pronounced. Thick steel-gray hair swept back over his head into a ponytail. A colorful blanket draped his shoulders against the cool morning air. As the dust settled, a young Native American woman stepped through the door. She wore a white western cut shirt with the sleeves rolled up to the elbows, jeans, and cowboy boots. Her smile evaporated when she noticed the others in John's car.

"Probably best if you all wait here. I didn't exactly mention to her that this was a work visit. She can be a little feisty."

John walked toward the makeshift ramp leading up to the porch as Chooli waited for him with crossed arms.

Alex focused her attention and listened. She could hear most of the conversation.

The woman lashed out. "We don't see you for weeks, then you call and want to come out. Great, I thought you were coming to see him. But you end up bringing a bunch of gawking tourists here?"

John looked at the ground. "I'm sorry, Chooli. They're not tourists, they're FBI agents working on the Pima Predator case...possible connection to *yee naaldlooshii...*"

The woman looked confused then amused. "Really? Just here for work? It's a legend, a myth. This is pathetic."

Exasperated, John pleaded, "Can we just talk with Sicheii for a few minutes?"

The woman shook her head and whispered in John's ear. His shoulders slumped, and the big man seemed to shrink a few inches.

Walking back to the car, Alex detected sorrow etched on his face.

John opened the car door and leaned in. "Okay, just found out Sicheii has been having good days and bad days, mostly bad days now. He hasn't spoken since last night. Chooli said he needs his rest and we shouldn't get him upset."

Sarah nodded. "Maybe we should pay our respects and leave. From what you've told us, this topic is pretty frightening. I don't want to be the reason this man's health fails."

Before John could answer, Marc asked, "What about her? Does she know anything about the legends?" He motioned toward Chooli with his head.

Alex saw a flash of discomfort cross John's face. "Uh, yeah, Chooli might. Let me ask her if she'll talk with you."

John slowly walked back to the porch and after a short conversation, he and Chooli approached the car. There was an icy air about her. She stood, arms folded across her chest, near the hood of the sedan with the investigators.

Terri started. "Thanks for talking with us. Chooli, right?"

The woman nodded.

"I'm Terri Watson with the FBI. This is Detective Marc Peterson, FBI agent Sarah Holmes, and behaviorist Alex Stepanova. We wanted to learn about the skinwalkers."

Chooli scoffed. "It's a legend. We put that crap on t-shirts to sell to tourists. If you're here looking for help to catch your killer, you must be pretty damn desperate."

Marc jumped in, "We understand, it's an unconventional approach, but–"

"But some legends may seem real to people. Enough so, that they believe them and, in this case, may emulate a skinwalker," Terri finished.

John asked, "Did Sicheii ever say anything about them?"

Chooli shifted her weight, uncrossed her arms, and slid her hands into the back pockets of her jeans. She looked to the desert and took a deep breath. "Yes. He told me a story several months ago, back when the killings here started making the press. Look, he wasn't well at the time. I don't know how much to believe."

"What was the story?" Alex asked.

Chooli closed her eyes and began. "He told me the–, you know, *yee naaldlooshii,* were real. He said he had never seen one, but his grandfather did."

Terri's eyes sparked, and she leaned in slightly. "What did he say about them? Did he describe them?"

Chooli ran her hands through her ebony black hair. "He said it happened many years ago, when his grandfather was a young man. His grandfather was on a horse in the desert, hunting or something, and saw it, across a dried river bed. It was like a wolf but much bigger. When it saw his grandfather, it–it stood up on two legs and stared at him. He said his grandfather's horse got frightened and started to run. He said his grandfather looked back and saw the, I don't want to say the name, the thing chasing him. It was on all fours now and gaining on his grandfather, at a full gallop. His grandfather got back to the village safely but saw the thing on a bluff looking down at him."

The group stood silent.

Chooli finally said, "Look, I told you he wasn't well. It was probably a bad dream."

"That could be. But did he ever talk about where they came from? What do the legends say about their origins?" Sarah asked.

"The legends say they are dark spirits that come from evil witches or medicine men. But he said the legends were wrong. He said the real creatures came to our land with the Spanish. When the Spanish soldiers and missionaries came, the things came with them. They attacked our people and animals. Some of our people then became like them, and it got folded into our beliefs. Why are you so interested in this stuff? You don't really believe it, do you?" Chooli asked nervously.

Terri pressed her. "What do you know about them? How do they act?"

Chooli began speaking as if she was reciting a text she had read. "The legends say the–thing that walks on all fours lives inside the man, just below the surface. Eventually, the thing becomes too strong, and the man can't hide it anymore. He becomes the thing–an animal in a man's skin."

She seemed to snap back. "There, that's all I know. I don't want to talk about this anymore, okay? It's just a damn myth." She looked over her shoulder at the porch. "He was a sick old man having visions. That's it."

Alex saw Terri wince slightly at Chooli's description of the skinwalker.

Marc nodded. "Thanks, Chooli, for talkin' this with us."

Chooli nodded without smiling. "I think you should all greet Sicheii. I told him yesterday John was going to stop by, and I think it gave him a spark. A quick hello and goodbye would be best."

On the porch, John knelt next to the frail figure. He touched his hand and spoke softly to him in Navajo. The old man's eyes remained closed, but he managed a slight nod. Under the watchful eye of Chooli, one by one the group knelt and greeted the elder. Alex was last. She had no words to say and simply touched his hand.

His eyes suddenly opened and he looked at her, surprising Alex. His lips moved but no words formed. After a few seconds, the eyes closed again as a tear ran down his cheek. When Alex stood, Chooli was staring at her. "He hasn't opened his eyes since yesterday. What did you do?"

Alex stared back at the woman. "I can assure I did nothing to provoke him," she said calmly.

An odd silence settled on the group. Marc stepped in between the two women. "Okay, how's about we all saddle up and get back to the city?"

Chooli decided perhaps she had underestimated John's friends. At the car, she made a point to shake all their hands. As she gripped Alex's hand, she felt an energy run up her arm. Alex leaned in and whispered so only Chooli could hear, "I am very sorry for your grandfather. I can tell he is a good man. You should not be rash in dismissing his words nor the legends."

Chooli nodded slowly, eyes wide. She watched the car leave as she rubbed her right arm.

After almost twenty minutes of driving, John eased the car back onto the paved road. Everyone seemed lost in their own thoughts. Alex and Terri seemed particularly quiet.

Sitting in the front seat, Marc decided to break the silence. "I have to admit, I'm a little surprised you can drive, John." he said, looking straight out the window.

John gave him a quizzical look.

"I'm kinda shocked you can sit down. I mean it looked like Chooli chewed your ass pretty good when we first pulled up."

John laughed. "Yeah, she was *not* happy with me. I honestly can't blame her. I haven't been around much. I keep telling myself, after I wrap up this case, I'll spend more time with them. But then–"

"Another case comes along, doesn't it?" Terri noted from the back seat.

"Yup. That's exactly it. I'm guessing you all know what I'm talking about," John agreed.

The three law enforcement officers all nodded.

Alex had been mostly quiet after the meeting. Despite her silence, she exuded a restless energy. Peering out the window in the back seat, she spoke up. "Detective Lightfoot, I see there are antelope in the distance. What other large animals does your desert hold?"

John glanced back in the mirror. "Yeah, those are pronghorn antelope, and then we have bighorn sheep, javelina, a type of wild boar, and mule deer, out there as well. When I was a kid, I used to go hunting once in a while with my dad and grandpa."

"I see. How very interesting," Alex said pensively.

As the group entered the hotel lobby, Alex turned to Terri. "Agent Watson, I would like to borrow the rental car for a few hours this evening."

Marc overheard the conversation. "Sorry, you're not on the lease. Whatcha need? One of us can drive you."

Alex looked him in the eye. "I have a need for a hunt. I have never hunted such animals as these, nor experienced the desert, and wish to do so. It has been several weeks since I have– accommodated this exigency."

Sarah's face registered a moment of shock. Terri's did not. Marc rubbed the top of his head and closed his eyes while he answered. "Uh, okay. I gotcha. How about I drive ya out there and you can run it off a little? Do what you need to do."

Terri chimed in, "I think I should go as well. I don't like the idea of one person sitting alone in a car on a dark desert night. We have another predator out there."

Sarah swallowed hard. "Well, if you two are going, I may as well go too."

Alex smiled. "I did not expect to have such a hunting party escorting me. I can assure you, I will not be far from the car, should an unexpected visitor approach you. Allow me to change clothes, and I will meet you here in the lobby, say in fifteen minutes."

Marc eased the car off the pavement and onto a dirt side road. He had no idea where to go to provide Alex with the best opportunity for prey, but this seemed like a good spot.

He disabled the dome light before Alex opened her door and stepped out barefoot. She removed her sweats in two fluid motions and placed them on the seat. The silvery moon reflected off her pale skin as she walked toward the open expanse.

Sarah whispered, "I never thought about it before, but does she always get naked before a hunt?"

Marc chuckled. "Yeah, shocked me too, the first time."

"It's to protect her clothes. When she transforms, she would tear those clothes to shreds." Terri added.

Sarah nodded. "Makes sense."

A broad smile appeared on Alex's face. She paused and stretched her arms wide. The cool night air and darkness embraced her like old friends. She rolled her head once, cracking her neck. The transformation started.

Her body felt hot. The air crackled slightly, and there was a faint whiff of ozone, as there always was. She didn't fully understand the physics behind the process, but believed the transformation tapped into a different plane of existence. Her body convulsed slightly as the muscles expanded. Divinely excruciating pain permeated her teeth and bones but lasted only a few seconds. Her skin felt like it was on fire as the hair burst forth. Then it was completed. Her green eyes dilated fully and scanned the surrounding area.

Hunting prey animals was different from hunting humans. She suppressed the urge to roar. This prey would recognize the sound of a predator and run for their lives. She knew they were likely very fast and agile. Unlike animals that faced danger regularly, humans often froze when confronted.

Her senses were electric. So many new scents and sounds. Her brain began to build a three dimensional model based on the sensory input. She could hear an animal she was unfamiliar with in the distance. It sounded as if it was digging in the ground. She began to trot toward some scrubby trees. Beyond the trees, the mesas loomed, black silhouettes against the deep purple sky.

Terri, Marc, and Sarah sat on the ground, back-to-back, twenty yards from the car, their blades resting on their laps. "Everyone stay sharp," Marc whispered as his eyes scanned the dark. If there was another predator out here tonight, it would not be ideal to be sitting in the car, where their visibility and hearing would be impaired. Best to know what was coming and have room to maneuver, if necessary.

Sarah whispered back, "If I was any sharper, I'd cut myself."

It had been just over an hour since Alex left them. A short time ago, they thought they heard a high pitched squeal, but couldn't be sure. The desert ground had now cooled and started pulling heat from their bodies. Marc was just about to suggest they get a blanket to sit on when he saw her.

She was angelic as she strode toward them. Her white skin glowed in the soft moonlight. But as she got closer, he could see she was covered in dark blood from her mouth to her navel.

They all stood silently. Marc looked at the ground while Terri handed Alex a bottle of water from the case they had purchased on the way out. Alex washed off most of the blood before Sarah handed her her sweats, which she donned nonchalantly.

"All good?" Terri asked.

"Yes, Agent Watson, it was most satisfying. Thank you," Alex said with a slight nod.

"So, um, what did you find?" Sarah asked.

"I believe Detective Lightfoot called it a javelina," Alex said. The group's blank faces stared back at Alex. "A type of wild boar. It was a large male." The group nodded.

Sarah's face appeared slightly squeamish. Alex touched her shoulder. "I can assure you, Agent Holmes, it was very quick. The animal did not suffer."

Marc looked at the group and clapped his hands. "Alrighty then. This was fun, but let's load up and head back to the hotel."

The warm water of the shower felt soothing, and Alex allowed herself a luxurious extra few minutes under the steamy spray. She knew the hunt was necessary. And she did not lie to Agent Holmes; the kill had been quick. The raw flesh satisfied her and the release of the beast left her feeling balanced. But several things bothered her. Displaying this behavior was not likely to encourage Terri to make the transition. Nothing she could do about that. Life as a werewolf was complicated.

Also, having Detective Peterson and Agent Holmes see this side of her felt strange. Of course they knew what she was, but seeing her covered in blood after a kill was–alienating. She was a "part of the team," as Detective Peterson had put it. But displaying this side of her only drove home the point she was different from them. So different.

And then the old Native American man, Sicheii. His reaction to her touch earlier left her unsettled. He clearly sensed something about her. Was the reaction joy or fear? So many thoughts. Too many. Best to leave these alone tonight. The perceptions of others were out of her control.

Toweling off, she checked the time, it was 11 p.m. back in Philadelphia. It was late, but she dialed the number nonetheless. A calm came over her as she heard Cigus's cheerful voice. "Hello, Alex! How are you doing, dear?"

"I am fine, Cigus Varney. I should be asking how you are?"

"I am feeling better each day. In addition to my recovery, I am happy to report that I have not killed your plants yet."

"That is good news. Both for you and my peace lilies."

Cigus laughed and then a silence fell. "Are you really fine, my dear?" he asked.

Alex let out a breath. "Many people are counting on me, and I fear I may not be what they seek. Can you tell me I am good again?"

Terri, Marc, and Sarah met up in Marc's room. He poured himself a scotch. "I have a can of Guinness and an IPA in the mini-fridge for you if you want."

"That is very thoughtful of you," Terri said with a laugh. She poured the dark liquid into a pint glass and waited as the head settled.

Sarah popped the tab on the IPA and took a sip from the can. "So, what did we learn today, other than Alex is a stone-cold apex predator? I have to admit, knowing and seeing are two very different perspectives."

Terri shifted in her chair. "Yeah, it's a little disconcerting."

Sarah shook her head. "No, not that. It's freakin' *awesome*. I mean, she's incredible. To be so comfortable in your own skin is powerful stuff. I'm not a hunter, but I understand a girl has to do what a girl has to do. Yeah, she has a nasty side, but don't we all? Hers just comes with a heaping dose of mystical shapeshifting energy and carnage."

"Are you getting a girl crush?" Marc teased.

Sarah chuckled. "I might be."

Terri smiled and relaxed. Her stout had settled, and the creamy head arched slightly over the lip of the glass. She took a long pull. "Okay, other than that. What did we learn today?"

"Well, it seems our killer has been active here for a long time," Marc said as he sat at the desk.

Terri nodded. "Maybe, or we're looking at multiple skinwalkers over the years. Alex said she didn't think they were immortal so maybe we're looking at a series of them."

Sarah took another sip of her IPA. "That would make sense. They may have been here for generations. If that's the case, there must have been news stories in the past. I can start looking through the archives and see if I can find anything.”

“True, but I don't know if that'll help us immediately,” Terri countered.

“Yeah, drawin' a family tree for this asshole may get us there eventually, but how long would that take?” Marc asked.

“What if I work with Alex on it? We can create a specific boolean search and get through it pretty quickly,” Sarah offered.

Terri nodded, but she was already thinking of the next prong of their investigation.

“I like that, but there is something else we may want to search for. Remember when Alex pointed out all the killings were face to face? She mentioned the killer isn't just killing for food. There's a thrill they derive from it.”

“That thrill-killin' is rampin' up by the looks of it. I think he or she is gettin' bolder.” Marc added.

“Exactly. They're hunting with impunity. Feeling invincible and superior.” Terri thought out loud.

“Alex did say the transformation process was–I think she used the word 'intoxicating.'” Sarah recalled.

“Right. So what if our killer is on social media bragging about themselves?” Terri said, taking a sip from her deep brown beverage.

“I like that thought.” Sarah perked up. “We can search for posts on the days after the attacks and narrow it down a bit. It's still going to be a tough slog though. Assholes with superiority complexes on social media are way too common. I'd start with the troll sites, 4chan and 8chan, but there are thousands of users there.”

“Maybe Alex can give you a hand there, too?” Marc pointed out.

Sarah nodded. “Worth a shot.”

Terri paused over her drink for a few seconds. "What do we think about fully briefing John and Ed?"

"You mean, like *really* briefing 'em?" Marc asked.

Terri looked at Marc and Sarah. "Yeah. You guys have been here longer. What's your read on their readiness to hear our tale of monsters and mayhem?"

"My read is that they aren't there yet," said Sarah. "And honestly, we don't have anything convincing we can point to. We can't show them Alex. Short of that, we have a legend, a pile of mangled bodies, and, in their eyes, a wild story. I remember the first time you told me. I was skeptical as hell."

Marc nodded. "She isn't wrong. Let's see if we can ID this guy and then think about tellin' 'em. If we tell 'em too soon, and that Captain of theirs gets wind of it, we'll be sent packin' with a state police escort straight to the airport. And then they're really on their own." Marc took a deep breath. "I don't like holdin' back, but I don't think we have a choice right now."

"Okay, that was my feeling as well, but I wanted to get your thoughts," said Terri. "Sarah is right. We can't divulge Alex to them. And without that, we sound pretty crazy. Let's hope we get this killer in our sights soon."

CHAPTER 17

*A*T A CORNER TABLE *in Starbucks, my eyes focus like lasers on the laptop screen. As I reach for my iced chai tea, I notice beads of condensation forming on the plastic cup, eventually gathering enough mass to stream down to the table top, where they've now created a puddle. I can taste the cinnamon and ginger. Damn, that is some good tea.*

My efforts at stalking the Criminal Investigative Division building have been an epic waste of time. The other day, I sat at the bus stop near the building as long as I could. I even went home, changed clothes, and came back to sit more. All I learned was there were too many people coming and going. Some in uniform and some in regular clothes. Like the two women getting dropped off with luggage. What was that all about? Were they moving in? It wasn't a productive use of my time, and it placed me on surveillance cameras. I need to focus my efforts if I want to have any hope of a successful hunt.

I've previously read the news articles covering the Pima Predator's activities with great satisfaction. What a great name. In addition to being a living god, I'm a bonafide celebrity. But that isn't the purpose of today's reading. No, today I'm looking for other details.

A Captain Cutler is predominately quoted in the stories. Although tempting, I've watched enough cop shows to know this guy was not doing the real work. He was most likely a paper pusher and an ass kisser, if Hollywood was to be believed. I continue to scan the numerous articles, taking a moment to appreciate the quantity of kills. I have been a busy boy.

Here's something. At a crime scene in July, two detectives were quoted as saying, "No comment," and they were named: John Lightfoot and Edward Stackhouse.

Stackhouse. I know that name. This needs to be explored further. Could I be so lucky?

I feel a smile tug at the corners of my mouth. Luck's got nothing to do with it. This is just the universe confirming my superiority.

A wave of excitement runs through me. Deep inside, a restlessness starts to bubble.

Having cleared the CID lobby, now only receiving a curt nod from the Scroogelike elderly gate keeper, the group climbed the stairs and made their way toward the war room.

Just outside the door, Ed appeared. "Hey guys, Johnny got some bad news. Sicheii, the old head y'all met with the other day, he died last night. He was a good old dude. I got to know him through John over the years. Just wanted you to know."

Inside the war room, they found John busying himself re-reading reports from the psychiatrist's murder. Terri was the first to speak. "Ed told us about Sicheii. I'm sorry."

Marc and Sarah followed suit with their condolences. Alex realized she was bad at these kinds of interactions but managed to say, "From all accounts, he seems to have been a very insightful and genuine man. I would have liked to have met him in his prime."

Then she remembered something. "A friend once told me, as long as we, the living, remember the dead, they aren't really gone."

She glanced at Terri after she spoke and saw a slight smile on her face.

John cleared his throat. "Thank you. I'm gonna miss him. But for better or worse, we all have work to do. There's still a serial killer out there to catch."

Terri knew all too well what he was doing: compartmentalizing. Wall the grief off for now with work. The status of the dead won't change. He could grieve later.

"Right. So let's get to it," she said.

Sarah and Alex started the deep internet searches. Ed set them up in a separate office space with a pair of undercover computers. The IP addresses were registered to a fictitious company rather than CID. These computers were mostly used by undercover officers working child exploitation cases.

Sarah wasn't relishing the dive into the world of 4chan and 8chan. The hatred and twistedness residing there was disturbing. She'd been down these rabbit holes before, working as an analyst assisting domestic terrorism cases. It was a very dark place.

"I have created a bot to assist us, Agent Holmes. I have provided it with the pertinent dates and several key words we discussed. The bot will search independently and free us to work through the boolean search of the newspaper archives," Alex said.

Sarah was a little stunned. "Uh, sure. That's great." Alex sure had mad computer skills.

By noon, several interesting articles had emerged. There was a story from August 1957 about several cattle being killed and mutilated over a span of months. The sheriff was quoted as saying it looked like the work of a wolf pack. An article from 1969 described the bodies of a pair of hippies being discovered near their van in the desert. They had been mauled by a large animal. In 1980, a man hunting said he came across the carcass of a bighorn sheep by a river. He noted the footprints in the mud near the remains were deep and massive. It made the news because he was sure it was a bigfoot.

Sarah printed out the articles. As Ed walked into the room, she slid them into a folder.

"So how's the hunt goin'?" he asked casually.

"There's no joy sifting through these hate channels. It might shock you to know there are a lot of sick puppies out there," Sarah quipped.

Ed laughed, "I'm guessing you are only seeing the tip of the iceberg. These are the ones that can type. Imagine how many are out there not posting?"

Sarah frowned. "Well, that's depressing."

Alex focused on the computer screen. She was in the zone. After a few tweaks, her bot was working perfectly. Unfortunately, it was working too well. The volume of potential hits made it difficult to sort through with any precision. After an hour of reading, one's eyes and mind became tired and lazy. She thought for a moment, then altered the search words to include the word "mortal."

She now focused the search on a particular username on 8chan. "I believe I have something of interest for you both," she said, sitting back.

Sarah slid her chair over, and Ed leaned in as Alex spoke. "The day after the killing of the trooper and the young female on the highway, a poster described 'the mortals getting what they deserve.' The poster also stated that one dead cop is just a good start."

Ed frowned. "That's f'd up, but not surprising."

Alex continued. "Correct. But this same poster talked about the death of a certain psychiatrist and questioned the ability of mortals to understand the supremacy they are facing. This post was uploaded at 12:35 a.m on the night of the killing. What time did the news break on that story?"

Sarah furiously plowed through her notes, but Ed knew the timeline.

"Sonofabitch," he said. "It was well after that. The call didn't come to the PD until around 1 a.m. Keep digging on this one!"

Sarah scribbled the username: Rutty2000

Ed turned to exit and find John but met him coming into the room. The two men nearly knocked heads.

"Medical records got released," John said. "I'm going to drive over to the office to pick them up."

Sarah could hear the men talking excitedly as they ran down the hall. She turned to Alex. "That was some shit-hot searching! I'll get with Terri and start the process for a subpoena to the service provider to get the information on that username."

Alex smiled. "Thank you for the compliment, Agent Holmes." She paused. "These computers are securely undercover, are they not?"

"I believe they are," Sarah answered.

"Then if you will give me a few hours or so alone, I believe I can provide you with those details." Alex retrieved a thumb drive from her bag.

Sarah was confused for a second then it hit her. "Oh, right. Gotcha. Don't need to know how you're going to get that. I'll just go fill Terri and Marc in on the developments."

The team poured through the psychiatric records but the process was not as straightforward as they had hoped. The patient lists, going back seven years, were tagged with diagnosis codes. Terri had pulled up a copy of the Diagnostic and Statistical Manual of Mental Disorders, the DSM-5, on a computer and cross-checked it with any promising leads.

Alex quietly slipped into the room and handed Sarah a piece of paper with the handwritten name Thomas Rutledge.

Sarah flipped ahead to the R section and found his records. "How about this one, Rutledge, Thomas: F60.0, F60.2, and F60.8.

Terri read the corresponding codes aloud. "'Paranoid Personality Disorder, Antisocial Personality Disorder, and Narcissistic Personality Disorder.' Whoa. This is interesting. What does his chart say?"

Sarah dug into the folder. "Patient first came to Swanson at age 17, under order from a juvenile court. Patient exhibited extreme irritability and aggressiveness. Patient also exhibited patterns of extreme antisocial tendencies, deceitfulness, and an exaggerated sense of self-importance. Patient was prescribed antipsychotic medications and seemed to respond to treatment. Patient has an extremely high IQ and was able to complete college and gain employment." She paused as she flipped to the end of the record. "Patient has regressed. Aggressive behavior and narcissistic tendencies have increased. An increase in the medication has had no effect. Patient has missed the last several appointments and stopped responding to messages. I fear the patient is in a downward cycle." She looked up at the group, "That last entry was about six months ago."

"I'm no shrink, but this sounds like our man," Marc said.

CHAPTER 18

T HE UNMARKED STATE POLICE van slowly rolled to a stop on the dark street. Marc recognized the faint final guitar riffs of AC/DC's "Thunderstruck" trailing off as the back doors swung open. The ten helmeted men dressed in black silently climbed out of the van as Marc directed them up the street. They moved in a line up the sidewalk a half a block to the apartment complex. Ed was there with the apartment manager, holding the door open. The search team, parked farther up the street, remained in their cars.

John was posted upstairs, keeping eyes on the target door. Apartment number 216 was a third of the way down the hall. The group of men in black flowed past him in a stack, weapons trained down the hallway. Ed, bringing up the rear of the conga line, stopped by John. Marc, Terri, Sarah, and Alex lined the wall behind him.

Marc watched as the tactical team silently made their way down the hall and eventually hugged the wall near the door. He suddenly recalled a similar scene from Fallujah, Iraq. His heart raced and the hallway started to spin. He shut his eyes tightly and willed himself to stay in the present. When he opened them, he saw the point man give a hand signal. A large man with a ram silently moved to the front and stood before the door.

The point man hammered his gloved hand on the door several times yelling, "Police! Open up!"

After waiting a few seconds, the two men exchanged looks, and the point man nodded. The ram slammed home directly on the deadbolt lock. A loud crack echoed as the wooden frame splintered and the door swung inward. Immediately the SWAT team poured into the apartment, rifle-mounted flashlights piercing the darkness as they screamed, "Police!"

Alex had been told by John and Ed to stay around the corner. She found this darkly humorous. I'm the one here to save you, she thought, but go ahead, do it your way. Her initial protest to her placement during the entry was cut short when Terri gave her a look. She begrudgingly accepted her place. Now listening intently to the voices down the hall for any sign of trouble, she was prepared to make the transformation if necessary. But the only voices she heard were the SWAT team members calling out "Clear."

It had been twelve hours since the name Thomas Rutledge was found in the psychiatric reports. An emergency court order demanding the IP address and subscriber information of the 8chan poster confirmed what they already knew: Thomas Rutledge was their main suspect. An arrest warrant was immediately issued, and the SWAT team quickly planned their assault.

The SWAT team exited the apartment and were replaced by the search team. Alex was allowed to enter with the rest of the investigators after the initial photographs were taken. They removed their vests and prepared for several hours of searching.

"Whew. I'm surprised the neighbors didn't complain about the smell. This place looks like an animal was living here," one of the photographers commented as he snapped pictures.

The apartment was in an extreme state of disarray. Dirty dishes filled the sink and dishwasher. The trash can was overflowing with take-out containers. Most disturbing, the walls were covered with violent images, almost childlike in their simplicity but very unsettling. Some were drawn with a pencil, others with some sort of marker. Several of the depictions were drawn with such intensity that the drywall was gouged.

"Wow. Good luck getting his security deposit back," Sarah said as she studied the walls.

Alex along with Terri and Marc made their way to the bedroom. The bed was unmade, and clothes covered the floor. When no one was looking, Alex discretely leaned over and sniffed the sheets. She stood straight up and turned to Terri. The expression on her face was solemn and serious. She nodded and whispered, "He is what we thought."

A pit formed in Marc's stomach. Up to this point, their work had been a mostly academic exercise. Now, they were standing in the den of the creature. A creature who had just killed the only person trying to help him.

The evidence collection team continued to comb through every corner of the four-room apartment, bagging and logging every item meticulously. With so many bodies working in a small space, the area became cramped almost immediately. Terri, Sarah, Marc, and Alex stepped out into the hall to get out of the way.

"I don't like that he isn't here. Do you think he got spooked?" Sarah asked.

"His car is still parked in the back, midnight blue BMW SUV," Marc pointed out.

Sarah thought for a second. "Out of town for work?"

"Possible," said Terri. "Let me make a couple of calls and see if we have any former agents working corporate security that might be able to shed some light on our guy." She pulled out her phone and walked down the hall.

Alex examined the smashed door. "Although, it won't tell his whereabouts, the condition of his den may tell us a few things."

"What kinda things? I've got my own ideas, but shoot." Marc urged.

"I believe he is spiraling, as you pointed out. His two lives are becoming one. He is having a difficult time separating the wolf from the man. I may suggest this is exacerbated by his clinical condition," Alex whispered.

"Yeah, that's what I was thinkin' as well," said Marc. "He looks to be runnin' headlong toward a big climactic finish."

"What might that finish look like?" Sarah asked hesitantly.

"I dunno, but I'm guessin' it'll be hellish," Marc said, looking back at the apartment door.

Terri returned to the group, "So our guy isn't on a business trip. He was fired a few days ago for assaulting his manager. He never showed up for his HR interview and they can't reach him by phone."

Marc nodded to Alex. "Spiral."

Terri looked around the group. "We need to brief John and Ed."

"Agreed. Not sure how this is gonna go, but we need to tell 'em," Marc said.

"You're kiddin', right?" Ed asked, his grin of amusement melting away.

John stared at Terri. "You really believe that?"

"Look, I know it sounds crazy. But we faced this in Philadelphia. We saw murders like this. And Marc and I saw the creature. It's no joke," Terri implored.

The decision had been made to not expose Alex. It wasn't an easy decision. It was feared if word of her identity got to the wrong ears, there might be attempts on her life and carnage in their wake. However, trying to convince John and Ed their target was a werewolf, with nothing but circumstantial evidence, was a tall order.

Ed pointed to the exit. "You all need to step out and get some air or something. You're talkin' like crazy folks."

"You have to believe us, for your own safety. You have to try to understand what you're up against," Sarah pleaded.

Ed scanned their faces. He was stunned by the serious expressions staring back at him. "Look. You might've seen some things in Philly that you can't explain. I wasn't there. But I will tell you this guy, Thomas Rutledge, is just a man. A sick killer, but still just a man. I'm not buying any boogie man stories."

He turned to his partner. "John, you're not buying into this, are you?"

John remained silent.

Ed shook his head. "Oh, man, now you got Johnny believing in these ghost stories."

"I'm not saying I believe it, but I'm listening. It may not be as crazy as it sounds." John said quietly.

A male evidence technician poked his head out of the door and called down the hallway to them. "Hey, we got something here. You better take a look."

John held up the group in the hall. "We'll table this conversation for now. No word of this in front of anyone else. Understand?" he whispered.

Inside the apartment, the man held up a plastic bag containing a piece of paper with a handwritten list of names. Several names on the page had lines written through them and a date next to them.

Ed studied the paper. "Any of these look familiar?" he asked.

"Oh my god. It's his hit list." Sarah gasped as she recognized several victims' names.

"It seems so," said Marc. "Look at the bottom."

The name Ezra Swanson was written in black ink, then lined through in red with the date of his murder next to it.

"There are about twelve names on here that aren't lined through. Those people are in real danger," Sarah pointed out.

Ed laid the document on a table and photographed it with his phone. "I'm on it. I'll head back to the office and start trying to identify them. We have to locate them fast and tell them they need to become scarce, like today."

"I'll go with you and lend a hand. If you guys find anything that might help us, call me," Sarah said as she shouldered her ballistic vest and followed Ed.

John pointed to a laptop computer found on a nightstand in the bedroom. "Okay, let's get that computer to the forensics lab like now. I want to be reading it by the end of the day," John barked at one of the computer recovery team members, who had bagged the laptop for transport. The young man scooped the laptop up and ran for the door. "Now *that* is the sense of urgency I expect."

Robert strolled through the Smithsonian's Museum of Natural History. It was a nice time to come here. During the off season, it wasn't overrun with tourists and their children. He didn't like to be around families and laughter. Too often, it opened doors to places he did not want to peer into.

He logged onto the free wifi and checked his burner phone. A short text message appeared from an unsaved number. "Nephews are en route for the surprise party. Make sure the guest of honor doesn't become suspicious. Have a plan to clean up after."

He deleted the message and powered down the phone as he made his way to the Egyptian exhibit. He thoroughly enjoyed learning about the mythology of ancient cultures.

Jerri's phone buzzed and vibrated on the counter. The sudden noise startled her, and she almost dropped her bagel as she lunged for it. The caller ID told her it was Lisa, from her office. Hopefully, it was the call she had been waiting for.

Two weeks ago, she contacted the Arizona Bureau of Natural Resources and asked them if they had any reports of odd animal mutilations over the last two years. There had been a fair amount of tap dancing involved to explain to the woman in Arizona why a medical examiner in Philadelphia was interested in suspicious animal deaths, but she managed to swing it. Jerri laid on the charm, and the woman finally agreed to send Jerri the reports and any samples they might still have.

Those hair and tissue samples arrived the week before and were immediately sent to the University of Pennsylvania for analysis and comparison with the samples recovered from the Pima Predator's victims. Fortunately, the techs at Penn were less curious and didn't ask why the chief medical examiner was requesting DNA analysis of animal tissues. Having learned a little about Alex's behavior, Jerri was playing a hunch the killer in Arizona likely supplemented their hunting with large domestic and wild mammals.

"Hey Dr. Williams," Lisa said. "Sorry to bother you so early on a Saturday, but I just got the results from Penn and you had asked me to call you if they came in." She was a good tech but junior. There was no better way to learn the job than working weekends in Philadelphia.

"Can you tell me what the report says?" Jerri asked.

"Sure. Most of the positive results came back to coyotes as the primary predator or scavenger. Several results were inconclusive due to degradation of the sample. But two of them were surprising. It was a couple of the bighorn sheep samples from a few months ago. They detected wolf DNA, or at least that was the closest match in the database it said. Those samples were compared to the first set you sent over, the human victims. They are an almost identical match."

"Almost identical?" Jerri asked.

"Yeah, that's what the overview says, ninety-nine percent match. This is for the Arizona murders, right? Weird that we're getting so many animal DNA hits."

Jerri was ready for the question. "Yeah. I'm trying to help them weed out other cases of cross-contamination so they can narrow down their suspects."

"Gotcha. I'll leave the package on your desk."

"Okay. Thanks, Lisa. I'm going to swing in this morning and take a look."

Her husband, Blaine, yawned as he walked into the kitchen in search of coffee. He seemed a little annoyed when Jerri told him she needed to run into the office. His protest over the rim of his mug: "What kind of an emergency can there be? They're already dead."

At her desk, staring at the test results, she could finally scratch the itch that had been bothering ever since the call from Lisa.

She carefully compared the two genetic tests, and, at first glance, they appeared identical. But as the report stated, upon closer examination, there were slight differences. She sat back in her chair, processing what she was seeing. If the same killer were responsible for killing the animals and people, the results should be exact. Maybe the samples were corrupted? Then it hit her: she'd seen samples like this before in a recent genetics class she attended.

The search team had left about an hour before, leaving the investigators to sit in the apartment, waiting for someone, anyone, to come and repair the door. They couldn't leave until it was secured. John held his phone in front of his face as he grilled some unfortunate soul on the whereabouts of this alleged carpenter and why he wasn't here.

Alex sat quietly, gazing at the walls. Despite her acute sense of smell, she didn't seem to be bothered by the unpleasant odors of rotting food and filth. The others were not so fortunate. John had tied a red bandana around his face, resembling an old time train robber. Marc had pulled his t-shirt up over his nose. Terri felt as if the sick greasy smell was clinging to her skin and hair. She tied one of Alex's scarves around her face. For once, she could smell the soap and laundry detergent Alex used. It was actually quite pleasant.

John sat at the kitchen table, laptop open, working on a piggyback search warrant. The team had found the keys to a storage locker in a kitchen drawer. The trick would be to find which storage facility they belonged to. John knew that would have to wait until after Thomas Rutledge was apprehended but decided to use the down time productively.

Terri had an uneasy feeling and paced the apartment. Marc seemed on edge too. He caught up with her by the living room window. "Whatcha think?"

"It's definitely our guy, but I can't help but feel we're missing something," Terri said, eyes scanning the room.

"I know. Me too." he said, rubbing the back of his neck. "Lemme see the picture of the hit list again."

Terri pulled the image up on her phone and handed it to Marc. He slowly scrolled until he got to the bottom. "Doug Bowman." he said, handing it back.

"What about him?" Terri asked tiredly. She recognized the name as one of the victims but the significance was escaping her.

"Doug Bowman. He ain't on this hit list. He worked with Ed's sister at the warehouse. He was the guy killed in the restaurant parking lot." He lowered his voice, "Just killed, no–you know, impromptu gnawin'."

Alex heard the discussion and came over. "You are correct, Detective Peterson. That particular victim did not show any signs of predation. He was simply murdered." Alex's brow furrowed. "That case showed signs of a planned murder, albeit sloppily, but planned nonetheless."

"If it was planned, his name should be on this damn list," Marc said pointing to the image.

While Marc was talking, something caught Terri's eye. She walked across the room to a small picture on a shelf. Holding the framed photograph, she studied the scene: two small boys with crew cuts standing with an older woman on a farm or ranch. Cattle lined a feed trough in the background. One boy was smiling, the other staring blankly. Otherwise, they were identical.

Marc's phone rang. "What's up Dr. J?" As he listened, his face grew grave.

Alex peered at the photograph over Terri's shoulder and asked, "Brothers?"

Marc ended the call with Jerri and turned to Alex and Terri. "Worse. Twins." He called into the other room. "Eh, John, you need to hear this."

As John stood, the carpenter appeared in the broken doorway.

Kenneth Rutledge sat at his small kitchen table, sipping his orange juice. The ingredients for chocolate chip pancakes sat out on the counter. They were his favorite. When he was a kid, he and his other half would eat a mountain of them at his grandmother's house. It was a nice memory from an otherwise difficult time.

When his parents disappeared, he and Thomas moved in with her. They were 11. She was kind enough, but he could never get over the feeling she liked his other half more. Thomas was the smart one. Everyone knew it. Grandma seemed to play it up too. Even though Thomas was the one always getting in trouble at school, she bragged about him constantly.

Ken heard rustling from the couch in the next room and soon Thomas appeared in the kitchen. It was fun having him over for a sleepover the night before. He was excited when Thomas called and said he wanted to come over. But when he got there, Ken got worried. Thomas told him that Grandma had been talking to him and told him to take an Uber over. He looked different, almost wild. His hair wasn't combed, he slept in his clothes, and he had started to grow a beard. Worst of all, his eyes seemed cold and vacant.

"Got anymore OJ, Ken?" Thomas asked as he stretched his arms over his head.

"Sure, Tom. In the fridge."

Thomas didn't come over very often, unless he was insisting Ken go hunting with him. Like the last time, when Thomas dragged him out to a spot on the highway. And then that policeman showed up. Ken shivered at the memory.

Last night was different. He wasn't talking about hunting. He just wanted to talk about Ken's friend at work, Trina Stackhouse.

Ken stood and moved to the counter. "If you want, I can make us some pancakes, Tom."

"Yeah. That'd be good. I'm starving," Thomas said, scratching his belly. "And then we need to get moving."

Sarah quickly typed the expanded search parameters for the database check. Within a few seconds, it populated.

"Shit! Here it is. Kenneth Rutledge, date of birth is January 1, 1995. Thomas's DOB was December 31, 1994. They shared a common address five years ago."

Terri had her phone on speaker as everyone listened. "Copy Kenneth Rutledge, common previous address with Thomas, DOB one day later."

John shook his head as he looked at the notes Terri scribbled. "Damn. Different years. One born before midnight and one after. Goddam twins. How the hell did we miss that?"

Marc grimaced and rubbed his head. "Shit. We got target-fixated and rushed."

Something sounded familiar to Sarah. What was it with that name? Was it just there had been so much talk about the name Rutledge?

She silently scanned the public records report and when she got to the employment section, she gasped. "Oh my god, oh my god! This is bad."

"What is it?" Terri could hear the panic rising in Sarah's voice.

"I remember where I saw that name. Kenneth Rutledge works with Trina at the warehouse! The same place Doug Bowman worked!"

Terri was processing the information as fast as her fatigued mind could operate. "Okay, that explains why Doug wasn't on the list here. We probably have two people, twins involved. We'll need you and Ed to start a full work up on the new suspect."

Sarah spluttered, "No, you don't understand. Ed isn't here. He left about twenty minutes ago to pick up his sister at work. Her car was in the shop and he was worried about her. He's at the warehouse!"

Thomas stared out the windshield of Ken's 2001 Nissan Sentra. He picked at a deep crack in the foam padding of the dashboard, dried and discolored by the Arizona heat. The sun slowly dropped below the Phoenix skyline and the creeping darkness caused some of the old mercury lights in the parking lot to begin to flicker as they warmed up. Ken sat silently behind the wheel, periodically glancing at the employee door.

"Let me know when she comes out," Thomas said flatly.

A group of workers emerged from the door, drawing Ken's attention. He sat back when he realized Trina wasn't among them.

"Why do you want to talk to Trina?" Ken asked, shifting nervously in his seat.

"I told you. Her brother is one of the cops after us. You saw the news. They're at my apartment right now, running around like ants that found a candy bar. I just wanna talk to Trina and explain things to her, so she can tell her brother. Maybe they'll back off. All right?" Thomas said convincingly.

Ken looked down at his lap and spoke quietly. "I don't like this. I wish things were different. I wish it was like it was when we were kids, before mom and dad disappeared."

"Well, that isn't the way life works," Thomas said pointedly.

Ken turned to his brother. "But if you hadn't killed those people, the police wouldn't be chasing you."

Thomas stared out the window. "Us. They're chasing us, Ken. They're probably at your apartment now too. We have to stick together. Remember, you're a living god too."

"I suppose." Ken shifted in his seat again. "Look, I'm not too sure about this 'living god' thing."

Thomas shot him a look.

Ken felt the simmering rage inside his brother. "I mean, it is cool to have all that power, but–I don't wanna kill people. I'm ok with hunting bighorn sheep and stuff. I like that. Maybe cows or something, you know, like Grandma did."

Thomas grew annoyed. "Dammit Ken, you know as well as I do, Grandma hunted people before she got old. She showed me the trophies in her shed, and they weren't prize-winning steers." Thomas sighed. "I bit you so you could finally be something."

Ken looked at his lap.

"What? Were you going to live like a pissant all your life? Driving a piece of shit car and working like a dog in a warehouse? Grandma saw something in me. In us. You should be thanking me every goddamn day," Thomas snapped.

Ken seemed to shrink into the seat. "No, No. I appreciate you changing me. I do. It's just the people. I know you said they were cattle for us and all, but it doesn't feel right to me. Some people are nice. I like deer and stuff better."

Thomas shook his head. "You're pathetic, Ken. I hand you the world, and you want to run through the desert and chase fucking antelope."

There was a long silence then Ken asked, "Why did you kill Doug?"

Thomas tried to calm himself. Looking out over the parking lot, he said, "Because you told me he was riding your ass. I felt your shame and anger. You needed to understand you don't have to take that. I wanted to show you what power you could use if people pissed you off. We don't take crap from anyone."

Ken turned to his brother. "Sure, he got on my case once or twice and I got mad, but he wasn't all bad. He had a family and kids. What about them now?"

Thomas was silent. A dark thought started to form in his mind. Perhaps Ken wasn't meant for this life. Would he ever be the ally Thomas had hoped, or would he become a liability?

The employee door opened. A solitary figure was silhouetted in the escaping light of the door frame. "Is that her?" Thomas asked.

Ken glanced at the figure. He hesitated. "Yes, that's her."

Ed impatiently sat in his unmarked Ford Taurus, tapping his fingers on the wheel. Of all the days for my baby sister to need a ride, he thought, it has to be today. Under normal circumstances, she would have taken an Uber home. In fact, she suggested it. He overrode her and said he would drive her home. He was always protective of her, often more than she liked. But with Thomas Rutledge on the loose, he was not taking any chances. He'd drive her home and then get back to the office. So much to do, but they were closing in on him. Ed could feel it.

The flash of light from the door opening caught his attention, and he saw Trina striding out of the warehouse. The sun had set and the blue glow of the parking lights cast a strange glow over the lot as they warmed up. Moving from barely lit to darkness, she made her way across the parking lot. He started the engine and put the car in gear when he saw a figure get out of a car and approach her. His senses heightened.

Panic swelled in his chest as he saw the figure grab Trina's wrist. He punched the accelerator and covered the few hundred feet quickly, skidding to a stop next to them.

"State Police. Put your hands over your head!" he screamed as he drew his SigSauer .45. A second man got out of the Nissan Sentra and stood next to the first. They looked almost identical. The only difference was the one holding his sister's wrist had a scruffy beard and uncombed hair.

Trina looked at the second man, "Ken, what's going on? That's my brother, he's a cop. Don't do anything stupid."

The figure released Trina's wrist. He looked at Ed, and grinned. "Brother? Well isn't this my lucky day."

John drove while Marc dialed. Voicemail. "Damn it, Ed, pick up!" Marc said to the phone.

The tires screamed in protest as the big block Dodge Charger roared around a corner. The red and blue lights in the grill reflected off the rears of the cars in his path just before John passed them. Terri and Alex, buckled in the back seat, gripped the overhead handles tightly. Marc focused on the phone and called again.

Ed kept his weapon trained on the men. In the background, he could hear his phone ringing in the car. "I said put your hands over your heads, both of you. Nobody has to get hurt here, Ken. Just do what I say." Years as a trooper had taught Ed how to read volatile situations. He decided to try to lower the temperature of the encounter, but something about the first man was unsettling. "Okay, everybody just calm down, and let's talk a little bit. I know he's Ken. What's your name?"

The man sneered. "My name? Thomas. Thomas Rutledge. I thought you would have guessed that by now."

Ed's stomach dropped. He motioned for Trina to get behind him. "Get in the car, Trina."

"Ya' know, I met a state trooper once," Thomas said mockingly. "I think his name was Pearl. He died screaming. Didja know him?"

"Ken, please, just listen, this is my brother," Trina pleaded from Ed's car. "He doesn't want to hurt you."

Ken looked uncomfortable. He turned to Thomas. "Maybe we just let them go?"

"It's too late for that" Thomas hissed. "If you won't do it, I will. We don't have all night here." He took a step toward Ed.

"Get on the ground! Now!" Ed yelled.

"Or what? You're gonna shoot me? Let's see how that goes." Thomas took another step forward. The sound of two rapid shots rang out. Ed put two .45 rounds into Thomas's chest. But he didn't as much as flinch.

With another step, Thomas shoved Ed, sending him backwards onto the car door, slamming it shut.

Ed tried to bring his gun up, but Thomas caught his wrist and twisted it. He heard a pop, then searing pain in his wrist as the gun fell with a metallic clunk to the pavement. He screamed, then mustering all the strength he could, he swung his left elbow hard into the side of Thomas's head. There was a loud hollow crack and Thomas's head snapped over, then came right back.

Terror swelled in Ed's chest as Thomas smiled, blood staining his teeth. "That was a good one. I like your fight."

Thomas's eyes glowed with a red hue and his face began to twist. When he snarled, Ed saw the teeth. The canines were suddenly long, and the jaw started to protrude.

Ed yelled to Trina, "Get the hell out of here! Drive! Now!"

Trina hesitated as she watched her brother struggling. She could see Ken staring blankly at the fight. Then she caught a glimpse of Thomas's eyes and face. Panicked, she threw the car in drive and stood on the accelerator. White smoke enveloped Ed and Thomas momentarily as the sedan screamed from the parking lot.

Thomas turned to his brother, his voice now deep and gravelly. "Are you going to stand there like a statue, or are you going to do something. She's getting away."

Ken watched as the taillights disappeared out of the lot.

Thomas shook his head angrily. "You're an idiot, Ken. Just like I thought."

Distracted momentarily, Thomas released his grip on Ed, who dropped to the ground gasping and scrambling to retrieve his gun.

"Don't say that, Tom. I am not," Ken protested.

Lying on his back and aiming with his left hand, Ed emptied the magazine into Thomas. Holes appeared in the man's jeans and shirt as the bullets tore home.

Thomas snapped his attention back to Ed, lying on the pavement. Looking down at him, he ripped off his torn shirt. The pain from the impact of the bullets fully unleashed the monster. His mind clouded with a white hot rage.

Ed gaped in awe as Thomas reached down and, with a clawed hand, dug one of the bullets from his abdomen. A small trickle of blood appeared but stopped as quickly as it started. He held the lead mushroom up to his face for examination before tossing it at Ed.

Throwing back his head, he let out a roar. Thick gray brown hair began to cover his flesh.

Ed's mouth fell open as Thomas seemed to swell, thick muscle rippled under the fur. What was a man was now a massive growling beast. Red eyes fixed on him.

Marc continued to call, and at last the phone was answered. He thought he heard crying. "Ed, is that you? Listen, get Trina, and get the hell away from the warehouse."

Through the sobs, a woman's voice answered. "No. This is Trina."

"Where's Ed?" Marc asked.

There was a slight pause. "I think they killed him, back at the warehouse."

A lump formed immediately in John's throat as he reached over and took the phone. "This is John, Ed's partner. Are you ok, Trina? Where are you?"

"Yes, but Ed–he was trying to protect me and then–"

"Trina, where are you? We'll come to you."

"Uh, I'm at 40th and University at a red light." she managed to relay between sobs.

"Okay, take a left. About a mile or so up the street, there's a Waffle House. Pull over there. There's a Holiday Inn and Hilton there. Park in the back. We'll be there in two minutes."

"John, he was fighting with a guy in the parking lot of the warehouse. Ken Rutledge's brother. Thomas, I think he said his name was Thomas. Ed tried to stop him, but–oh my God, he started to turn into–something, a monster. I wanted to help, but Ed told me to get away and —"

"It's Okay. You did what you had to do. Just pull into the hotel center. There's lots of people around there. You'll be safe. We'll be there in a few."

Everyone in the car heard the conversation. A silence fell over the group as John sped to the Waffle House lot.

Tears rolled down John's cheeks as he got on the radio and reported an officer was likely down at the Amazon warehouse parking lot, 3003 South 38th Street.

When the transmission was finished, he tossed the mic on the floor as a primal scream poured from his throat.

CHAPTER 19

THE SCENE AT THE hospital was chaotic and heartbreaking. Ed's body had been recovered from the parking lot and rushed to the trauma unit in hopes the doctors might be able to perform a miracle. They could not, and Ed was declared dead upon arrival.

Trina was hysterical. Between sobs, she demanded to see Ed, refusing to believe her big lovable brother was gone. Finally John, who had seen the body, took her by her shoulders and looked her in the eye. "Trina, don't do this to yourself. You don't want to see him. Not like this." He then pulled her close and held her as she broke down.

Back in the war room, John slumped in his chair, eyes closed. Exhaustion and pain had finally caught up to him. "Tell me *exactly* what we're dealing with?"

Alex spoke up. "A lycanthrope."

John stared at her. The look in his eyes showed he had no intention of trying to figure out what that word meant.

Terri entered the room at that moment. She had been down the hall checking on Trina, who was in John's office sleeping, a female trooper posted outside the door. The doctor at the hospital had prescribed her Xanax to help her sleep. "A shapeshifter," she said directly.

"A goddamn skinwalker?" John asked.

"Yes. commonly known as a werewolf. Two of them, it seems." Alex said matter of factly.

John looked around the room. "Werewolves? Really? I thought they only came around during a full moon or something."

"Actually, the moon has no light, it's just reflected sunlight. They can transform anytime." Terri stated.

John nodded mockingly. "'Course they can. Why the hell wouldn't they." He paused a second, then continued, "So, you guys came out here knowing there was a werewolf running around?"

"Yeah. Pretty much. You understand why we couldn't say anything before today." Marc offered quietly. "We were hoping to find it, I mean them, through your investigation."

John looked around the room. "And then what?" John said angrily.

"Kill them." Terri said coldly.

John scoffed, "With what? This thing has already been shot to shit."

"We have a weapon." Marc said, looking at the floor.

Before John could ask what the weapon was, Alex jumped in. "There is another matter at play here I feel should be addressed. It sounds, from Trina, this lycanthrope, Thomas Rutledge, has targeted her. If that is the case, there is the possibility that there may now be a–what would be the best way to describe it, a spiritual entanglement between them."

"A what?" Terri's mouth fell open.

"A psychological entanglement might be the better description." Alex looked down at the table.

"What are you saying? He can read her mind or something?" John asked. "This is all getting too goddamn weird."

"No. Not read her mind per se, but–feel her. If Thomas has this trait, he may be able to feel what she feels and he may be able to find her," Alex said without looking up. Everyone was silent.

Alex continued, "Sometimes, when a lycanthrope has an emotional connection to a person, prey or—a potential mate or even just strong emotional bonding, there may be a psychological attachment. It is difficult to describe, but the focus of this attachment may sense it through dreams."

Terri suddenly remembered the vivid dream she had involving Alex. What did that mean? She tried to calm her mind. Stay on task, she thought to herself.

"You mean, he might be able to track Trina, with this psycho attachment or whatever it is?" Marc asked, sounding a little worried. He caught Terri's attention and gave her a 'What the hell?' look with his eyes.

She recognized the look and silently shook her head.

"Yes, I'm afraid so," Alex said quietly.

"How's that even possible?" Marc asked.

Sarah chimed in, "There is a thing called quantum entanglement, where two particles can be separated by distance but still be connected. In fact, they cannot be distinguished from each other even though they occupy separate space. It is a thing in physics." Everyone turned and looked at her questioningly. "What? So I like to read sciency stuff, too." she said.

John shook his head, "Wait a minute. So you're telling me I have twin werewolves running around my state and now one of them has locked onto my dead partner's sister? And just how the hell do you know this stuff?" he asked, turning to Alex.

"You do not need to know the details, but suffice to say I am familiar with these kinds of creatures," she snapped. "Now, do we want to do something about getting Trina somewhere safe?"

Marc spoke to John. "I'm thinking of somewhere remote. Maybe we try to put some miles between Trina and them. See if we can break this connection. Plus, the city and suburbs are too congested. These guys could get close to us before anyone noticed." Marc refused to look at Alex. He was pissed off that she withheld this information from him.

"I think I know a place." John said as he reached for his phone.

CHAPTER 20

MARC PULLED THE RENTED Camry off the gravel road onto a long dirt driveway. As he slowed to make the turn, the home seemed more quiet and remote than the first time they were here.

In the backseat, Trina was still feeling the effects of the sedative from the night before and dozed most of the drive, head leaning on Sarah's shoulder.

Near Sicheii's house, he recognized Chooli's pickup truck. She was waiting for them and stepped off the porch. When the car came to a stop, she strode toward them carrying a lever action .30-.30 rifle on her shoulder.

"Thank you for agreeing to help us, Chooli," Marc said, as Sarah and Trina came to his side.

She removed her sunglasses and hung them from her shirt pocket, then asked, "Where's John and the others?"

"They're staying in the city, hoping to eliminate the threat there." Marc replied as he hefted his go-bag and Trina's duffel.

Trina's eyes were hollow, her face worn with sorrow and shock, as she looked at Chooli "Thank you." she managed to say.

Chooli's face softened as she took Trina's hand. "You are welcome here. I am sorry for you. Let's go inside."

The temperature was rising quickly, but inside it was still cool. Sarah noted Sicheii's possessions still filled the house. His wheelchair and a small oxygen tank sat near the hospital bed. Pictures of his family hung on the wall over the bed. She could see a smiling John and his family in a large frame. It felt strange to be in the house of a recently dead person, like a violation. Items that were dearly important to him still sat where they were, but without their owner, were now just things in a house.

"Sorry about Sicheii," Marc said as he looked at the bed.

Chooli nodded and motioned for them to sit on the sofa. Sarah dropped her go-bag near the arm of the sofa and helped ease Trina's onto the cushions.

Chooli carried a kitchen chair into the living room and faced them. No one sat in Sicheii's large recliner. She turned to Trina. "I met your brother a few times, with John. He was a gentle giant, full of heart. He'll be missed," Chooli said gently. "You should be safe here."

Trina nodded silently.

Chooli turned to Marc and Sarah. "So Sicheii was right, *yee naald-looshii* has returned."

Trina looked at her, confused, "Yee what?"

Chooli continued. "It's Navajo. It means one who walks on all fours, a skinwalker. You saw it, didn't you?"

Trina's face registered shock at the recollection. "Yes. I saw him, it, whatever it was. I saw it start to change. My brother fought with it and–I wanted to help but–"

"There was nothin' ya could've done," Marc said quietly, looking at his boots.

Tears welled in Trina's eyes.

Sarah spoke up. "Actually, we believe there are two of them, twin brothers." She turned to Trina. "There is a chance that they may try to track you."

The fog was clearing, but Trina didn't understand what Sarah was saying. "Track me?"

Marc spoke up. "Apparently, when one of these things zeroes in on a person, they can sorta follow them. Some kind of entanglement thing."

Trina's mouth hung agape.

"Have you had any odd thoughts or dreams?" Sarah asked gently.

Trina looked surprised, "Yes, I had a very weird dream on the way here. How did you know?"

Sarah frowned as she looked at Marc, "We've been told when the entanglement happens, there may be premonitions."

Chooli leaned in, "What do you mean, premonitions? Like visions or something?"

"Yeah, sort of. I think they usually come in the form of dreams." Marc replied. "Trina, what can you tell us about this dream?"

"I was walking through the warehouse alone. It was dark and I felt like I had to fix the lights. As I made my way, I heard off and on scraping on the cardboard boxes. I turned and—something was there. It was walking toward me, shredding boxes with these claws as it stared at me. It was big and covered with hair. I—I thought it was from the pills the doctor gave me to sleep. It seemed so real, though." She began shaking.

"Understood. It's okay." Sarah put her hand on Trina's shoulder as she looked at Marc. The connection was there.

Marc turned to Chooli. "As remote as we are, there's a chance these two assholes may slip the dragnet in the city and find their way here. We need to plan for that." He instinctively took out his cell phone to check for any messages from Terri or John and saw he had no bars.

Chooli saw him check. "There's no reception out here. The only place you can get some signal is up on one of the mesas. Other than that, it's the land line." She pointed to the yellow wall phone in the kitchen.

Marc nodded.

Chooli's eyes narrowed. "I have a question. How do you two know anything about skinwalkers?"

"We're familiar with them, lycanthropes." Sarah said calmly.

Before Chooli could ask what that was, Marc chimed in. "Werewolves. We've dealt with this before."

Chooli nodded. "Your friend Alex. I know."

Marc and Sarah stared at her in shock.

"What?" Trina looked around the group.

Chooli leaned back in the chair. "Sicheii must have felt it when he met her. I sensed something when I touched her hand. I didn't know what it was about her at the time, but it makes sense now."

Marc and Sarah looked at each other with resignation. "So much for secrets," Sarah whispered under her breath.

Trina looked stunned. "You mean that lovely woman is a—one of them?"

"Yeah, she's a shapeshifter, but if there is such a thing as a good one, she's it." Marc said.

"She's saved our butts on a couple of occasions. I can personally attest to that." Sarah pointed out.

Trina shook her head. "Am I the last person in the world to know there are damn werewolves running around? How is this possible?"

"I'm sorry, Trina. We know this all sounds like complete insanity. I'm sorry we're hitting you with this all at once," Sarah said softly.

Chooli looked at the wheelchair across the room. "Before his stroke, Sicheii would talk about the universe always trying to balance itself. Hot and cold, light and darkness, good and evil. It's almost like he knew you guys were coming."

Marc looked at Chooli. "In the last couple of years, I've learned not to dismiss anything. But I gotta tell you, that's too deep for my thick skull right now. My goal is to keep everybody in this room in one piece."

Chooli nodded.

"So, with that in mind, we've learned some things in dealing with Alex. And based on what we've seen here, they seem on point for your Arizona variety of werewolf. First of all, bullets have little to no effect on them." Marc said, nodding toward the rifle Chooli had resting by the front door.

Trina spoke up, "He's right. I saw Ed shoot it. It did nothing."

"Well, that fits with the legend we have as well," Chooli said as she leaned in. "So what does kill them?"

"We aren't one hundred percent sure, but Alex noted old weapons are most effective. Edged weapons and possibly fire."

Chooli thought for a second then got up and went to a closet. She returned with a small compound bow and quiver of arrows. "What about this?" she asked.

"I like the way you think," Sarah said with a smile.

"Sicheii got it for me when I was a little girl. I used to hunt rabbits with it, but I haven't used it in years," Chooli said as she walked back to her chair.

"I'd say that qualifies as an old weapon," Marc said with a grin.

"We also have these, if it comes to it," Sarah said as she drew the large seax blade from her bag.

Chooli smiled. "I like the way you think, as well."

Marc glanced out the front window. The landscape was level and open before him. His mind went back to his time in Iraq and Afghanistan.

This place was a nightmare to defend. There were too many ways for Thomas and Ken to approach. With their simple weapons, they'd never be able to hold them off. They needed a tactical advantage. With no time to construct defenses, they would have to look to one of the oldest deciding factors in any combat situation: the terrain.

Marc turned to Chooli. "I saw some hills around, is there anything back there?"

"My great-grandfather's old homestead is tucked in there. It's pretty rough and isolated."

Marc stood. "That might be better. We should pack up what food we can and move there. Bring some extra clothes, Chooli, we may be there for a few days." She rose and headed toward the spare bedroom she had been using while she was staying with Sicheii.

"Mind if I look around to see if there is anything that might be useful?" he asked.

"Be my guest," Chooli said over her shoulder.

Marc called out from the kitchen, "Is there electricity at this homestead?"

"Yes, I think it's still hooked up," Chooli replied. "And a water pump. The family used to use it as a hunting cabin."

He returned a few minutes later with a box of items, most noticeable were three five-pound bags of flour, a box of kitchen matches, a spool of picture-hanging wire, and an oscillating floor fan.

Sarah looked at the box and cocked her head to the side, "Um, flour? What are you going to do with that, bake them some bread?"

Marc laughed, "I have a plan. Grab that oxygen tank as well."

CHAPTER 21

TERRI CHECKED HER PHONE, there were no messages from Marc or Sarah.

John glanced over. He saw the concerned look on her face. "There's not much for reception out there."

She slipped her phone into her cargo pants pocket. "Makes sense."

The FBI command center had been activated overnight and hummed with activity around them. It was a cavernous space packed with desks and computers and bodies. John was struck by the resources that had been cobbled together in a matter of hours. Like everything in the Bureau, there was a plan. Once the Special Agent in Charge, the SAC, authorized the activation it could be operational in less than an hour. Analysts and agents had designated desks and responsibilities. Task force officers and representatives from all the local and federal law enforcement agencies had desks reserved for them with placards.

Large smart boards around the room displayed key information. On the center board, newly minted wanted posters with the faces and biographical information of Thomas and Kenneth Rutlege stared out at the group. In large red letters they read, "Armed and Dangerous. Do Not Approach. Notify Command Authority if Located."

SSA Mike Carson entered the room. His smooth head glistened under the fluorescent lights. He scanned the room and soon spotted John and Terri. Weaving his way through the throng of bustling bodies, he made his way to them. With no words, he embraced John in a strong bear hug. As he patted his back vigorously, she heard him whisper, "I'm so sorry about Ed."

John nodded. "Thank you, Mike."

"We're gonna get these sonsabitches," Mike said as he released John.

Before John could acknowledge the sentiment, an analyst approached Mike. "The emergency cell phone tracking subpoena was signed. We just got the order to the phone company. They should have cell tower pings back to us in about ten minutes. Thought you'd want to know."

"Good deal. We got tac teams geared up and ready to roll. Just tell us where these guys are and we'll release the dogs," Mike replied evenly. "I'm going down and jock-up with the team." He spun on his heels and briskly strode toward the door.

A concerned look appeared in John's eyes as he looked at Terri. "What'll happen if they corner them?"

Terri shook her head. "Nothing good. We need to be ready to move on the location when it comes in." She held up her hand radio. "I'm on the tactical channel, so we'll get the location the same time they do."

"Yeah, and what then?"

"We'll have a little time before they hit the place. They have procedures they'll follow. We just have to get to Thomas and Ken first."

John shook his head. "That wasn't the 'what then' I was talking about." He lowered his voice. "How do *we* deal with them?"

"Let's get moving. We can talk about this in the car," Terri said as she took out her cell phone.

In the relative quiet of the FBI building lobby, Alex sat reading *Meditations*, by Marcus Aurelius. She was not really reading. She tried to appear nonchalant as she occasionally turned a page, but inside, she was barely containing the boiling cauldron.

She had failed. Ed Stackhouse was dead, killed by one of her kind. She didn't know Ed well. But what she did know, she very much liked. Feelings of remorse and pain were relatively new to her. What would she feel if something happened to Terri or Marc or Sarah?

Her eyes found a quote: "How very near us stand the two vast gulfs of time, the past and the future, in which all things disappear."

We only have the instant in between, Alex thought.

She took a cleansing breath with closed eyes. The buzzing of her cell phone brought her out of her short meditation.

After a quick glance at the message, she packed her things and awaited the arrival of Terri and John.

A yellow traffic sign flashed a warning: "Police Emergency Ahead. Be Prepared to Stop."

That was all Thomas needed to see. He deftly maneuvered the Sentra into an alley behind a strip mall and whipped out his phone. A dark cloud came over his face as he pulled up his Waze app. The routes to the south, toward the Mexican border, were all blocked. "Cops aren't as stupid as I thought," he said under his breath.

Scrolling through the maps, he found a path out of the city. Suddenly, a pit formed in his stomach as he stared at the screen. *Those bastards at Apple are listening,* he thought. "Gimme your phone, Ken."

"They're pinging all around the ASU campus," Terri relayed to John. "They got cell phone tower hits on South McCallister."

"Jesus." John said as he pulled the car onto the street. "PD is gonna have to lock that whole place down. If they're cornered with a lot of people around, what are they gonna do?"

"Yeah, I'm afraid to think about that. At least it's winter break. Not too many students and faculty around," Terri offered. What would happen? There would certainly be casualties, civilians and law enforcement. There would be cameras too, so sending Alex in would be very risky.

In the backseat, Alex seemed unusually serene. "From personal experience, there will be almost no faculty present on the university grounds. A very small number of students will likely be there, foreign students and those few taking winter courses."

John glanced in the rearview mirror. "Good point. Hey, you guys never explained what this weapon you brought with you is. Is it some top secret government thing or what?"

Terri paused for a second. "Yeah, it's sensitive. I don't know if we can deploy it on a campus. If they break the perimeter, we can use it."

"What the hell kind of thing is it? I need to know, now!"

Removing her sunglasses, Alex looked at John in the mirror, then spoke. "It's me, Detective John Lightfoot. I am the weapon."

The car veered as John whipped his head around. "The hell you say? You're the—what the hell are you?"

Terri swung around and stared at Alex. "Alex has a very unique skill set. She's seen this before and knows how to deal with these creatures," she said while staring at Alex.

"Skill set? What the hell kind of skill set do you have to deal with werewolves?" he asked.

Terri replied, "One that we aren't at liberty to explain. I'm sorry. You will have to trust me on this one."

John grimaced. He had a thousand questions all popping at once. But Terri's tone was clear. She wasn't going to answer anymore. "Alright. I guess I'm in for a pound at this point. What do we do next?"

"Let's get to the rally point and see what the situation looks like," Terri said. The radio crackled, and a calm woman's voice instructed all tactical units to proceed to the intramural fields. "That's where we need to be."

Alex had one more thing she wanted to express. "I would like to apologize to you, Detective Lightfoot."

He glanced at her in the rearview mirror. "For what?"

"I failed you and Detective Stackhouse. I am sorry he is dead. I should have been more attuned to the threat our quarry posed," Alex said quietly.

He didn't look back as he took a deep breath. "Well, we all could've done some things better. You guys tried to warn us but–. Look, I don't know if the outcome would have been any different. Sometimes, it's just your day."

The rally point appeared ahead and it was clear that the circus was well underway. The campus was in the process of being locked down. An emergency shelter-in-place order had been distributed to all cell phones in the area and on the university's social media. Three helicopters thumped through the air immediately above the sprawling campus. Several more news choppers circled at a distance.

John leaned over to Terri and whispered. "I have a bad feeling. This isn't making any sense. They're just driving around the campus?"

"Terri nodded. "I'm with you. This doesn't feel good."

John pulled up a map of the area on his phone. "Shit. I think they're on a bus."

Terri's face went pale. "At least their phones are."

Alex surveyed the hundreds of uniformed officers hurrying to their assigned locations, with more arriving every minute. "A very clever way to throw the dogs off their scent."

Once the vehicle stop was initiated by a state police tactical team, Thomas and Kenneth Rutledge's phones were discovered in a McDonald's bag in the rear of a campus Flash bus. Records showed Thomas Rutlege had attended classes there and was thus familiar with the area. Captain Cutler convinced the brass that a full search of the campus and surrounding area needed to be conducted. It was the last location the suspects were known to have occupied. In short order, the small army of law enforcement officers spread over the campus and began searching every building. To speed the process, additional resources were pulled from units blocking roads not leading to Mexico. The thump of rotor blades from multiple helicopters overhead was continuous throughout the search. It wasn't a bad call, just the wrong one.

Hours later, it became apparent the pair was not on the campus. A thorough review of CCTV videos didn't reveal any images of the pair entering any buildings, and none of the search teams found any trace of them. Following the trail of earlier cell tower hits, investigators discovered the suspects' Nissan Sentra, located near a bus stop several miles from the campus.

Gabriel Ortiz took a long pull of water, causing the plastic bottle to crinkle. Sitting on the hood of the police car, he relayed how he came to end up in the trunk of a late model Nissan Sentra. "It happened so fast. I just parked and got out to go to work, and this dude came out of nowhere. He snatched my keys and grabbed me by the neck. I thought he was gonna kill me. I said I got a wife and baby girl at home. I said, 'Take the truck, man.' I was sure I was gonna die. But that was when the other dude stepped in, must have been his brother or somethin'. He grabbed the first dude's arm and said somethin' like "Stop it. I don't want anymore killin'. Let this guy go."

He took another gulp of water. "The first dude looked like he still wanted to kill me, but he ended up wrapping me in duct tape and stuffing me in the trunk. Dude just tossed me in there. Really strong."

"Did you know either of these guys?" the officer asked.

"No, man. I never seen them before in my life. That first dude was scary. Like seriously homicidal crazy looking."

The officer pulled up a photo of Thomas Rutledge on his phone. "Was this one of the males?"

Gabriel nodded vigorously. "Yeah, that was the first dude."

Thomas drove the blue GMC Sierra pickup out of the city. Before ditching his phone, the Waze app had shown him all the major roads south to Mexico had long delays. Roadblocks. The routes north were lighter but still probably had roadblocks. But there was a path through a residential neighborhood near a golf course that put him close to open desert. The Sierra easily made the transition from pavement to open ground. Within minutes, they were alone on a dusty road as Phoenix faded into the horizon behind them.

Thomas spoke after several minutes of silence. "You shouldn't have stopped me back there, Ken. That guy is gonna tell them what car we're in."

Ken shifted in the seat. "He didn't do anything to us. He had a family."

Thomas checked the rearview mirror. "That isn't my problem."

"I just pictured Trina. She was so scared and upset. She's my friend. I just want to find her and make things right," Ken said softly.

"Ken, you can't make things right. Her brother tried to kill me, and I had to kill him," Thomas said matter of factly.

"He was only trying to protect her! You didn't have to kill him!" Ken was on the verge of tears.

"These people are here to either humor us or feed us. That's all. They aren't our equals or peers or friends. Everyone is below us. You have to understand that," Thomas stated. "Grandma knew it."

Ken slumped in the seat. He suddenly had a disturbing thought. "Thomas, what happened to mom and dad?"

Tom gripped the steering wheel and stared straight ahead. "I don't know. They just disappeared in the desert one night. That's what the cops said."

"Did Grandma kill them?" Ken asked.

Thomas didn't answer and didn't look at his brother.

"Did she?" Ken pressed.

"What do you think?" Thomas said calmly.

Ken looked away. "I think she did. I think she was angry because mom and dad didn't want us to spend too much time with her."

"Maybe, Ken. They should've listened to her. She was a killer," Thomas said coldly.

"I don't want to be a killer! I don't want this life," Ken screamed.

Thomas let out a breath. "Don't be a pussy. You're a werewolf, Ken. We're the top of the food chain. We can have anything we want. It's right there for the taking."

"Top of the food chain. Is that why we're running for the hills in a stolen car? This don't seem so great."

Thomas snapped, "It's just a fucking setback! Okay. Why are you always pointing out what's wrong? I'm the smart one, not the retar–"

He stopped himself. It wasn't that he was concerned with Ken's hurt feelings. Ever since he killed Trina's brother in the parking lot, he felt different about Ken. His brother was going to have to go. But with the cops looking for him right now, this wasn't the time or place to pick a fight.

He took a softer tone when he spoke next. "We'll regroup when we get to Mexico, after the cops take down the roadblocks. Until then, we'll hang out in the desert for a while. You can chase all the antelope and bighorn sheep you like. Sound good?"

Ken turned and stared silently at the landscape as they drove.

Thomas used the quiet to focus. He had never tracked someone before. He didn't even realize he could do it. Something happened when he touched Trina. They were now connected. He let his mind relax and he–felt her. He could sense she was in the desert. There was a Native American woman with her, and some white people. She was out there somewhere, near the mesas.

He pushed the accelerator and glanced at his brother. He felt no remorse at the dark thoughts bubbling in his mind. Trina was Ken's only real friend. She was the only one alive to have seen them together. If she was eliminated, he might be able to pass as Ken. If he got cornered, he could slow his speech and play dumb long enough to convince the cops he had nothing to do with any of it. Then, he'd slip away. Yeah, that might work.

Of course for that to be successful, Ken would have to–. He stopped himself. Gods have to do hard things sometimes. Don't think about it too much. Don't want Ken to get any ideas. Best for everyone if it's a surprise.

A calm came over him as he drove.

Marc stood in the doorway and surveyed the small cabin. The smell of dust and stale air told him no one had been in there in a long time. The wood frame homestead was about as bare bones as you could get. The front door opened directly into the living room. A small wood burning stove sat in the corner. A couch and a couple of chairs comprised the spartan furnishings in the cramped room. A relatively modern ivory colored fan, hanging from the ceiling, seemed out of place. The living room was separated from the kitchen area by a small dinette set. A gas stove and refrigerator rounded out the remaining visible furniture. Further back, down a narrow hallway, was a bathroom and two small bedrooms. A large propane tank outside provided fuel for the gas stove.

The location of the property was much more to his liking. Chooli's description of the area was accurate. It was surrounded on three sides by steep sloped hills leading up to flat-topped mesas. Chooli showed him a narrow path that led to the top. If it was necessary, they could retreat up there and make a stand. Their weapons would be more effective against Thomas and Ken while they were trying to climb. The driveway up to the house was long and dusty—anyone approaching by car would be visible at least a mile away.

Chooli moved to open a window. Marc stopped her. "Hold up. We need to keep all the windows closed."

She raised her eyebrows. "Okay, but it's gonna get nasty in here."

"Nasty might be what he's going for," Sarah commented.

Marc walked Trina to the back bedroom. "I have an idea. Maybe we can turn one of their advantages into a disadvantage. I want you to study this room, focus on the details. If they show up, I want you to think all sorts of warm thoughts for Ken, even Thomas. Warm, nice thoughts and this bedroom. Got it?"

She looked at him with a quizzical look but nodded.

Marc looked at the group. "Good. Now everyone else, we're going to change clothes. Maybe run around outside a little first and sweat them up. Then come into this bedroom and leave them in a pile."

Chooli smiled. "Bait."

Marc caught her eye. "Exactly."

Outside the cabin, Chooli and Sarah jogged around, working up a good sweat. Marc walked the ground, eyeing the steep inclines behind the structure. He climbed the trail to the top and surveyed the area. When he came down, he gathered the two women to a shady spot on the north side of the cabin. With a twig, he sketched out in the dirt their location, the road, the house, and the surrounding hills. Using the twig as a pointer, he started describing the plan.

"Okay, here's the way I see it. The bad guys are probably feeling pretty cocky. They'll drive right up to the door here. When we see 'em coming, we hightail it up this goat path trail to the top with Trina. We hold the high ground and defend the path up with everything we have."

"Sure, but how long can we hold them off?" Sarah asked.

"Hopefully, long enough," he said matter of factly.

He looked at Chooli and Sarah. Their faces were unsure. "Look, we have some advantages here."

Chooli chimed in. "Really? Like what?"

"First, we know them. We know how many of them are coming, we know the way they're coming, and we know what they are. Second, they don't know us. They don't know how many of us are here, and they don't know we have effective weapons."

As he said the words, Marc realized their weapons were untested. They were exactly what Alex had described, but would they work?

"Thirdly, we have surprise. They aren't expecting anything close to what we're gonna give 'em. They don't know I got a bunch of steely eyed death dealers by my side." He gave a grin and a wink.

Sarah and Chooli smiled back. He needed them to feel confident.

Marc stood. "Plus, I have one other trick up my sleeve. Let's get inside."

Thomas eased the truck to a stop in front of the small house. A dusty red Toyota Camry sat a few yards away. He was no expert tracker, but judging by the footprints left near the car, he could tell several people had gotten out. Ken stood by the truck and nervously kicked at a rock as Thomas walked up the ramp to the porch.

His muscles felt strong and alive as the transformation started. He threw his shoulder into the old wooden door and it easily gave way.

Launching into the house, he quickly realized it was empty. Closing his eyes, he inhaled deeply through his nose. He recalled Trina's scent. She had been here. Along with some others. He leaned over near the hospital bed in the corner. The sheets had been removed, but the mattress still clung onto the faint stench of medicine and death. It reminded him of the hospice where his grandmother died.

In a fit of rage, he tossed the bed across the room.

"I'm in a world of hurt here, Grandma. What do I do?" he whispered to himself.

Grandmother's voice answered in his head. *"You know what you have to do, Rutty. Track them. Find them. And then kill them. All of them. She and Ken are the keys. With them gone, you can be free to start over. You can do this, but you have to move quickly. Do it for Grandma."*

His grandmother's words disappeared as the wall-mounted phone in the kitchen rang with a shocking clang. Before the third ring, he knocked the yellow plastic box from the wall.

Outside, Thomas scanned the horizon. "Your girlfriend isn't here, but she was. She can't be too far."

"She isn't my girlfriend, Thomas. She's just a friend."

Ken looked at the dirt clod he had been kicking.

Thomas closed his eyes. He could feel her, it was strong. She was close. He started slowly walking the yard, peering at the ground as he stepped. After several minutes he found it. Tire tracks in the fine red dust leading to an old jeep trail to the west.

Terri slid a pile of papers to the side as John set the three cups of coffee on the war room table. Nearby, Terri's handheld FBI radio chattered. She was half listening to it in case something useful materialized. It did not.

Likewise, John's State Police radio, tuned to a specific channel for the manhunt, occasionally burped an alert or update. Thus far, no credible leads had come in. John, Terri, and Alex were all reaching the same conclusion. Thomas and Ken had somehow evaded the search and gotten out of the city.

John took a sip of his coffee. It wasn't fresh, but at least it was hot and had caffeine. "I think we better give a call out to the house. Let Marc and Sarah know what's going on back here. Make sure they know to be on their toes out there."

"Absolutely," said Terri. "But if I know Marc, he's already set up a plan A and plan B and is working on a plan C."

She brought the cup to her lips. Despite the addition of a liberal amount of creamer, the bitterness of the brew still assaulted her taste buds.

Alex paced the room slowly with her hands behind her back.

"Yes, he is quite capable, as is Agent Holmes. Were these simply men that they faced, I should not be worried in the least. But they aren't simply men."

She had forgone the coffee altogether but could smell the acerbity as John entered with the mugs. It was drip coffee that had been brewed several hours ago and did not appeal to her in the least.

John dialed the landline and put his cell phone to his ear. After a few seconds, a confused look appeared on his face.

"That's weird. Phone was ringing then it just cut out."

He dialed again and, this time, got a busy signal. "I can't get anyone at the house. I think we should head out there."

Terri frowned. "All right, let's move." She shouldered her ballistic vest and go-bag as she strode for the door. Alex was already two steps ahead of her.

"So what, exactly, *is* this plan?" Sarah asked.

Marc tore open the bags of flour.

"I'm thinking if they show up, we give 'em a helluva surprise. Then try to hold out until the cavalry arrives."

Chooli shot him a look. "The cavalry? Seriously?"

Marc thought for a second, then it dawned on him.

"Shit. Sorry, bad reference. How 'bout the rescue party?"

Sarah shook her head. "Read the room, dude," she mocked jokingly.

Chooli laughed. "Just messing with you. I'd take the cavalry at this point."

Marc carefully poured flour onto the ceiling fan. The white powder sat in mounds along the still blades. The remaining flour he poured onto a box set in front of the small oscillating floor fan he brought from Sicheii's house.

At the entrance to the hallway, he strung wire attached to a bundle of wooden kitchen matches placed on the matchbox strikers he had tacked to the floor. Near the matches, he placed the oxygen tank.

Sarah watched this process with great interest. If the circumstances were different, she would have found it amusing.

"So, I guess we're not baking a cake."

"Nope," Marc confirmed.

"Just what are you cooking up?" she asked as Chooli walked over.

Marc surveyed the room. "If it works, a small thermobaric bomb."

Terri continued calling the landline at Secheii's house to no avail. "Busy signal."

John nodded but didn't say anything.

The unmarked Dodge Charger chewed up the highway as he expertly maneuvered around the slower traffic. The pit that had started forming in his stomach back at the war room now felt like it was the size of grapefruit. What were they rolling into? Thomas's and Ken's whereabouts were currently unknown. Why was no one answering the phone at the house? These two facts may not have been related, but something told him they were.

Marc watched out the front windows for any signs of a car approaching. Chooli said no one except Sicheii and her came to the cabin anymore. Anyone driving toward them was likely trouble.

Sarah sat with Trina in the back bedroom. There was a window there they would use as an egress point if a car approached. Marc didn't want Trina to know anything about the trap they had laid in the other part of the house. He didn't know how strong the psychological connection was between her and the skinwalkers, but he didn't want to take a chance on tipping them off. Better if she didn't see anything of it.

Chooli stood on top of the mesa directly behind the house, her weapons at her feet. Shielding her eyes from the blazing sun, she had an excellent vantage point. Scanning the landscape below, she saw it. A dust cloud, faint but moving along the road leading to them. She called down to Sarah and Trina.

"Chooli just saw someone approaching. We better move." Sarah called to Marc in the front room.

"Copy," he calmly replied.

He grabbed his go bag and made his way toward the back bedroom, carefully stepping over the wire. Once on the other side of the wire, he reached back and opened the oxygen tank valve a quarter turn. In the hallway, he opened the fuse box and turned the power on to the front room. Slowly the ceiling fan began to spin up and the floor fan started to oscillate in an arc. The room soon filled with a thick white haze of aerosolized flour.

Climbing out the window, he could see Sarah and Trina already scrambling up the steep slope of the mesa. Trina had her eyes closed as Sarah guided and pulled her up the narrow path.

He took one last look back. "This better work," he said to himself.

Thomas pulled the truck into the yard. The small shack sat quietly before them.

"This is it," he announced as he stepped from the vehicle. He closed his eyes and focused. The only sound was a fan, faintly humming inside.

"I don't want to do this," Ken protested.

"Don't bitch up on me now, Ken. Let's go," Thomas said as yanked Ken from the car. The rage that started at the first house never ebbed. He knew what he needed to do. Grandmother had told him.

Standing near the porch, he paused. He felt an impression of a bedroom. They were hiding in the back of the house. Perfect. He threw open the door and was immediately hit with a white powder. Taking a step back, he sniffed the air. "It's only flour," he called back over his shoulder. Beyond the starchy smell of flour, was the pungent odor of sweat.

"Trying to hide from me, are you? We'll see how that works out," he growled, striding through the room. Ken hesitated on the porch.

Thomas felt a slight tug at his foot as he made his way into the hallway. Glancing down, he saw a small flash erupt near the floor.

The explosion didn't have the sharp crack like C4 or other high explosives. It was a slower, deeper 'whoomp'. The overpressure blew out the windows in a flash of orange fire. The roof lifted slightly as the walls buckled outward and then the whole structure collapsed in flames.

"Holy shit!" Chooli exclaimed.

Sarah lay on the ground next to Marc. "Um. Tell me again, what did you do in the Marines?"

Marc was focused on the burning pile of debris. The trap had worked, but he couldn't be sure the explosion was enough to kill them. His eyes searched for any movement.

Without turning toward her he said, "If we get out of this, I'll tell you." He reached for his cell phone.

"Deal," Sarah confirmed, watching the flames lick skyward.

Suddenly, the propane tank, covered in burning wood, erupted in a fireball. They all ducked instinctively.

Chooli stared at the burning remains of the house. "They have to be dead, right?"

From the backseat, Alex lurched. "Detective Lightfoot, you need to accelerate. We are running out of time."

Terri's brow furrowed as she looked back at Alex. Retrieving her phone she did in fact have a pair of text messages from Marc. She read aloud: "Moved to hunting cabin. They are here."

John punched the accelerator. "I know what he's talking about. They must be on top of a hill back there if he got a message to you."

Twenty minutes later, he leaned forward and looked up as he approached Secheii's house. Wisps of gray black smoke rose over the tops of the mesas to their right.

Terri craned her neck to look up at the smoke wafting skyward in the distance. "Is that coming from the area of the cabin?" she asked.

"I think it is," he replied as he pulled the car onto Sicheii's driveway.

Alex saw the smoke as well. "They are in trouble. How far is the house?" she asked.

"It's about five miles of driving but straight across the hills, only about a half of a mile," he said, accelerating onto the jeep trail.

"I will go this way. It will be faster," she said as she unbuckled her seat belt and opened the door. She hit the ground, rolling several times.

John slammed on the brakes and looked back. "What the hell?"

Terri watched as Alex stood and began to run toward the distant hills and faint smoke column. The change was happening as she ran. Soon Alex was fully transformed, running on all fours.

"She's good. Let's go," Terri said to John.

His eyes were wide and his mouth hung open.

"Let's go!" she yelled, bringing him back to the present. He pressed the accelerator to the floor and the Charger jumped to life again with a roar, bouncing over the rough terrain.

Thomas could feel the fire around him as he pushed the blackened boards away and stood. His ears rang and his vision was blurred. His nose stung from the offensive odor of charred wood and burnt hair.

As he tried to walk, an achy pain shot through his chest. Something had struck him hard in the blast. He looked down at his feet and saw a charred oxygen tank. He massaged his cracked ribs as he stumbled toward his brother sprawled on the ground.

A few yards away, Ken, too, began to stand. The blast had sent him reeling backward and drove a large splinter of wood through his right thigh. Once he put weight on it, his leg collapsed and he writhed in pain. Thomas reached his brother and, with one pull, yanked the bloody shard of wood from his leg. A high-pitched shriek echoed off the box canyon walls.

"That really hurt,'" Ken said meekly.

Thomas looked at his brother and laughed cruelly.

"Really? It hurt? You'll heal, and then we're gonna shred them."

Thomas looked at himself. Most of his clothes had been blown or burned off. His flesh had been torn by the explosion and burned by the fire after. He was recovering, but slowly. The injuries were substantial. The transformation faltered while he recovered. It would take some time to be back at his full strength.

His vision cleared a bit as he stood over his brother. He scanned the tops of the mesas. "You will pay for this! It's gonna take more than that to kill me!" he screamed, streams of saliva flying from his mouth.

As he spoke, something whizzed and lodged into his side with a slight thud. A searing pain exploded as he glanced down and saw an arrow shaft sticking out from his side. Instinctively, he reached down and jerked it from his ribs. His vision went red with pain. The scream that came from his throat rivaled his brother's.

Ken looked up at him, "I told you it hurt."

Thomas scrambled behind the Sierra pickup as Ken ducked down behind a pile of shattered lumber. Thomas realized the arrows wouldn't kill him, but did hurt like hell. All of these injuries were stalling the transformation.

Poking his head above the hood, Thomas saw a Native American woman perched on a hill, notching another missile.

"You're dead! I will tear you to pieces!" he screamed in rage.

He motioned for Ken to come to him. An arrow narrowly missed his brother as he limped to Thomas. "Listen, we are going to change as soon as we can. You'll go straight up there," he said pointing to where Chooli stood, "and I'll circle around them."

Ken gave him a worried look. "I don't want to do this."

Thomas growled, "You'll be fine." He knew Ken was going to suffer making his way up the steep wall while arrows rained down, but so be it. Better Ken take the pain than him. Thomas reasoned the wounds may weaken his brother and make the second grisly task easier.

The two sat, backs against the truck, for several minutes while the healing process completed. Only their panting breath interrupted the silence. At last, Thomas could feel the transformation starting.

"Go now!" Thomas roared and pushed his brother toward the slope.

As soon as they emerged from behind the truck, another missile whipped toward them, narrowly missing Thomas's head.

Marc's stomach dropped when he saw the two men in their full monstrous forms. He hoped the explosion and fire might have delayed them longer. It only bought them twenty minutes.

One was halfheartedly running straight up the slope toward them. The other was moving around the side of the hill trying to outflank them.

"Damn he's fast," Marc said under his breath.

"What do we do now?" Chooli asked, the fear rising in her throat.

"You and Sarah stay here. Hold the hill and the path. I'll track the other one and try to keep him off the top. She drew the bow and took aim at the skinwalker clawing his way up the steep embankment. The arrow found his shoulder and a howl of pain reverberated through the canyon as he tumbled back down.

Chooli notched her last arrow and said a silent prayer when she saw something barreling across the canyon floor. She squinted and gasped. "There's another one."

Sarah saw it too and whispered, "It's Alex."

Alex saw the skinwalker pick himself up from the ground and pull the arrow out of his shoulder. He stared up at the top of the mesa and roared in painful frustration. She was running at full speed and closed the distance in a few strides. The skinwalker must have heard the pounding of her feet and turned at the last second, just as she slammed into him. The two forms rolled across the ground, roaring and snarling.

From around the corner of the mesa, Thomas heard Ken howl with pain and knew his plan was working. Then he heard a deep thud followed by unfamiliar vicious growls.

He looked back, and to his shock he saw Ken squaring off with another werewolf. This one was female and very big. Ken was in for a fight. Change of plans. He thought briefly about joining the fray directly, but decided instead to try to get behind the new challenger fighting Ken. If his brother died in the fight with this new werewolf, so be it. Ken's usefulness had come to an end anyway.

A voice, soft and familiar, echoed in his head. "Tommy, you didn't listen, and now the hunters are here. Kill them all, then you can disappear into the desert. Make grandma proud of you."

Marc watched from the top of the small bluff as Alex slammed full speed into one of the skinwalkers. He didn't know which one. The two bodies rolled several times from the impact. The skinwalker got up, holding his ribs where Alex had impacted him. The two circled each other slowly, growling and snarling.

Out of the corner of his eye, Marc saw movement near the burning house. It was the other skinwalker, stealthily maneuvering to get behind Alex.

"No, no, no," he said under his breath.

He slid his blade back into the sheath and started to make his way down the steep bank on his side, using his legs to ward off any large stones in his path. Sarah saw him.

"Where are you going?" she half whispered.

"Alex is in trouble!" he called back.

His slide was less skilled than he had hoped. His foot slammed into a large rock and catapulted him. He went down the rest of the slope rolling in a cloud of red dust.

Sarah turned to Chooli. "Alex is in some kind of trouble. Marc is heading down. I'm going too. You guys stay here."

Chooli held her last arrow. " Like hell I am! This is my ancestors' fight. I am going with you!"

Trina suddenly appeared. "Me too. I'm not staying up here alone."

Even before the car skidded to a stop, Terri got a quick glance at the battle unfolding. Alex had squared off with one of the skinwalkers. Marc, large blade in hand, was running in a half-crouch across the ground. He wasn't focused on the fight Alex was engaged in, but on something else. Terri followed where Marc was staring, and, just before the red dust obscured her view, she caught a glimpse of gray brown fur.

John leaped from the car and took cover behind the engine block. Drawing his pistol, he aimed over the hood. Expecting to see Terri take a position near the trunk, he was stunned when he saw her running full speed toward the burning house with a large blade in her hand.

Marc crouched behind Chooli's pickup and watched the other skin-walker creep around the corner of the smoldering building. The skin-walker was intently focused on Alex, as she battled his brother.

Alex had no idea of the peril that was only yards away. Marc gripped the knife with white knuckles. His aching lungs craved oxygen from his sprint, but he forced his breathing to be slow and silent. This was the battle he was hoping to avoid: attacking a shapeshifter alone and with no advantage of terrain. Even with the element of surprise, he knew he was probably going to get killed. But he was determined to draw some blood first and give Alex a chance. The skinwalker took two cautious steps toward the fray and was right next to him. He had to move. Now.

Lunging at the beast, he slashed. The blade bit deeply into the flesh, opening a bloody gouge on its back. With the downward thrust, he heaved the blade up to the hilt into the kidney area.

"Surprise, fucko!" he screamed.

The skinwalker howled in pain and spun. A backhand blow left Marc sprawled on the ground. A massive paw reached back, initially fumbling to find the blade, it finally pulled the knife from its back. Tossing the bloody blade away, it snarled at him. Marc had played out his hand in a final act of defiance. The inevitable was coming now.

He glanced over to Alex. Now alerted to the second skinwalker's presence, she looked at him briefly before charging at her opponent. He thought he recognized a look of appreciation in her eyes.

Turning his attention back to his wounded foe, Marc saw the eyes narrow and the massive teeth glisten as it snarled at him.

Suddenly, Terri appeared. She leaped and slammed her blade into the thickly muscled upper back of the beast. A slight metallic ring told him Terri's blow had struck a bone. Marc's relief suddenly turned to horror as he watched the skinwalker whip Terri to the side and snap her left leg in his jaws. A high pitched shriek curdled his blood as the skinwalker's teeth tore into her flesh. With a jerk of his head, he tossed her like a doll ten yards to the side.

The beast turned back to Marc, fresh blood and saliva dripping from its jaws.

Terri hit the ground hard, knocking the wind out of her. She gasped for air as she looked at her shattered thigh. A small geyser of bright red blood spurted from the wound. She realized her femoral artery had been severed. Her hands shook as she struggled to remove the tourniquet from her vest. Despite the pain and rising panic, she managed to get it around her thigh near her groin and pulled it tight.

Things started to get blurry and slow down. In the distance, Sarah screamed. She heard Alex roar with rage and then whimper. She tried to torque the strap tighter, to stop the blood flow, but she felt tired. Her hands were weak and wouldn't respond. A chill settled over her. God, it got cold fast. She closed her eyes.

She could hear the din of battle all around her. Then it occurred to her she was somewhere else. Was this a dream? Was this what dying felt like? She found herself on a grassy plain, a gray sky hung low. The screams of the dying surrounded her. The clash of steel weapons and wooden shields clamored. She was someone else, an ancient warrior. Deep inside her, a voice cried out to her in a strange language. Somehow, she understood it: *Get up and fight! This is not your day to see Valhalla!*

Suddenly, an intense heat passed through her body. A series of spasms jolted her off the ground. The air around her seemed to crackle with an unseen energy. In a flash, her eyes popped open and she gasped. Snapping her hands to the tourniquet, preparing to crank it tighter, she realized the bleeding had stopped. Cautiously flexing her leg, she was amazed to find it responding.

A calmness settled over her as she stood. She loosened the tourniquet and let it drop to the ground. She ripped open the Velcro of her ballistic vest, which suddenly felt constricting, and tossed it to the side. She picked up the blade at her feet and recovered Marc's blade as well. Uruz and Tiwaz filled her hands. The weapons felt natural, like extensions of her body. She stared intently at the skinwalker before her. She saw him toying with the others as they feebly slashed at it. Twirling the weapons in her hands, she set upon the beast.

They had retreated behind Chooli's pickup. The skinwalker moved steadily toward them. Marc realized it was amusing itself as they tried to ward it off. It easily dodged their thrusts and slashes. Sarah swung her blade in short arcs but was unable to connect. It seemed the skinwalker was now aware of the danger the edged weapons posed. The beast reached out and snatched Chooli's bow, snapping it in two. She wielded her last arrow like a small spear. Trina held a piece of jagged lumber. Marc reached down and grabbed the only weapon available, a rock, and took aim. Then he heard a banshee-like scream come from behind the skinwalker. As the beast turned, he caught a glimpse of Terri.

"Holy shit," was all he could mutter.

Sarah saw her too. "Oh my god."

Terri stood, arms at her side slowly spinning the blades. Her face twisted into a menacing grin.

Thomas was confused. Hadn't he already taken care of this one? He roared and charged the woman who mocked him. She easily slid to the side, dodging his charge. He felt a cold sensation on the back of his thigh as both blades slashed deep cuts into his leg. The coolness immediately gave way to scorching pain.

Thomas fell to the ground, his right leg now useless. He screamed in frustration as he struggled to stand. He looked at the woman before him, slowly spinning the twin silver blades, now stained with his blood. She was different. The look in her eyes was simmering, controlled rage. Not only was she not afraid, but she was–confident.

For the first time he felt fear. It started in his stomach and moved up into his throat. The icy feeling left him unsure. She looked at him and motioned, inviting him to attack her. She spoke a language he didn't understand. This one was different.

With his injured leg, escape was not an option. Kill her, and he had a chance. Mustering all the rage he could, he crouched then launched himself at her.

The roaring monster lurched forward. His bloody teeth bared and clawed hands flung wide. Terri cooly stepped back one pace and, in a flash, brought the blades up, slicing deep parallel channels the length of his torso. The downward stroke was immediate and as smooth as a breeze. She buried the twin blades deep into his chest. A whimper trickled from the skinwalker's throat as he slumped to his knees before her. Pulling the blades from his ribs, she smoothly crossed them and slashed his throat, nearly severing his head. She watched the massive form topple. It was over.

Marc and Sarah were frozen. Terri turned to them and was almost unrecognizable. Rippling muscles stretched the limits of her clothes. Her blonde hair hung across her face. Blood mixed with earth to form a hellish mask. Unblinking wild eyes stared at them as she huffed fast and deep.

After a second, they recovered and rushed to her. Sarah immediately knelt to check on Terri's wounded leg. She ripped back the torn fabric of her pants and gasped. The wound was healed. She looked up at Terri who only stared silently, panting.

Marc suddenly realized he didn't hear any sounds from Alex and the other skinwalker. Grabbing Sarah's blade, he started running toward the scene of the fight, expecting the worst.

Ken fell to the ground, his broken body bleeding. Pain filled his head but one thought suddenly burst forth: his brother was dead. A peace fell over him. His soul no longer felt the rage and disappointment of his twin. He no longer felt the pull to please him. The desire to try to make Thomas love him was gone.

He looked up at the werewolf before him. Bloody teeth menaced him as she drew back her right hand for a strike. Crimson stained razor claws silhouetted against the blue sky.

Ken closed his eyes and tilted his chin upward. He wanted it all to end. Please just make it quick, he thought.

Marc breathed a sigh of relief when he saw Alex approach. She was naked and covered in dirt and blood. Large teeth marks were visible on her left leg and she walked with a limp. Deep scratches crossed her torso but appeared to be already healing. As she walked by she put a hand on his shoulder.

"Thank you, Detective Peterson. That was very courageous."

He gave a slight nod.

Alex went to Terri, who was still standing. Her breathing was slowing, but still on the verge of hyperventilating. Alex looked her up and down then closed her eyes as she leaned in and inhaled deeply through her nose. She opened her eyes and gave Terri a look of recognition, then held her close.

"Oh my dear, Terri. I am so sorry."

The blades slipped from Terri's hands as she collapsed into Alex's embrace. Burying her face in Alex's neck, sobs wracked her body.

Chooli retrieved a blanket from her truck and wrapped it around Alex and Terri.

Unsure of what they had just seen, Sarah and Marc exchanged looks. They were soon joined by John and Trina.

John surveyed the group. "Everyone okay?"

"I think so," Marc replied tiredly, the adrenalin subsiding and exhaustion settling in. Looking down at his shaking hands, he clenched them into fists.

Alex held Terri's face in her hands and looked into her eyes. "You are okay. We are all okay, my dear."

Terri's breathing settled as she started to calm.

John knelt down by the body, now a man. Thomas Rutledge's eyes stared up into the blue sky, the shock he felt at the moment of his death etched on his still face.

Chooli stood next to him. "The dark spirits have left him. He is finally at rest."

John stood, "What about the other one?"

Alex, still holding Terri, answered without looking, "He is hurt, but alive. He is no danger. It is not in me to kill innocents. I sensed he did not want this life. He is not a killer. I suspect you will find he did not participate in the murders."

"And how do you know that?" John asked.

Alex turned to John. "I have tasted his flesh."

John rubbed the back of his neck and grimaced. "Okay. Yeah, I guess I'll have to sort that out."

Sarah nudged Chooli and Trina. With a nod toward Alex and Terri, she announced, "Alright, let's get you two cleaned up. There is a hand pump behind the house. Unless Marc blew it up." As they ushered the bloody pair of women off, she noted Alex's limp had vanished.

Watching them walk toward the water pump, John asked, "Can you tell me what the hell just happened?"

Marc chuckled, "You are now in a very exclusive club, my friend. I'd tell you not to tell anyone about it, but no one'd believe you anyway."

The upbeat country music thumped and twanged through the bar. Their server, Becky, delivered a round of drinks to the table in the back: a Scotch, a Guiness, one hoppy IPA, one Budweiser, and a glass of Chardonnay. The Chardonnay was from California, a respectable wine region, but no Burgandy.

Alex had asked for a French vintage but was told in Becky's sweet Oklahoma accent: "We're just a honky tonk bar, ma'am. We don't have all the fancy wines." Nonetheless, Alex discovered it was a pleasant glass.

John stood and raised his bottle of Bud in a toast. "I want to thank you for putting your butts on the line for us all here." He wasn't accustomed to making speeches. Looking around the table, he couldn't help but notice the absence of one.

"And here's to Ed, the best—" Emotion suddenly swelled in his chest. The words choked in his throat as his eyes filled with tears.

Putting his arm around John's shoulders, Marc raised his glass of Scotch, "To Ed."

In unison the group toasted, "To Ed."

"He was a good man," Sarah said, putting her hand on John's arm as he sat.

"Thanks. He was all that. I'm gonna miss him."

John gave a weak smile and drained his lone beer. "I'm gonna leave you all. I've got a ton of work ahead and frankly, I'm beat. Tomorrow's Christmas Eve, and I haven't spent much time at home. Then I gotta get with Chooli and plan Sicheii's funeral, so I better scoot."

Collecting his white straw hat from the table, he stood and paused. "And somewhere in there, I have to figure out what the hell to do with Ken. I'm not entirely comfortable knowing there's a—you know, werewolf, running around out there." He glanced at Alex as he finished.

Catching his look, she smiled reassuringly. "I can assure you, Kenneth Rutledge has no stomach for, shall we say, the more urban hunting. He knows he is best suited to the occasional foray into the wilderness. When I spoke with him, he said that is what his grandmother did, later in life. Well, that and the occasional bovine. Kenneth is no killer, and without his brother's influence, he should be able to adapt to a more docile existence. You will have no trouble from him, Detective Lightfoot."

John's brow furrowed slightly, "Alex, there are so many damn questions I want to ask you. But honestly, I don't even know where to start. So I'll just table it for now and wish you all a good night and safe travel home. Oh, and have a Merry Christmas as well."

"That is probably for the best, Detective," Alex replied. I am not sure I could answer your queries anyway. There is much I do not know myself.".

Terri took a sip of her Guinness and wiped her lip. "To be fair, what we do know is actually classified. Someday perhaps, we can share more with you, John."

Terri was getting back to herself. The shock of the confrontation in the desert and her transformation had worn off. She kept waiting for her memory to evaporate, the way Alex had described during her initial transformation. Terrified of losing herself, she kept repeating, "I am Terri Watson, Special Agent with the FBI. My father was James Watson." After several minutes, she realized her memory was intact. To her relief, she also noted she didn't feel the urge to take a bite out of anyone. She felt like herself, only different, more perceptive perhaps.

She noticed the Guinness had a particularly interesting flavor. She could taste the roasted malt like never before. She also could smell the moisturizer Becky, their server, used. Curel, probably to prevent her hands from drying out as she washed glasses throughout the night.

John donned his hat and nodded. "Understood. I won't tell anyone. Besides, like Marc said, who the hell would believe me anyway."

He shook everyone's hand one more time then departed. As he left, he handed $300 to Becky, telling her the table in the back was not to pay for any drinks as long as there was any money in the kitty. Anything left over was hers.

Marc looked at Terri.

"How ya doin' Ter? You ok?"

She smiled. "Yeah, I'm good."

Sarah took a sip of her IPA. "You scared the hell out of us, girl. Good to have you back."

Marc rested his elbows on the table and held his Scotch glass in both hands. "So, did ya know, before the bite, that you–you might be a–"

"A shapeshifter?" Terri asked.

"Yeah, a shapeshifter," he said slowly.

Terri met Alex's eyes as she spoke. "We suspected it."

"We?" Marc and Sarah asked in unison, looking at Terri, then Alex.

"Alex had told me I might have the marker." Terri looked down. "I didn't want to believe it at first, but here we are."

A silence fell on the group for a few seconds before Marc hoisted his glass in the air. "Well, Ter, the way I see it, if one kickass shapeshifter's good, two kickass shapeshifters is better!"

Alex laughed. "Very succinctly put, Detective Peterson."

Craning her neck, Terri peered toward the kitchen area. "It's weird, though. I have this craving for raw meat. I wonder if they'd let me chew on a steak back there."

Sarah's face went pale. "Are you serious?"

Terri smiled. "Naw, I'm just screwin' with you."

"Nice one. You got me," Sarah said with a laugh.

Becky brought over another round of drinks. When Marc reached for his wallet, she explained they were already paid for.

Putting his wallet back, he turned to Sarah, "You know how to two-step?"

"Um, I'm from West Point, New York, so no," she said with a smile.

"C'mon, I'll show ya." Marc stuck out his hand.

"And how do you know how to two-step?" Sarah asked as she took his hand and walked to the crowded dance floor. "I'm gonna guess your Philadelphia-raised Irish mother and Scottish father didn't teach you."

Marc held Sarah's left hand and slipped his arm around her waist. "Eh, no. But they did send me to dance classes as a little kid. I learned some tap, ballroom, and country two-step in a neighbor's basement. No ballet though. Couldn't bring myself to wear the tights."

He started to lead her around the floor. "They said it would come in handy someday. So I figured, maybe today was that day."

"Marc Peterson, you are a man of mystery," she said with a laugh.

Terri took a large sip of her stout. "I have a question, Alex."

"Yes?"

"Why didn't I—back in the desert today—why didn't I turn into a full—?" Terri stopped.

"You are asking me why you did not fully transform into a lycanthrope? Are you disappointed?" Alex asked.

"No, not disappointed, but curious. If you know," Terri explained.

Alex shook her head. "I am sorry, Terri. I do not know. It could be yours is a more organic transition process, and that is the way it normally is. Perhaps the next time you may become fully altered. Or you might be of a family of partial shapeshifters, and you may never fully transform."

"Are there such things?" Terri asked hopefully.

"I am hoping you can tell me!" Alex said with a laugh. "Do you have any memories of past lives?"

Terri nodded. "Yeah. When I transformed, or didn't transform, today. I had a memory of being in a battle. I could feel an ax in my hand and a helmet. All around me was chaos. I had been wounded, and another warrior grabbed me by the shoulders and screamed at me in–I assume ancient Norse. Here's the kicker, I could understand it. Every word. They told me I needed to get back up and get into the fight."

"That would make sense. You come from a Nordic line of shapeshifters. There are likely more memories still hidden in the mist. You may find some are—" Alex hesitated.

"Are what?" Terri asked anxiously.

"Some may be from the wolf, the skinwalker, that bit you. You may have memories from his lineage as well."

Alex was reluctant to share this possibility. She didn't want Terri to worry unnecessarily. But it was too late. Terri's face registered horror.

Alex took Terri's hands in hers. "Dear Terri, I don't know if that is the case or not. It seems I have experienced this from the wolf's lineage that triggered my transformation. But it may not be in your future. If it is, you will gain an insight into his line and understand where they came from. As we now know, we are not alone in this world and that information may be useful."

Terri nodded. "Yeah, you might be right. All knowledge is good, even the scary kind."

Squeezing Terri's hand, Alex noted, "You have nothing to be frightened of, my dear. *You* are now the frightful one."

Terri smiled and looked at her drink. "Thanks."

Terri and Alex sat silently, watching Marc and Sarah dance several songs in a row. There was a lightness to them, and Alex could hear their laughter over the music. A slight pained look appeared on her face. She spoke without turning to Terri.

"Do you remember the conversation we had on the way to the airport?"

"The one about Marc?" Terri asked, as she too watched the dance floor.

"Yes. I now know I was presumptuous. You may forget the request I made of you," Alex said quietly.

Terri slid her chair close to Alex's. "I'm sorry, Alex. Life is messy sometimes."

Alex continued to watch them dance. "Yes, I suppose it can be." She turned to Terri. "You know, it was not going to be romantic, with Marc. I prefer the company of wom–" Alex stopped herself. "I simply wanted to start a family. I feel so alone."

The hurt on Alex's face caused Terri's heart to ache. It was her turn to comfort. She reached over and took Alex's hand. "You are not alone and you have a family. We are your family." Terri felt the warmth of Alex's hand and she suddenly remembered the dream she had. Starting in her chest and quickly moving to her face, Terri felt her own flesh begin to feel flush.

"Thank you, Terri." Alex stared into Terri's eyes.

"Also, I, uh, already submitted the paperwork to the office to close you as a source. So–that's done."

Terri didn't look away from Alex's gaze.

"I see," Alex said slowly.

"So, um, what do we do now?" Terri asked, feeling herself fall into the beautiful green pools of Alex's eyes.

Alex smiled as she raised her hand and brushed Terri's cheek.

"I hope you kiss me."

Marc and Sarah caught a glimpse of Terri and Alex leaving the bar hand in hand. Marc's phone alerted to a text message from Terri: "C U in the morning." He smiled to himself as he put the phone in his pocket. Sarah looked up at him and smiled too. She pulled his body close to hers and laid her head on his chest as they swayed to the slow music.

CHAPTER 22

Aᴌᴇх ᴡᴏᴋᴇ ᴇᴀʀʟʏ ᴀs the morning glow filled the hotel room, the cheerful promise of another day. She could feel Terri's arms still wrapped around her. A peace fell over her as she listened to Terri's breathing, remembering the night they spent together. At that moment, she saw her future. It was bright and joyful. She had found her pack—and her soulmate.

The dark thoughts of revenge she had been harboring faded. It was such an unpleasant emotion, one that could not coexist with happiness and contentment. She still felt bad for the fate of her parents, but she knew following vengeance was a path that would likely lead to her doom and possibly the death of her new pack.

Terri stirred, and Alex saw her blue eyes flutter open. A smile crept across her face to meet Terri's. Alex leaned in and kissed Terri's forehead. "Good morning, my dear."

"Morning," Terri said sleepily. She had slept better last night than she could remember. Beyond the excitement of the previous night, she felt comfortable and, strangely, safe with Alex. Not just in a physical way, but emotionally. She didn't realize how much she craved that until it was lying next to her.

"What time is it?"

"Seven. We have time to lounge a bit yet this morning," Alex announced as she pulled Terri closer to her. "If you will indulge me for a few minutes, I feel I should give Cigus a call and let him know we are safe and coming home today."

"Absolutely. I need to check my email anyway," Terri said, but didn't really make an effort to move. "Then we can shower and get some coffee downstairs."

Alex leaned over and retrieved her phone. Cigus picked up on the second ring.

Cigus anxiously paced the floor as he had since 6 a.m. A worry popped into his head: he may wear a path into Alex's ornate Persian rug. He opted to take a seat on the sofa. An unassigned anxiety hung over him today and he felt a sense of fear and dread. He'd been thinking of his friend, Alex, constantly since she'd left to–to do something he didn't fully understand. But he knew it was dangerous. She hadn't called the night before, as was her routine, so he'd had a fitful night's sleep.

The sound of his cell phone mercifully interrupted his thoughts. He glanced at it and saw it was Alex. Perfect timing! he said to himself.

"Hello, my dear Alex! I am so happy to hear from you. Is all well with you and your friends?" he asked anxiously.

"Yes, Cigus Varney, we are all well. The situation has been resolved, and I am happy to say we will all fly out this evening." An unconscious smile creased her face as she spoke with Cigus. "How are you feeling?"

Cigus chuckled. "Me? I'm feeling very good. I went for a walk yesterday and I was just getting myself together for another one today. It is chilly but clear here. A little brisk air is good for a person. I have to say, you sound very chipper this morning, Alex. It is good to hear."

Alex laughed. "Yes, I feel very chipper indeed, Cigus. And I am happy to hear you're feeling stronger."

"My dear Alex, I cannot tell you how happy I am to hear you are well. I have been doing some rather deep philosophical thinking here and I am eager to talk to you about it when you return!"

Alex heard the doorbell to her home in the background.

"Just a second, there is someone at the door." She heard Cigus heft himself up with a slight grunt and make his way to the front door. "It looks like a pair of delivery people with a package. Let me set the phone down and sign for it."

Alex quickly tallied up the items she had ordered for her trip. All were accounted for. "Cigus, I am not expecting any packages. They will come back if they cannot deliver it." Something was off. "Cigus, please do not open the door. Cigus!"

Now fully awake, Terri sat up. Her brow furrowed as she looked at Alex.

Alex muted the phone and put the call on speaker as they both heard Cigus fumbling with the lock.

The two men dressed in brown could hear the lock being turned. One held a large cardboard box and the other a clipboard with a signature pad. Their mundane expressions belied the fact they had braced themselves internally. They knew this target was dangerous and very hard to kill. All of their targets before were deadly, but the Augur was very specific about this one.

To their surprise, an elderly man appeared in the doorway. "Delivery for Alexandra Stepanova," the man with the clipboard announced.

Varney detected a thick Italian accent. "She is not available right now. I can sign for it."

"And you are?" asked the man with the box.

"Cigus Varney. I'm a friend of Ms. Stepanova."

The man with the box peered past Cigus into the home. He did not see any sign of their target, but he could not take the old man's word that she was not present. He pulled his hand from under the box and sprayed an aerosol at Cigus's face.

The move stunned the old man. Before he could react, the odorless mist from the silver can hit him squarely in the eyes, nose, and mouth. Within a second, his knees buckled and his head wobbled. An odd thought tumbled in his rapidly fading consciousness, "How strange that the UPS man is wearing purple rubber gloves–"

The two men stepped into the residence and dragged the unconscious Cigus into the foyer before closing the door behind them. From within the box, they each retrieved two new silver cans and quietly searched the house. The old man was telling the truth. Alexandra Stepanova was nowhere to be found. They returned to the prone figure in the foyer, his chest rising slightly with each breath. The man who had been holding the clipboard retrieved a hypodermic needle from his cargo pants pocket, removed the cap, and plunged it into Cigus's neck. The breathing stopped shortly thereafter.

They spoke Italian to each other as they discussed ransacking the home to make it look like a burglary gone wrong.

Alex was listening, barely breathing herself. She had stopped speaking when she heard Cigus open the door. She heard their conversation, then Cigus gasp, and then the door close. The sound of footsteps, loud then fading, told her the men were searching her house.

And then she heard them speaking and recognized the Italian. "We should make a mess of the house to look like—uh, a home invasion," one said.

"No, leave the old man here. It will look like a heart attack, and there will be no investigation. We may then get another opportunity to finish the job."

Cigus was dead. She could infer from the conversation she overheard and—she could sense it.

Terri watched as Alex's face went from shock to rage. Her eyes smoldered with fury, and her jaw clenched.

Alex turned to Terri and said in a controlled steady voice, "They've killed Cigus."

Before Terri could say anything, Alex held her hand up. She listened closely to one of the tinny voices coming from her foyer.

It was almost a whisper. "*Requiem aeternam dona eis Domine, et lux perpetua luceat eis.*"

"Is that—Latin?" Terri asked in a whisper.

Alex was stunned as she nodded slowly. "Yes. It is the prayer for the dead."

Terri leaped from the bed, grabbing her cell phone as she ran into the bathroom. Frantically, she placed calls to the Philadelphia Police and

Philadelphia FBI office in rapid succession. She then called Marc. After a few rings he picked up.

"Yo, what's up Ter?" he asked sleepily.

"We've got a very bad situation playing out. Alex just called Cigus, back at her house. He was murdered while he was on the phone with her. I think she was the target."

Marc sat up in the bed. "Jesus Christ."

"I'm with Alex now. I've called the PD and my office. I warned them to alert the first responders to possible toxins or poisons, but you may want to call the PD as well to stress that. Also, can you call Sarah and let her know what is going on and meet us in Alex's room?"

"On it. Be there in five." Marc ended the call and looked over at Sarah, in the bed next to him, now wide awake as well and staring at him.

Alex heard Terri making calls from the bathroom. She unmuted her phone and spoke to the killers in Italian. Her tone was a menacing hiss, her message direct. "Hey, you fucking errand boys. Listen up. If you would like to meet me, I can arrange that. I have killed many of you before and would relish the opportunity to kill more. And I will guarantee, if we meet, you will curse your whore mothers for ever giving birth to you."

Over the phone, Alex heard swearing and then the door quickly opened and closed. They were gone. She disconnected from the call and sat her phone on the bed just as Terri stepped from the bathroom. Terri walked over and sat on the bed next to Alex. Sobs wracked her body as Terri held her close.

Terri thought Alex was crying because Cigus had been killed. That was certainly true; Cigus had quickly become a close friend. But Alex was also crying because she now realized the future she pictured was just a mirage. It would always hover before her in the distance, shimmering and beckoning her, but never attainable. She finally grasped what she truly was: a hunted animal. Any plans she wanted to pursue would have to be shelved until this was resolved. She also knew what that meant. Either she killed her pursuers or they killed her.

In those tear-filled moments after the murder of Cigus, with Terri holding her, Alex was already steeling herself for the fight to come. In the back of her mind, she coldly reasoned: when applied properly, perhaps revenge could be a useful emotion.

Mental exhaustion enveloped Terri like a net as she put her key in her condo door. The flight home was silent and excruciating. Alex, eyes closed and head resting on the seat back, barely spoke the entire flight. To the casual observer, Alex appeared serene. But Terri knew a torrent was raging under the calm surface.

Terri's own swirling mind proved difficult to contain. She filled ten pages of notes during the flight, careful that no flight attendants or fellow passengers read them. Getting the thoughts out of her head and on paper helped take some of the energy from the mental storm inside her. The notes ranged from actions to be taken to protect Alex, to investigative steps, and finally, to likely actors.

All she wanted to do now was drop her bags and take a shower before she went to the Philadelphia FBI office. At least step one from the list was accomplished. Alex was booked in the Ritz using Terri's undercover name and credit card. Having her safely out of the picture for the time being was critical for Terri and the others to focus on the tasks at hand. She knew this was only the beginning of the crucible that was to come.

One line of thought refused to be quelled. Someone was after Alex. Who? The Russians? That would be logical, but something didn't seem right. The murder seemed to fit the profile, but the conversation Alex heard didn't. Killers rarely recite a prayer after their grisly work, especially in Latin.

As the door swung open, she was greeted by Max, padding across the kitchen tiles. He suddenly stopped, arched his back and hissed. A deep unsettling growl emanated from his throat. Terri was startled by the reception, but then it dawned on her. She was now different.

Shutting the door behind her, she tried to convince Max she was still herself. Opening a new can of food, she slowly spooned it into his bowl. Large black eyes stared back at her from across the room. Lying on her back next to the bowl, she opened her arms, exposing her midsection and throat. Instinctively, she knew this was a sign of vulnerability.

Max carefully approached her. He sniffed her and they rubbed noses. Rolling on her side, she stroked his back and listened to the wet smacks and purrs as he ate.

CHAPTER 23

THE STORY OF THE strange Christmas Eve murder on Pine Street lingered in the Philadelphia news cycle for two days. It was the kind of headline that wrote itself: "Priest Murdered in Home Invasion Before Holiest of Days." An apartment fire in West Philadelphia that forced parents and children to run for their lives on the day after Christmas soon took the attention. No one was hurt, but the images of kids cradling new toys as their homes burned was much more dramatic.

Alex had grown restive in the Ritz. They needed to move her to a longer-term safe house location. Marc and Terri had talked about it and found a cabin for rent in Lancaster county. Ironically, the cabin was near the Wolf Sanctuary of PA. After discussing it with Alex, who had to laugh in spite of the overall situation, Sarah used her undercover ID to sign the lease. Alex's only question was regarding the Wi-Fi connection at the cabin.

The cabin was substantially smaller than Alex's town house, so she could only bring a few items. While Alex and Terri walked the house, determining what items to take and which to leave, Marc and Sarah stood guard on the sidewalk at the bottom of her steps. Two marked police cars blocked the street at either end.

This was the first time Alex had been back in her home since returning from Phoenix. The silence that greeted her at the door was not unexpected but felt eerie, definitive and deep. Her plants, wilted in their pots, seemed to be in mourning as well. She immediately gave them water.

She and Terri packed a few boxes and suitcases with items to take with them. Everything left would remain in the empty house until–. The time frame was undefined.

In the spare bedroom Cigus had been using, Alex's shoulders drooped. The job thus far had been hectic and mentally consuming. Now, she was confronted with Cigus's few personal possessions. She was prepared to walk away, when a brightly colored box poking out from under the bed caught her eye. It was wrapped in red and green paper: a Christmas present.

The tag read, "To my friend, Alex. May you use this in good health. Love, Cigus"

Terri came into the room as Alex knelt by the box. Putting her hands on Alex's shoulders, she watched Alex carefully pull the paper back.

"What is it?" Terri asked quietly.

Alex laughed out loud. "It is a cast iron skillet and a cookbook."

All the items she was taking with her were piled in the living room. Atop the pile, sat the gifts from Cigus.

Alex and Terri's heads snapped to the door when they heard Marc's voice outside. "Whoa there, young buck. Where ya goin'?"

A voice somewhat familiar to Alex replied. "I wanna see the lady that lives here. I gotta talk to her." It was a young voice.

Opening the front door, Terri saw Marc and Sarah blocking the path of a teenager. "What's your name, kid?" Terri asked.

Before the youth could answer, Alex said quietly, "Donte Crenshaw. His mother calls him DC."

The youth looked up and stared at Alex.

Donte sat on the sofa.

"I saw the picture of the man, the priest, in the news. They said he was murdered at this address. And I remembered him and–I remembered he was your friend."

Alex nodded. "Yes. He was my friend."

Terri quickly pieced together the facts and a look of shock bubbled up on her face.

Donte looked at his feet. "Anyway, I, I, just wanted to let you know I didn't have anything to do with what happened here. I've been helpin' my mom and doin' my homework. I'm gonna graduate next spring."

Alex smiled. "I am very pleased to hear that, Donte Crenshaw."

Donte stood. "Okay. So, anyway, I'm sorry about your friend. I'm gonna go now."

Alex rose and touched his chin gently, raising his gaze to hers.

"I can see you have much potential in this world, DC. Be careful to never let those near you try to diminish your light."

"Thanks." A smile tugged at the corners of his mouth.

After he left, Terri asked, "Was that the kid from the–incident?"

Alex smiled. "Yes. That was a most unexpected visit, but also very gratifying."

Marc poked his head in the front door. "Hey, the uniformed guys just informed me they're gonna turn into pumpkins in about fifteen minutes. Can't block the street forever. We gotta load up and go."

Alex hefted a box containing her laptops, plants, and a few personal items, including the cookbook and cast iron skillet from Cigus. Terri started moving suitcases as Marc and Sarah stepped inside to help.

Before closing the door for the last time, Alex paused and scanned the house. It was a good den, and she would miss it. But, it was time to make another. One that would be more concealed from these new hunters. One that would allow her time to think about many important matters. Matters such as how to track the dogs that killed her friend.

One month after returning from Arizona and it might as well have been the first day. No solid leads had turned up and the case was turning cold. Terri hung up the phone. SSA Marasco had just asked her to come upstairs to meet with the counterintelligence team for a call with FBI HQ. This would be her third meeting today and it was only 10 a.m.

Since the murder, the investigative pace of work had been frenetic. Terri was exhausted, both physically and mentally. She was pouring in the hours and it was taking a toll. Despite her fatigue, sleep had been elusive. Although she knew him and liked him, the death of Cigus had not hit her like it did Alex. The burning desire to bring the killers to justice was for a different reason. She had to protect Alex.

Alex. Maybe it was the fatigue, but at this minute, she missed her terribly. She could still feel the embrace when she left her. No time for that now, gotta stay in the game.

Suddenly, the large frame of Marc appeared in her cubicle door and handed her a cup of coffee. "Hey, I got some good news from John. Trina Stackhouse got her company transfer. She's moving to the Gulf Coast area, near her parents."

Terri took a sip of the hot beverage. "That is good news. I'd move somewhere new too, if I were her. What's going on with Ken?"

"John said he's probably lookin' at probation. All the murders were tied to Thomas. Then, with his saving that guy in the car trunk and–"

"And saving Chooli and Trina at the house before Thomas disappeared into the desert," Terri added. This was the cover story John worked up. An extensive manhunt continued for Thomas, but with no further killings and no credible sightings, the consensus was jelling that he likely perished somewhere in the arid expanse of the Arizona wilderness.

"Yup. That was some good work on John's part. Takin' all that together, John thinks Ken'll be alright," Marc confirmed.

Terri nodded, but couldn't even muster a fake smile.

Marc's brow furrowed. "You holdin' up ok, Ter?"

She closed her eyes. "No. I think I reached task saturation yesterday."

"You need to delegate some of this. You're not helping anybody if you're too tired to think straight. Carve it up. I'll deal with the PD and Jerri's people. Sarah can work with the criminal squads here. You focus on the spooks and the counter intel guys upstairs. Sound good?"

Terri finally managed a real smile. "Thanks. You're a lifesaver."

"Naw, I'm just a guy trying to help his partner." He took a breath before he continued in a whisper. "Hey, somethin's been eating at me. With all the crazy crap we've seen, and we've seen a lot, do you ever wonder what else is out there that we don't know about?"

Terri's expression turned serious. "Yeah, the thought has crossed my mind."

EPILOGUE

R OBERT SETTLED BACK INTO his chair and watched several other headquarters agents, supervisors, a deputy director, as well as a platoon of analysts begin to fill the seats around the large oval table.

It had been an exhausting period. At least it seemed that the situation in Arizona had been resolved. One less thing to worry about.

The most troubling part for Robert was the surprise party in Philadelphia. It had been a disaster. The guest of honor was a no-show and a civilian had been killed. A very unfortunate circumstance. The targeting for the op had been good, but the timing had been poor. Fortunately, his plan to get Armando and Luca home cleanly had been successful.

The Augur had visions and warned them this target was going to be a challenge. And now she was aware of the pursuers. She had actually spoken to Armando and Luca directly and heard their voices. Unsure where she was, the men were rattled until the moment they entered Dulles International Airport for their Vienna-bound flight that night.

The Augur was old and experienced, but this was a situation he had never faced. God willing, they would get another opportunity and prevail. They had to.

Robert checked his watch, since his phone was secured in a box outside the doors of the conference room. The teleconference was going to start in five minutes. On his yellow legal pad, he prepared for the meeting.

He headed the sheet of paper with: Conference call with PH FBI regarding current investigation into attempted murder of source.

Below that he wrote a few placeholder questions, the last one being: Current location of source?

Watching the remaining people file in wearing their cheap business suits and worn shoes, he smiled and made small talk. Despite the setbacks and fear, he oozed calmness. He had to make everyone believe it was just another day in the office.

CONTACT

I hope you enjoyed Skinwalkers. For updates on new projects and fun
content, you can follow me on:

Facebook: D. Werkmeister - Author
Instagram: Werkmeister.author
Website: thestorywerks.com
Email: dwerkmeisterauthor@gmail.com

Finally, a gentle reminder: Please leave a review. A sentence or two is all
it takes and it makes a world of difference. Thank you!

9 798991 499101